Maninder

The Summer of Gramps
by Terry Groves

Published By
Breaking Rules Publishing

Copyright © 2020 Terry Groves

All rights reserved. No part of this book may be reproduced, stored in a retrieval system or transmitted in any form or by any means without the prior written permission of the publisher except by the reviewer who may quote brief passages in a review to be printed in a newspaper, magazine or journal.

The author has used an outside source to edit this book.

Soft Cover - 10402
Published by Breaking Rules Publishing
Pompano Beach, Florida
www.breakingrulespublishing.com

Acknowledgements

No book is ever created in isolation. I would like to thank my best friend, Mark Laurie for being a constant support for my writing and such a wonderful source of inspiration. My son, Anthony Groves, and his partner Lisa Grightmire, for reading and listening to my stories and offering valuable feedback. My many friends and family for their constant encouragement and for reading me. Christopher Clawson and David Reavis at Breaking Rules Publishing for their faith and support.

I could not have done this without you.

Who's the Brat?

"Where the hell is that little brat?" Mike slowed when his grandfather's voice boomed on the other side of the mudroom door, his hand poised to grab the pitted, brass knob. The tap and clomp of the man caning his way across the kitchen vibrated through the floorboards, up the scarred wooden door separating them.

"He's not a brat." Grandma's voice, quick to Mike's defence, made him smile. "He's been trying to get on your good side, but he's convinced you don't have one. I'm getting concerned too."

"I need to make sure he's not stealing my stuff."

"And what might you have worth stealing?" She paused, and Mike pictured her working at the sink, peeling potatoes or cleaning vegetables. He wondered what he had done to make his grandfather view him as a thief. A chair scraped on the linoleum floor, another tap, some clomps, another little scrape. Grampa must have sat down. Mike felt a twinge listening in on their conversation like this, but they were talking about him. "And why would you call him a brat? He's been a nice young man since he's been here."

"Just look at the trouble he's caused Julia. She had to go to Mexico to rescue her marriage from all that kid's trouble."

Mike flinched at the mention of his mother's name.

"Bert, you don't know anything about that. Malcolm was called to Mexico to fix that dam project. Our girl just went with him. I think it's nice they can travel like that."

"Dumping the brat on us."

"You stop that, he might hear you."

The sounds on the other side of the door faded as Mikes mind wandered back a few years. . .

He and his friends, Uwe (a German name, pronounced 'oova') and Chuck had spent a summer Saturday afternoon at Fort Henry. The old for was within walking distance of their homes in Kingston and they had been there frequently.

In winter I wasn't open but the fact that it stood on a bluff, overlooking the city and St Lawrence River made it a frequent destination for sledding. This day though, there was no snow, just a lot of tourists. Mike found it interesting trying to picture how life must have been for the soldiers who manned it more than a hundred years before.

Walking through the battlements, touching the cold limestone of the walls and moat helped Mike connect with the past that fascinated him. The re-enactments, demonstrations, and tours helped feed his imagination, but today's guards smoked factory made cigarettes and drank from soda cans. This always broke the spell.

"Let's check out the gift shop." Chuck gave Mike a poke'.

"What for? I'm broke."

"Me too, but its cooler in there." Chuck shaded his eyes as he looked toward the sun.

"And we can check out the cheesy crap the tourists buy." Uwe offered.

"All right." Mike touched the wall again, feeling the rough stone rasp against his fingertips. He gve the wall a little kick, then followed his friends.

The store was dim and dank after the mid-day, mid-summer sun. Mike was afraid he would bump into something or someone while his eyes adjusted, so he moved with baby steps. He could hear Chuck and Uwe ahead of him, laughing together.

Tourists pressed in around him, picking things off the shelves, looking at them, then setting them back down. Kids asked for gifts, parents looked serious as though giving the ask consideration before shaking their head no, or guiding the small clutching hands to return the found treasure.

Mike looked over the wares, wondering why anyone would want this stuff. Cheap snow globes, fake beaver fur caps, spoons, plastic bows and arrows, none of this interested him. Then he felt closed in. Too warm, damp, his heart began beating faster. He looked for his friends, saw Chuck through the crowd.

Chuck looked at him, a strange smile bending across his face. Chuck's face lit up, his mouth opened a bit and he held up a feathered tomahawk. Keeping his eyes on Mike, he opened his jacket and tucked the tomahawk inside. Mike realized he was going to steal it.

Mike's mouth grew dry and his heart thudded. Why was Chuck doing that? Then Mike saw a brass cannon on a shelf. As though someone else was in control of him, he reached out, picked up the small item, noting its weight. This was no cheap trinket. It was probably real brass.

Before he knew what he was doing, the cannon was tucked into his back pocket and he headed for the door still wondering why he was doing this. Chuck and Uwe followed him into the bright sunlight, laughing, Uwe clamping Chuck's shoulder. Before his eyes had adjusted to the sun, Mike heard a voice

behind them.
"Just a minute there, boys."
And that was that. They were caught. He was a thief even though no one discovered that cannon in his pocket. He was in the company of thieves, Uwe had taken a package of Canadian flag stickers, so he was a thief by association. Had his grandfather heard of that? Had his mother shared that shame?

    Mike backed himself up to the outside door, picking his steps with care to not make a sound. He pushed on the outside door and let it slam. With heavier steps, he headed back to the kitchen door, grabbed the doorknob, twisted it then pushed the door open.
    "Hi Grandma, hi Grandpa," Mike hoped he sounded as though he was just coming in from outside and wasn't aware of their recent exchange. He glanced at his grandfather sitting at the old Formica kitchen table, one hand wrapped around a bottle of beer, the other holding his cane. Green linen shirt and green canvas pants, Grandpa wore the same clothes every day, like it was his uniform. They reminded Mike of the janitors at school. Old serious men, too serious to smile. He wondered when men became so serious. His father sometimes became serious, but he also spent lots of time smiling. Perhaps serious crept up on men when they weren't looking, took them over, like the pod people in the horror movie. Was Grandpa a full-fledged pod person? He wondered why this man thought he was a thief. It was true that he had a habit of getting himself into trouble, but he hadn't stolen anything in years, nothing he'd been caught for anyway. It was a question he couldn't ask without revealing his eavesdropping. Pushing it from his mind, he focussed on the issue in front of him.
    "Hello dear," Grandma was working on a bundle of green leaves in the sink. 'Spinach', Mike thought, 'yum, spinach salad.' "What have you been up to?" but it came out 'whatcha bin up to?'

"Picking up around the yard, hanging the garden hose and stuff. If its ok, I'll cut the grass tomorrow." He looked toward his grandfather.

"Have you used a power mower before?" the large woman asked without turning. Her shoulders rocked as she washed and tore at the leaves in the sink.

"You'll cut your foot off." Gramps snarled.

"I cut the grass at home sometimes." Mike lowered his voice and looked at the floor. "Dad's watched me."

"Well, he's not here. Too busy flying to Mexico."

"Bert, "Grandma's voice was sharp, the word shooting across the room. The old man sat silent. "Mike, go wash up. Supper will be soon." Gram continued but in a softer tone.

Mike headed into the bathroom, glad to be out of grandpa's sight. 'Grumpa', he thought, 'what a grump,' then smiled at his reflection in the mirror. The smile drooped into a frown as he remembered his parents leaving him for the summer when they went to Mexico. Dad had to supervise a dam construction project there that had gone bad, and Mom had gone to spend time with him. Mike knew part of the reason she had gone was so they could work on their relationship. By sixteen he had witnessed enough of their arguments and late-night discussions to know divorce had come up several times. He knew too, that some of their problems were a direct result if his own actions, misbehaviours. He wasn't sure just why he did some of the things he did, but he knew some of them were seriously bad. He also didn't know how to fix them. If spending the summer at Grumpa's kept his parents together, maybe he could endure it. Hoping that if he made himself helpful, Grandpa would like him, wasn't working. Grandpa didn't seem to like anything, except beer.

Mike turned on the taps as he looked at himself in the mirror. He made a face and watched his smile break wide open, but it felt heavy, fake. Rubbing his hands under the water, he didn't wait for the hot to make its way from the tank in the basement. The tank was old with rust spots, sitting on cinder blocks to raise it off the dirt floor. The cool, musty basement was full of spider webs. Mike turned the tap off before an eight-legged creature could crawl out of the pipe. Putting his happy face back on, he headed to the kitchen for supper.

Before bed, he flashed an email off, *Mom, can I come to Mexico with you. Grandpa hates me.*

Finding Bad

The next morning Mike went out to the yard to pick up things that shouldn't be run over by a lawnmower. He still wasn't certain that Grumpa would let him use that, but he hoped he would. There wasn't much on this hobby farm for a sixteen-year-old boy to do. No internet and certainly no Play Station. He was happy to do what he could to help out, anything besides sitting around doing nothing. And Grandma was nice. Maybe later he would walk into town for a swim at the pool, maybe meet some other kids.

"Grandpa's gone to work." Grandma said when Mike asked about using the mower. "I don't know when he'll be back, probably not until supper." She looked at Mike and he saw something in her eyes, disappointment? "I don't know if you should use it without him being here."

"I'll be careful." Mike had not spent much time with his grandparents. Aylmer was a long way from Kingston where he and his parents lived, so they didn't get together very often. Until now it had only been when Gram and Gramps drove the five hours to see their daughter, this was Mike's first time at their little farm. It wasn't really a farm, just an acre of land with a house and an old barn. A stand of corn along the lane between it and the house ended at a small vegetable garden beside the barn. The rest of the space was grass, dotted with a few fruit trees, crab-apples, pears, cherries, and peaches. "Please?"

"Well," Grandma wiped her hands on her apron. "I guess it will be alright. It's in the barn, just inside the door. You should find the gas can there too. When you're done, put everything back where you got it." Mike stepped toward the door before she could change her mind.

The yard seemed to get bigger the longer he pushed the mower around it, Mike thought about Gramps. He wasn't certain what he had done to make the man not like him, he just seemed to have a natural dislike. Mike was glad Grumps still worked part-time, a few hours a few times a week, at the public school in town. Mike wasn't certain what he did there, had only heard Grumps say he was going to the school to work, and Mike was afraid to ask. Imagine that, being afraid to ask your grandfather what he did at work. Anyway, him being away a few hours at a time gave Mike a measure of safe time.

At noon Grandma stepped onto the porch and waved at Mike. He had taken his shirt off, the sun was bright and hot. He wiped his forehead with the back of one hand, waved at her and let the mower's engine die.

"I have a sandwich here for you. And a nice cold glass of lemonade." Grandma shaded her eyes with a hand. "You must have worked up an appetite by now."

"Sure have. Pretty thirsty too." Mike walked toward her, pulling his t-shirt over his head.

"You are doing a good job out here." Grandma surveyed the lawn.

"Sure is a lot of grass. How does Gramps do it, with his bum leg and all?"

"He just motors on through it. Come on and sit on the porch to eat. Cooler in the shade."

"I was thinking I might go to the pool after I'm done."

"I think that's a wonderful idea. Wash up at the side tap there then have your lunch."

Grandma sat with him while he ate. Her knitting needles clicked as she rocked on the porch swing.

"I don't think Gramps likes me much."

"I think he just doesn't know you. Give him time."

"He seems pretty angry all the time."

"He has a lot on his mind."

"Hmmm."

"I remember when we first met." Grandma set her knitting in her lap and looked up into the crab-apple tree branches. "It was at the fall fair."

Mike looked at her, his sandwich forgotten in the soft tone in her voice.

"They had a barn dance in those days, was a big deal.

All us girls looked forward to it." She paused as though lost in the years, then her needles started clicking again. "All the boys would line up on one side and we would be on the other, waiting to be asked to dance." She sighed. "Sometimes those boys were so shy to cross that floor that us girls would dance together." She paused again; a smile gentle on her face. "But not Bert, no siree. He strode," she puffed out her chest and rocked her shoulders, "strode, out onto that dance floor grinning like so the top of his head might fall off. He hooked his thumbs in his belt and kicked out a few steps. He was showing he was ready to dance. Then he waited to see who would come join him. He was so handsome; his smile was worth a bag of nickels...which was a lot back then. I wasn't the prettiest girl there, but I had come to dance so I moved on out. We danced till we got married." Again, the old woman sighed. "Then the war came..." She folded her knitting into her bag and stood up. "But that's another story. You finish up your lunch, I shouldn't be delaying you from your work."

"Grandma," Mike wanted to hear more.

"Not now." She banged through the door, into the house.

Mike finished his sandwich, took his plate and glass inside and set them in the sink, then he headed back out to the yard work. He didn't see his grandmother. Her bedroom door was closed.

When Mike finished cutting the grass, he wiped down the mower. It had been perfectly clean when he started so he figured Grumps was particular about it. Since he didn't really get Grumps' permission to use it, he wanted to make sure he didn't do anything to set the man off. He even scraped out the grass from under the machine, around the blade. He replaced the tarp he had found covering the motor. He looked around to see if he was leaving everything as he had found it. He glanced around the barn, noting the four rough wood stalls that must have once held livestock. Now they were mostly empty, or storage space for yard tools and old boxes. The furthest one was in shadow but held something covered by an old, dusty tarp. Mike took a step toward it then heard car tires crunch on the gravel driveway. Grumps must be home. He headed out of the barn as though he had been doing something wrong.

"I see you cut the grass even though I said no." Gramps held onto the car door as he spoke. Mike swallowed hard. He wanted to run but knew he had to find a way to deal with his grandfather; they had the whole summer ahead of them yet.

"You didn't really say no." Mike tried to get the right tone into his voice so he wouldn't sound confrontational. "You warned me not to cut my foot off and look," Mike did a little tap dance, "both feet safe and sound." He finished up with a little flourish and a jazz hands wave.

"Don't be smart with me." Gramps tucked his shirt into his pants, pulled his cane from the car, slammed the door closed and staggered a bit as he turned toward the house.

"I'm not trying to be, sorry if I came across like that." Mike kicked at the dust in the driveway. "I put everything back the way I found it."

"You better have." Gramps didn't even turn to look at Mike.

Mike jammed his hands in his pockets and kicked at the ground again. He heard the house door open and, just before it closed, he heard Gramps call out "That kid...," then the door slammed shut, cutting off the rest.

Maybe a nice swim would help make him feel better, but he really didn't want to go into the house to get his swimsuit and towel. Maybe he would just walk to the pool and watch the swimmers. Maybe meet some kids his own age. He went to the kitchen window hoping Grandma would be at the sink. She was but was facing away, it looked like she was talking with Grumps. He could hear her talking but the words were muffled through the window.

Mike tapped on the glass and, when she turned to him, he pointed at himself and then made a swimming motion. She smiled and nodded her head. Then she held up on finger, *wait one second*, then pointed toward the front of the house. Mike headed to the porch there.

In a few minutes Gramma came out carrying his trunks and a towel. Grandmothers can be so smart. "Have fun." She smiled at him.

"Thanks Gram."

"Don't worry." She pointed over her shoulder with her thumb, indicating Grandpa.

"Sure."

"Nice job on the lawn." She spoke the words low but exaggerated the message with her mouth. And she smiled.

"Thanks." Mike turned and started the trek into town.

It was about a mile to the pool, but Aylmer was a nice place to walk through. It was as though time had skipped most of the town. There were so many reminders of older days, even the houses had a soft, comfortable feel about them. Large front porches, nice lines, and angles were so much nicer than the new houses that were gobbling up the neighbourhoods where Mike lived; all cold and clinical; efficient. The afternoon sun brought sweat out on Mike's forehead. Some trickled down his back. He remembered how cool it had been in the barn.

As he walked, he unfolded the towel, intending to roll his trunks into it so they were easier to carry. Something fell out. Mike looked down. A five-dollar bill lay at his feet. He picked it up. Grandma must have snuck it into the towel so he could pay his way into the pool. He hadn't even thought about that. He smiled and stuffed the bill into his pocket. Thirty minutes later Mike passed the money to the lady in the booth at the pool. He headed into the locker room, the smell of chlorine enveloping him.

Mike saw her as soon as he stepped onto the pool deck. The outdoor pool was surrounded by a twelve-foot fence. Beyond the fence was park land with a kiddie playground, sandboxes, monkey bars, swings, teeter-totters, and beyond that were two baseball diamonds. There were about twenty people in the pool, mostly younger kids but a few teenagers and some adults, probably parents of the kids. The playground was active, swings squealing, laughter and screams of play, lots of movement. There were ball games on each of the two fields. Mike heard a sharp crack, cheering and a sudden rush of movement, but he didn't really see any of this, he was looking at the teenager leaning against the fence.

She was tall for a girl, almost his own height. Her stance was casual, her light brown hair cascading past her shoulders in lazy curls. She was wearing a pink and black bikini and it was this that held Mike's attention. For a moment, the only things that existed in the universe were he, her, and the space between them.

"Outta the way," Mike was pushed from behind. He realized he had stopped in the doorway to the change room, dripping water from his rinsing shower.

"Yeah, sure. Sorry." He fumbled a few words as two teens stepped past him. Both were about his height, one had red hair, rusty red, curly and messy. The other had jet-black hair and Mike noted hair on his legs. Glancing down, Mike was fully aware that his legs were still bare, smooth as a baby. It wasn't as though he hadn't started down the puberty road, it just wasn't so obvious. The girl by the fence was obviously miles down that road, she filled the bra of her bathing suit very nicely. Mike gave himself a mental slap to keep himself from dwelling on that. He was well aware the effect those types of thoughts had on him. The last thing he wanted was to embarrass himself with something that was difficult to hide in a bathing suit. He noticed she was looking at him. She raised a hand and waved.

Mike raised his hand to return the gesture, a smile cracking his face until he realized she was greeting the two boys who had just pushed past him. He dropped his hand, then moved it behind his back. The three teens stood together talking. Walking to the pool, Mike found a clear spot, dove in and swam to the far end.

He stopped when he reached the end. He let his legs hang, placed his elbows on the pool deck and rested his chin on his forearms. From here he could see the ball games and enjoy the cold water seeping the heat out of his body. And not look at the three teenagers even though he really wanted to look at her again. A pair of legs stepped in front of him. Mike looked up.

It was another teenager, Mike looked higher, girl, higher, red bathing suit, white t-shirt with the word Lifeguard silkscreened in red letters across the chest. A lanyard with a whistle hung from her neck, sunglasses hid her eyes.

"No diving."

"Huh?" Mike squinted. She was only partially blocking the sun.

"No diving. See the sign." She pointed toward the wall of the change rooms behind him.

Mike looked. Sure enough, No Diving, was painted in large blue letters.

"Oh, sorry."

The girl crouched down, one hand moving to the whistle, but she just held it. "You're new." Mike thought she might be eighteen or so.

"Visiting my grandparents."

"We got lots of those in this town. Who?"

"Bert and Lana Weinstein. Know them? They live at the end of St Andrew."

"No. Don't think I do. I know most people in town though. What I meant though was who are you?"

Mike felt himself blush. "Oh right. Mike, Mike Tuthill."

"Ok, Mike Tuthill, no more diving. Jumping in is ok."

"What's your name?"

"Lifeguard." She smiled, stood and walked away. She gave him a look then turned to something else. Mike noted she had nice legs, strong and well-tanned. He looked back at the three teens, but they weren't by the fence anymore. The two boys were in the pool splashing each other, the girl was laying on one of the deck lounge chairs. Mike thought he might swim a few more laps and then maybe do a little sun tanning himself.

Ten minutes later Mike pulled himself from the water. He was breathing hard, water dripping from his body. The lengths had been good, but he had not been able to concentrate on his strokes, having to avoid the other pool users. There weren't any dedicated swim lanes, so he was forced to dodge the other swimmers.

He was happy to discover that the lounge chair beside the fence girl was still vacant, so he sauntered over and sat down. "Beautiful day." He offered.

"Huh?" She was laying on her stomach and had to turn her head to look at him.

"I said, nice day. It's a nice day."

She squinted and raised a hand to shade her eyes. "Yeah, guess so."

"Is there much to do in this town?"

"Like what?"

"I don't know, what do you do for fun?"

"Not hang out with teeny boppers."

Mike felt his face blush with blood and heat. It appeared small town girls can have big city attitudes. He was about to let her know that he was no bopper when a voice called behind him.

"Hey, Jeannie. Find a new friend?" The larger of the two teens, the red haired one, bumped Mike's chair with his leg as he approached. He waved his arms sending a cascade of water in all directions.

"Hey," Mike and Jeannie said at the same time flinching from the cold droplets. Jeannie turned over. "Jack, don't be a dork." She added.

"Just trying to cool you from the hot sun." Jack sat on the edge of Mike's chair. He half turned to Mike, "You don't mind do you?" With a small flick of his hand he indicated himself sitting.

"There are lots of other chairs." Mike offered.

"Go take one then." Jack stared at Mike.

"I didn't realize small towns were full of assholes." Mike looked at Jack then at Jeannie. She didn't seem quite as pretty now.

Jack stood up, "You better shut your mouth little kid."

Mike stood up, "You going to make me? Jack." Mike

wasn't feeling as confident as he was trying to appear. Although they were about the same height, Jack was quite a bit bigger than he was.

"Problem here boys?" The lifeguard who had chastised Mike about diving had wandered over unseen. She looked at Jack, then at Mike.

"No problem," Jack said, "someone was just leaving."

Mike shrugged then headed toward the change room. He didn't feel like hanging around here any longer. Ten minutes later he was walking back to his grandparent's wondering how the afternoon had turned out so bad. All he wanted to do was have a nice swim, maybe meet some new friends, get along with Grumps. It seemed everything he tried turned to crap.

He turned onto St Andrew Street. His grandparent's home was at the very end. The road ended where it curved into their driveway. At this end there were large, old houses, and the sidewalks were set back from the road. Between the street and the sidewalks, large maple trees grew. Mike couldn't reach around the trunks, they were so huge, and the bark was rough. They looked like they had been here a long time, maybe even before the houses. About sixty feet tall, their branches reached out over the street and lawns, cascading shade on the sidewalk. It was cooler here than on the main street, Talbot street, he had turned off of, and the shade was welcome relief.

As Mike walked, he studied the homes on his side of the street, marvelling at their solid looking construction and how every house was different. Different shapes, different building materials, different colours. Where he lived, most of the houses looked the same, cookie-cutter houses.

The further he moved along the street, the further apart the houses became. He could imagine how the street had grown up over the years, the town creeping outward, engulfing the farmland. Then he came to the Andrew house.

Mike didn't know if the house was named after the street or the street after the house or if it was all just a peculiar coincidence. Grumps had mentioned it when they had first driven by it. "Stay away from the Andrew's house." He didn't offer any more explanation and Mike didn't have enough guts to ask; he'd just nodded.

Now he took more note of it. The sidewalk ended just before the house which was set closer to the road than the rest of the homes. It had two short, bushy maple trees in the front yard, close to the house. The trunks of the trees were massive, but they were only about twenty feet high, as though stunted by neglect. There was a picket fence surrounding the property, but it hadn't been painted in years. Most of the colour was gone, faded and eroded by summer rains and winter snows. It had once been green, that much was obvious from the bits of paint that still clung to the wood in small patches. The house was yellow, dusty and unattended. The grass was long, the front porch steps uneven with wide gaps between the boards. The porch was surrounded by a short wall with snake scale wooden siding. Mike wondered if anyone actually lived in the place.

The trees were so close to the house, and they looked like old trees, that it seemed the house might have moved itself closer to them. It was hard to imagine anyone planting them that close. The leaves were so thick that the whole front of the house was dark, the light there must never get brighter than twilight. It seemed so appropriate that the sidewalk ended here, civilization not progressing any further.

Beyond the Andrew house was a greenhouse that was part of a large farm whose fields extended all around Grumps little hobby farm as though they were trying to eat it up. Past the greenhouse was the farmhouse, large, bright white, sitting in the middle of a tidy, green, well-tended lawn. Behind the house was a red barn with white cross members. There was a large gravel driveway and parking area where a number of green farm vehicles were parked. They all looked brand new, clean and shiny. Mike thought that here was someone who took care of their stuff. He thought about the dusty, dirty barn on Grump's property.

There was one more house, a red brick bungalow that

sat on a mid-size lot, before his grandparent's property. Across the street was a large, long barn that was part of the tidy farm, and beyond that was a cornfield. Between the barn and the street was a dirt trail wide enough for a tractor. A wire fence stood between the trail and the street. Long grass with tassels at the end grew up around and through the large squares that made up the fence.

After the streets of Kingston, Mike felt like he was in the boonies in this rural town. He kind of liked it though. It felt comfortable, homey, but he felt lost too. He hung his towel and bathing suit on the clothesline. This was another thing he hadn't seen much of at home. Everything went in the dryer there. There was a dryer in the back porch, but he hadn't seen it used yet. Grandma hung everything on the line.

Mike went into the kitchen, dreading some sort of confrontation with Grumps. "Hi Grandma," she was at her usual place at the sink. Mike could hear the TV in the living room and figured Grumps was in there. Good. Smells of something baking in the oven enveloped him in thick aroma. He took in a deep breath. It smelled like pot-roast. Mostly at home his mom assembled dinner, hardly ever made anything from scratch. But then, his mom worked.

She smiled, "How was your swim?"

"Good. Hard to swim lengths, no lanes marked for that, but the water was cold and the sun nice. I like the outdoor pool, but it must be a challenge in the winter." He grinned at her.

"At least it's not crowded then." She grinned back. "Why don't you go watch some TV with Grandpa?"

"Maybe," Mike said but thought 'not on your life. You don't even have cable. And to sit there with him...' "I might lay down for a bit."

"Sure," she said turning back to the sinks, "supper will be at least another hour."

Mike's bedroom was off the living room, beside his grandparent's bedroom. He thought it was odd that it didn't even have a door, just a curtain hung over the archway that separated it from the living room. It was a though it was never intended to be a bedroom, more like a den. Everything seemed a little odd in this old house. And the house was old, it must have been built in the 1930s. It had been added to, you could tell by the different construction materials and architectures. A room had been added here, part of the front porch enclosed into what Grandma called the 'Bird Room' but was just a storage area piled high with all sorts of stuff that Grumps had said were "things for kids to stay out of." Even the bathroom was odd, as though it had been something else, maybe a large closet that was turned into a bathroom. There was still an old outhouse about ten metres from the back door, but there was so much bushy growth around it that it was obvious it hadn't been used for a long time.

Mike walked into the living room because that was the only way to his room. He glanced at Grumps, hoping he was asleep, but he wasn't. It felt awkward saying nothing, so Mike said, "Hi Grandpa, what'cha watching?"

The TV was old, like the house. It was a floor model that stood on four legs and the picture was black and white. There was a couple dancing on the screen. The man was in tight pants and a puffy shirt and had a huge, phony looking smile. The woman was in a dress that lifted and blossomed out when she spun.

"Hrmph." was all Grumps said.

Mike paused a moment as though he might be interested in what was on, he wasn't. "Grandma says supper will be in an hour."

"Hope you didn't get into trouble in town."

Mike felt the hairs on his neck stand up. "Nope, just a swim."

"Hrmph."

Mike stepped through the curtain of his room. As it closed behind him it felt more like a vault door sealing him off from Grumps. The room wasn't very big and contained a queen size bed. There was only enough room left for a bedside table that had a drawer and a shelf. Mike's clothes were in his suitcase, tucked under the bed. He rolled onto the mattress, opened the nightstand drawer and took out his smartphone. He had to be careful how he used the phone. His parents had cautioned him that, although he had a data plan, he couldn't be using it to stream music or videos. It was so they could keep in touch by email and text since there was no internet in his grandparent's house. He could do some Facebook to keep in touch with his friends but, if he used up his monthly data limit, it would shut down until the start of the next month.

He checked for emails, none, then checked Facebook, he wished he didn't because Uwe and Chuck, were having fun and he was missing it. He put the phone away, lay back and drifted off to sleep.

After dinner, Mike had been right, pot-roast, nice and crispy on the outside just the way he liked it, they sat in the living room watching TV. Grumps had complained at dinner, too tough to chew. Grandma and Mike had exchanged cautious smiles. It seemed they just didn't have anything in common, not even food. The picture on the TV was grainy with lines that distorted everything every few minutes. Grumps didn't seem to notice. Mike recognized the host of Jeopardy. He hated that show, they gave you the answer and you had to come up with the question. He sat and watched it anyway. Grumps called out answers, or rather questions. Mike noted that he got a lot of them right.

When the show was over Mike announced he was going to bed. He wanted to check his emails again, and reading would be better than another hard to see show on TV. Grandma leaned forward and accepted his kiss on her cheek. Grumps just grunted and waved his hand indicating that Mike was in the way of the TV.

In the glow of his smartphone, Mike read the email from his mother. *I know Gramps can be a bit tough to take. Try to get to know him. Mexico is just not an option right now. Luv Mom.* Mike's heart burned. He had really hoped he could join them, escape. Grandma was great, nice, kind, always smiling but Grumps made everything so difficult, so mean.

Mike thought about how he had only been here a couple of days so far, there was still two whole months to go. He sighed, letting his shoulders droop. Then he picked up his book and started reading.

An hour later Gram touched the curtain that acted as a door. "Good night, sweetheart. Thanks again for the nice job you did on the lawn."

"Good night Grandma." Mike set his book on the bedside table, turned off the lamp, and pulled the covers over his shoulder. It looked like summer 2008 was not going to be memorable. He never thought he would wish for summer holidays to end.

New Friends

Dawn roused him with the aroma of frying bacon. Mike hesitated a few minutes, savouring the smell but dreading facing Grumps. What nasty thing was he going to say today? Grumps bedroom door was open and Mike could see he wasn't in there. The bed was made, crisp and tidy. Dreading the next few minutes, he walked into the kitchen. Grumps wasn't there either.

"Good morning Gramma." Mike smiled, "you sure make this place smell great."

"Why thank you, sweetheart. Just preparing breakfast. Grampa is out at the barn," she glanced toward the barn, "he will be in in a few minutes. Go wash up and brush your teeth."

Mike headed into the bathroom. When he came out Grumps was at the table. Grandma had set out a plate of toast and was serving up the bacon and eggs. Mike steeled himself. "Good morning Grandpa. You were up early."

"Early is before sunrise." Grumps picked up a piece of bacon and took a bite.

"Bert, use your fork." Grandma admonished him. There was a lilt in her voice that told Mike she was chiding him, edging toward his humour.

"Bacon tastes better from your fingers." Grumps spoke, his voice flat.

Mike sat down, picked up a piece of bacon with his fingers and tasted it. Gramma waved a hand at him, *put that down* it said. Picking up his fork, he took another bite. "Grampa's right, better with fingers." Mike smiled at his grandfather.

Grandpa frowned, "You thought I was wrong?"

Mike's heart burned. No longer feeling like eating, he still did because Grandma had gone to all the trouble of cooking the food. Chewing slow, looking only at his plate, Mike remained silent.

Grandma kept up a busy chatter during the meal,

talking about the sunrise, the dew on the grass, how unlikely it was to rain that day. She started to gather the dishes, "Bert, are there any jobs that Mike can help you with today?"

Work with him today? Mike hated the sounds of those words. Even when he was working so hard to be pleasant with this man, all he was getting in return were nasty comments. Spending any more time with him wasn't something to look forward to.

"Humph. Don't need no snot nose pestering me all day. Can't entertain himself?" Grumps turned to Mike, and it felt like the first time the man had really looked at him. "What would you do at home?"

Mike felt himself fluster. That question was unexpected from Grumps and Mike stumbled on how to respond. "I don't know." He paused, wanting a moment to think.

"Forget already?"

"No," Mike's thoughts raced in how to answer, "I guess I would work on my computer, maybe play my X-Box, go out with my friends. You got no internet, not even a computer."

"I ain't about to get no computer nor one of those game box things so..."

"Bert, he did a good job on the lawn and he wants to help." Grandma gave Mike a quick glance, a little smile.

Grumps chewed on his toast as though it was leather. Around and around his jaw worked. Mike could hear him breathing through his nose. Then he said, "sweep out the barn." He turned to Mike and stared at him again. "I guess you can clean up in the barn some. Think you can do that?"

Mike swallowed. "Sure Gru...Gramps. Sweep out the barn. I can do that."

"I have errands to do." Bert stood up and left the table, took his coat and ball cap from the hook by the back door, snapped the cap on his head and headed out.

"There now," Gramma said after the door banged closed. Resting her elbows on the table, hands clasped in front of her face as though praying, she smiled at Mike. "I know it's not the most exciting job..."

"I don't mind the job Gramma but I'm pretty sure he said that just to get rid of me. Why does he hate me? What did I do to him?" Mike felt his emotions choking him, stinging his eyes. He stopped talking because he didn't want Gram to know he was on the verge of crying.

"He doesn't hate you Mike." She reached toward him, laid her hand on his arm, "he hasn't had much chance to deal with young people. Doesn't understand you. You don't understand him. Sometimes you need to make a hard effort to get to know someone, let them know you."

"Wasn't he young once?"

"Oh yes," she smiled, and her eyes stared off into a past full of memories, "he was young once," she paused a moment, "but that was a long time ago. Lots of life in between then and now. Help me with these dishes." She pushed herself away from the table.

As Mike cleared the table, then dried the dishes Gram washed, he thought about what she said, wondered what it all meant. Of course, Gramps had been young once, everyone was. And yesterday she had said something about the war getting in the way. Mike had heard about people going to war and coming back changed. It was still happening even though Canada's missions were now mostly peacekeeping.

"Where does Gramps go?"

Gramma looked at him, soap suds up her forearms. "Here and there. Visits his friends. Still works too, just part-time though."

So he has friends, Mike thought. "Yesterday, he was a bit unsteady when he came home, is he diabetic?"

"No, not diabetic. Sometimes he visits too long with his friends. He is always careful though."

Mike wasn't certain what she meant by that but he didn't pursue the matter. Ah, Gramps sometimes drank and drove.

"Where does he work?"

"At the school on John Street."

"That's the public school? Doesn't he have to deal with

kids there?"

"Oh, I don't know. Odd jobs, fixing things. Doesn't talk about it much."

Mike let the topic go. If he got the barn done, he would have time to go to town and check out some things. After he put away the dishes, Mike folded the tea towel and hung it on the oven handle, swept the floor and gave his Gramma a hug.

"Thanks Grandma."

"Thank you. It's nice having a hand with the dishes." She hugged him back and Mike allowed himself to linger in that moment.

"I better get at the barn." She mussed his hair, then he headed out the back door.

Mike pushed the barn door open. It was a door in a door. A person size door cut into the sliding tractor size door. A simple bolt through a metal loop latched the big door closed. The smaller door only had a thumb latch. 'Small towns,' Mike marvelled. Back home everything got locked tight or it would disappear. Dust wafted out.

The lawnmower was where he had left it on the right-hand side, covered with the old tarp. He looked around. Sweeping the floor would be easy enough except that it was big and he would have to work around the timbers that made up the stalls. He noticed though that there was lots of dust, grass, straw pieces on the timbers of the stalls, clinging to the thick wood that made up the cross-members of the ceiling. Lots of cobwebs and traces of bird nests, spider webs. There was a second story too that Mike hadn't seen but knew the staircase at the back of the barn led to it. He thought he should check up there first. Not much point in cleaning up down here if messes up there would only seep down and clutter it all up again.

Mike creaked up the steps and unlatched the rough wooden door at the top. He pushed it inward and stepped into the dark, cool interior. The only light up here was what worked its way around the doors at each end or through cracks between the planks of the walls. Years of weather and lack of paint must had allowed the boards to shrink, leaving space for shafts of light to bring a dusky twilight into the hayloft. Mike unlatched the doors on each end of the barn allowing full light to flood the space, likely for the first time in years. Two pigeons flapped their wings then flew out the door. Mike stood for a minute in the doorway just looking out across the fields, house roofs, laneways that spread out in front of him. For that moment he forgot everything that had been laying on his mind. Life was still good. He turned back into the barn.

The space up here was cavernous and empty. A few pieces of rusty equipment that Mike could only imagine the use for looked abandoned and forgotten. A lot of straw, dust, and more bird nests and droppings decorated everywhere. The ceiling rose in a slow curve twelve feet above his head. Mike gazed around, gauging how to tackle this job. He wanted it to be a good, complete job, show Grumps he wasn't slacking.

He went downstairs, found a push broom and a sweep broom and headed back up to the loft. As he worked Mike thought about what Grumps might do all day, what had made him into the man he was now. Mike taped the handles of the two brooms together so he could reach all the way to the peak of the roof with the sweep broom. Dust and things he didn't want to think about rained down on him. Chaff and spider poop swirled, burning his eyes, Mike laughed when he realized what the dust clouds were, then clamped his mouth closed to keep it out.

Gramps had gone to war when he was only a little older than Mike was now. Mike pondered that, trying to imagine how difficult it would be to be in so much danger, so far from home. Then he wondered what Gramps had done in the war. Was he a soldier? Did he carry a rifle? Had he stormed the beaches of Normandy? Vimy Ridge? No, Vimy was World War I and Gramps had gone to WW2. Mike realized he didn't know very much about that war.

It had been a topic in history class, but they had only studied a few chapters. Someone in his class spoke about his father, who was in the military now. He had to go to

Afghanistan for six months. Mike didn't know much more than that about a five year event. He needed to know more.

By the time Gramma called him for lunch, Mike was pushing a pile of sweepings toward the loft door at the back of the barn. He wiped sweat from his forehead and looked around. There were clouds of dust in the air but the space was looking tidier. He trudged his way down the steps, then gazed around the lower level. There was no way he would get this all done today. Just to finish the loft would be a challenge, and it was getting hotter out. Oh well, Mike shrugged his shoulders, it wasn't as though he had much else to do and it was cooler in the shade inside the barn.

Mike brushed himself as he walked across the backyard. Puffs of dirt and dust rushed away from his hands. He thought he better stop at the outside tap and wash up before heading into the house. While he was rinsing off, Grandma came to the backdoor.

"Let's eat on the front porch. Oh my, the look of you." She smiled, "You look like those coal miners, not quite as black though. I think you must be doing a good job out there, you've brought all the dirt out with you." She laughed and smiled, and Mike felt his heart glow.

He walked around the house and found her sitting on the porch. A plate with sandwiches, cut into triangles the way he liked, two glasses of lemonade and some napkins were on the table between the porch chairs. Mike sat and took a sip of lemonade. "Mmm."

"Dusty work." Gram said.

"Did I get it all off?" Mike looked down at himself.

"The shower will do that later. You are fine for now. Almost done?"

"No. This job is a lot bigger than I thought and I still have the bottom to do."

"The bottom?"

"Yeah, I got most of the loft done."

"You're doing the loft? You sure are not afraid to work. I think Gramps was only expecting you to sweep the floor. The bottom floor."

"Yeah, maybe, but I want to do a good job."

"Eat, Mikey, eat." She waved at the sandwiches and he picked one up and bit into it.

He hated being called Mikey. That had been ok when he was a kid but he was sixteen now, but coming from Grandma, it felt ok. He thought back on yesterday at the pool. The kids he had met there didn't seem too friendly, somewhat mean, the one was more of a bully. Mike was familiar with those. At school he had run into enough. You didn't have to do anything, just be there, to get on their wrong side. Most of them were dumb to the nth degree. Maybe they were bullies to in an effort make up for that.

"You going to the pool later?" Gramma asked as though she had been peeking into his thoughts. Mike picked up another sandwich.

Mike hadn't even thought of that but responded, "Maybe if I get the loft finished." Uncertain why, he didn't want her to know about yesterday's conflict at the pool. He had a bad enough reputation at home for finding trouble. No point in confirming it here.

"I hear the Lucknow girl is a lifeguard there. She's about your age. Maybe a little older but not much."

"Really?"

"She's quite pretty."

"Grandma."

Grandma patted his leg. "I'm just saying." And then she smiled the way she had when talking about the dancing. Years fell from her face. "Hearts need distractions."

After lunch Mike headed back to the barn. When he stepped inside the doors and surveyed the work still ahead of him, he felt his energy drain out. It had been hard working above his head to clean the rafters that morning and he was feeling it; his shoulders and arms ached. It was tempting to just sweep the floor down here and call it finished, but then he thought about Grumps. How would that show that man he wasn't just a runt kid, a brat. He picked up the sweep broom and headed back upstairs.

Two hours later Mike heard the stairs creak. A moment later Gram stood just inside the doorway.

"My, my, my. I haven't been up here in a coon's age." She looked around. "I have never seen this place look so good." She looked at Mike who was pushing a pile of dirt out the loft doorway. "Why don't you knock off for the day, go for a swim."

"You read my mind Gram." Mike rested his hands on the broom handle. "I think I've done all I can up here. This old barn must have seen some times. Must have a few stories it could tell."

Even in the dim light Mike saw the colour rush up the woman's neck. "Oh, I hope it keeps its secrets to itself." She smiled and looked around again, "Those would be stories for another day," She headed back toward the stairway. "if ever. I've put your swimsuit and towel in the back porch. You might even find some cookies there too."

"Cookies?"

"You think you're the only one with missions to do? I will leave money for the pool in the back porch for you."

Mike listened to her clump down the wooden steps then gathered the brooms and headed down himself.

Mike found a five-dollar bill on a folded change of clothes on the washing machine in the back porch. It wasn't really a porch; it was an enclosed room that may have once been an open porch. The inside walls were just bare studs, boards were only on the outside. The porch protected the stone steps that led to the low basement. It also contained rough wooden shelves full of jars of preserves. And the washer and dryer were out here too. It would be cold here in the winter with no inside walls nor insulation. The backdoor was just a flap, boards fastened together with hinges added. A spring-loaded rocker arm, that opened and closed with a snap, held it closed.

Beside the clothes Gram had left on the dryer was his bathing suit and a towel. He changed right there to keep the barn dirt out of the house. He took his dirty clothes outside, shook them out then dropped them into the clothes hamper beside the washing machine. Tucking the money into his jeans pocket, Mike rolled his swimsuit into the towel and headed up the driveway. He munched on one of the cookies she had left him.

The smell of chlorine from the pool wafted over him as he passed The Chuckwagon, a small restaurant with a log cabin exterior. He had been enjoying the aroma of French fries and grilled burgers that emanated from the place when the pool smell invaded. Then he could see the squat building that held the shower rooms.

There was an arched bridge between the Chuckwagon and the pool. It was about twenty feet long, built of painted steel. Catfish Creek flowed six feet below it. The faded, green paint on the bridge flaked where rust bubbled here and there. Mike paused and looked over the edge into the water gurgling below. He wondered if there were any catfish in the swirling waters. He couldn't see, the trees that pressed in close shaded the shallow water. If Uwe was here, he'd be dropping a hook in there for sure.

The light breeze didn't abate much of the sun's warmth. The wind more pushed the heat than cooled it and Mike thought this must be how a roast felt in his mother's convection oven. He looked forward to the cool water. A few lengths would help stretch out the muscles his cleaning job had helped him discover.

While he was changing, he heard a towel snap, felt a dart of air flick his back. "Hey, new kid." Mike turned to see red-haired Jack standing there, his towel held by one end. "Back for more I see."

Mike turned back to what he was doing.

"Lose your tongue?" The voice was closer.

"I'm just here for a swim."

After a brief pause Jack said, "Hey, I think you got me wrong." He stepped closer and Mike took a step away, still not looking at him. "We might have got off on the wrong foot yesterday, sometimes I can be a little...." He let the words hang between them.

Mike turned toward him, opened his mouth but then closed it again saying nothing. His quick wit had gotten him into trouble before and he wanted none today. He piled his clothes into the locker, snapped the lock closed, picked up his towel and moved to step around Jack. Jack's friend was in the doorway to the pool and now Mike was between the two. Bad spot. 'Between a dork and a hard case' flashed in Mike's mind and he clamped his tongue...that trouble thing swimming back up.

"I mean it. No hard feelings. I was a dick and I'm sorry."

Mike turned back to Jack. Jack stood there, hand out, head cocked to one side. Mike looked in his face, Jack's eyes were soft.

"Alright," Mike reached out and gripped Jack's hand. "I'm Mike." Jack gave it a shake then let it go.

"That's more like it. I don't think you've been introduced to Alan. He's my bud." Jack looked over Mike's shoulder. "Alan, this is Mike."

"Alan." Mike nodded in his direction.

Alan stood aside and Mike headed for a shower.

"Hey Mike," Jack spoke while Mike rinsed off, "were doing something a little later. Maybe you would like to join us?"

"What's that?" Mike turned the taps off.

"Just a little adventure. Show you what we do for fun around here."

"How be I think about that?" Mike draped his towel over his shoulders and headed out to the pool deck.

"Sure. We'll meet you by the ball diamonds if you want to go."

On the deck, Mike tossed his towel onto a lounge chair then headed to the pool. He stood on the edge, prepared to dive then noticed the lifeguard looking at him. He gave her a quick wave then jumped into the pool. She waved back, but he didn't see it.

The cool water felt even better than he had expected it to. There were a lot of kids in the pool, screaming and splashing and laughing so Mike's lengths were again, interrupted a lot. He didn't mind though, the work in the barn had tired him and he felt good about his exchange with Jack. He didn't trust him but that look in his eyes when he offered his hand seemed legit.

Then his thoughts turned to Grumps. Mike stopped swimming and let his feet find the bottom of the pool. He stood and brushed the water from his face with his hands. The sun glared down, reflecting off the water in a million bright flashes. The sounds of the other swimmers faded.

He hoped his work in the barn would show Gramps he wasn't a brat, that he could do good work. He needed the man to like him. They had the whole summer ahead of them. They should be doing things like fishing for catfish, not fighting like cats and dogs. Mike pushed himself back into his strokes, letting his mind wander to better places. He missed his parents. They had only left a few days ago, but leaving him with relative strangers, even if they were his mom's parents, left a huge hole in his life. Gram seemed great; was easy to talk to, wanted to please him, and appreciated the efforts he was making to get along. But Gramps. . . he continued swimming.

He missed his friends back home. Not that he had a lot, but Uwe and Chuck were always there filling in the gaps, coming up with things to do, or just making hanging out fun. Now he was only getting messages from them, and not that many. Since they were always together, they didn't have much need for emails or texts. All three of them had got jobs at the Tasty Grill for the summer. Uwe and Chuck were working now, but he had to cancel when his dad got called to Mexico. Now he wasn't even going to have any money at the end of the summer. But did it have to be that way? Mike stopped swimming again. Maybe he could get a job here.

After his swim, Mike stood on the pool deck just watching all the surrounding activity. The kids and their uproar made him feel more at home. The number of kids surprised him.

"They come from all over." Mike turned to the lifeguard who had come up behind him.

"Huh?"

"The kids. I saw you watching them. There are a lot of farms and farm communities around here. The winters are cold, so," she paused and raised her eyebrows, "so, lots of kids."

Mike stood for a moment; his mouth open as he tried to understand what she was saying. She waggled her eyebrows, then he realized what she meant. He felt the heat creep up his neck. "Oh, oh, yeah, sure." Mike tried to laugh it off but felt awkward.

"I'm Suzie."

"Mike," he started, but she finished for him.

"Tuthill." Mike stared at her, "You told me yesterday."

"And you remembered."

"Not much changes around here," Suzie glanced around, "New tends to stand out."

Mike stood staring up at her wanting to say something but not knowing what. He had always been shy around girls, uncertain how to talk to them. He was about to say something about small towns when she said, "You like to do lengths. You swim pretty good. If you like, I could give you some pointers."

"Sure," Mike didn't know what else to say. After a moment, during which he pondered what might be wrong with his style he added, "that would be great."

"I help coach the kids swim team, help with swim lessons."

Mike frowned, she thought he was a kid?

Suzie blushed. "I didn't mean that. I mean, I help with the kids, but I didn't mean you were a kid. I just mean I'm learning to watch for good form, ways to correct that. If I help you, I'm helping me."

Mike smiled and Suzie let out a laugh. He guessed she was a little nervous too. "Ok, sure." He said. "Maybe the next time I come."

"Alright," Suzie looked around, "I better get back to the rest of the pool."

Mike went back to swimming, feeling good about her watching his style but curious about what he might be doing wrong.

Walking across the bridge after his swim, Mike remembered Jack's offer. He looked at his watch. It was getting close to supper time. He decided that, as much as he would like to go with them on their adventure, especially since Jeannie might be there too, he shouldn't be late for supper. No telling what Grumps would say about that.

Jacking a Car

"God damn it." Shouted words and a slamming door woke Mike. He recognized Gump's voice, checked the sun coming in the window and thought it was about 7 a.m. 'Didn't that man ever sleep in?'

"Bert!" Mike heard his grandmother, "The boy."

"Damn him too. Is he going to sleep all day?"

Mike sat up and rubbed his face, then his hair. It felt wild. He pulled on his pants and shirt and socks then headed to the kitchen. By the time he got there he was aware that a tire on the car was flat.

Grumps was holding the phone, his face was red. He had a blue and white CAA card in his hand. "An hour!" He yelled into the receiver, "I need to get to work." He glanced at Mike then turned away. Grandma stood at the sink. Mike could tell she was upset.

"Grandpa," Mike waited a moment for the man to look at him, he didn't. Mike stepped toward him, reached out and touched his shoulder, careful, as though he might be burning hot. Grumps twisted his head toward Mike, his eyes squinting, full of anger. Mike cringed a bit. "If it's just a flat tire, I can put the spare on. You have a spare?"

Grumps put a hand over the mouthpiece. When he pulled the phone away from his ear, Mike could hear a tiny voice speaking through it. "Of course I have a spare. You think I'm daft?"

"No, of course not. I just...it's just, I can change the tire for you. We learned about car maintenance in school."

"So, they do teach you something. I know how to change my own tire." Grumps glanced toward his wife.

"Now Bert. Remember your back."

"Woman," Grumps started but Mike spoke before he could.

"You can watch me, make sure I do it right." Mike really didn't want Grumps supervising him, but he had seen enough arguments develop between his parents and he could see one brewing here. "Come on Gramps, it'll be fun. Just you and me against the wheel." Mike smiled and raised his eyebrows to appear sincere even though he didn't feel that way.

Gramps looked at him. Mike looked toward his grandmother and saw relief in her smile but her eyes were worried. Finally, Gramps said, "Alright, but you better know what the hell you're doing."

"Bert." Grandma said.

"I'm sure the boy's heard worse than that."

Mike brightened. It was the first time Gramps has referred to him in a non-derogatory way. Being called a boy wasn't heartening, after all, sixteen is practically a man, but Mike was happy to not be the brat.

"Alright, let's do it." Mike headed to the door.

As he approached the car, Mike saw the rear driver tire was indeed flat. "Wow Grandpa, you sure did that one right."

"Hmph." Gramps was limping along behind him. Mike heard the porch door slam closed. Then there was a beep from behind him and the car trunk popped open. Mike looked inside.

The trunk was immaculate. The black carpeting didn't show any dirt or threads or even dust. Mike gulped realizing that gramps was as meticulous with his car as he was with his lawn mower. He would have to be careful not to mess things up.

"The spare is under the mat." Gramps pointed into the trunk.

Mike lifted the carpet and saw the tire. It was a space-saver, tiny tire, fastened in place by a large butterfly nut. Mike spun it off then grabbed the tire. At this angle it was heavy and awkward to pull out.

"Don't drag it over the paint. Lift it."

Mike did his best but bumped the tire on the lip of the trunk.

"Careful."

"I am."

"More careful." Gramps touched the metal lip where the tire had bounced a bit as though soothing it. Mike dropped the tire beside the car then reached back into the trunk for the jack and lug wrench.

"Careful." Gramps cautioned again.

"Is the parking brake set?" Mike asked. "Don't want the car to roll."

"Block the front tires." Grumps directed, "You'll find some in the barn."

Mike knew that setting the brake was enough but he didn't want to get into it with Gramps so he headed to the barn.

"And hurry up. I'm late already."

Mike sighed and started trotting.

After blocking the front tires Mike picked up the lug wrench to pry the hubcap off.

"Watch it." Gramps said, "Don't scratch the rim." After a moment he added, "Get a rag. Put a rag in there so it doesn't scratch."

"Gramps."

"Do it." Gramps waved the back of his hand.

Mike headed to the barn again to get a rag.

After removing the hubcap Mike went to loosen the lug nuts.

"Wipe them off first." Gramps directed, "If there's sand on them it'll scratch the paint on the wrench."

"Gramps."

"Do it. You gotta take care of your tools. I thought they taught you this in school. Or was it some other kind of carjacking they were teaching you?"

Mike wiped off the nuts then loosened one. He was surprised by Gramp's reference to car theft. Did he think Mike was that much of a hooligan?

"Aren't you going to jack up the car? Cripes"

"Yes, want to loosen the nuts first. It's easier that way."

"Easy shmeezy." Gramps turned away.

Mike sighed and continued loosening the other nuts.

Then he set the wrench on the ground so he could position the jack.

"On the rag. On the rag."

Mike looked at Gramps, who was looking at him again.

"Put the wrench on the rag. Haven't you learned nothing?"

Mike set the wrench on the rag.

"Make sure you get that in the right spot; where there's a space in the edge on the frame."

"I know Grampa. I see it."

"Make sure you do."

Mike set the jack in place then turned the screw on it by hand until it snugged against the frame.

"You better put a board under that."

"Mike looked up at his grandfather. "Huh?"

"Under the jack so it don't sink into the dirt."

"It's solid enough here."

Gramps looked him. Mike stood up, brushed his hands on his pants then headed back to the barn.

"Hurry up."

Mike started trotting.

By the time Mike was putting the jack back into the trunk he had made three more trips to the barn including one to get a large garbage bag to put the flat tire into. "Don't want any of that dirt in my trunk."

Glad that task was over Mike closed the trunk lid being careful not to slam it. Gramps stood looking at him.

"What?" Mike asked.

"Wipe it."

"What?"

"The edge of the trunk. You've left fingerprints on it."

Mike looked and saw a couple of small smudges on the paint. He picked up the rag from the ground, gave it a shake then moved to the trunk.

"Not that one." Grumps yelled. "That's dirty, it'll scratch the paint."

Mike's shoulders sagged then he trotted to the barn one

more time.

Finally, Gramps got in his car and started the engine. He rolled down his window and Mike stepped forward to receive the thanks that had to be coming. It would be nice to hear that at least once from this man.

"Don't forget to put all that other stuff back where you found it." Gramps pointed toward the blocks and plank and things that Mike had gotten from the barn to do the job Gramps' way.

"Sure. Of course." Gramps backed up, turned then headed out of the driveway. Mike gave him a weak wave then began gathering up the stuff in the driveway.

After he had put everything away, Mike headed back into the house.

"How did you make out?" Gramma turned from the stove.

"Got it done but wow, is Gramps ever picky about how to do things. It took way longer than it needed to." Mike turned into the bathroom to wash up.

"He does have his ways." Mike didn't close the door so he could hear her. "You deserve a special breakfast for coming to his rescue."

"Don't know that I was much of a rescue." Mike scrubbed at the dirt on his hands. "In the time it took, the CAA people would have been here."

"Maybe but then you two wouldn't have done it together."

"He didn't even say thanks." Mike dried his hands on the towel hung by the sink.

"Well, he hasn't been big in that area. He does notice though. You can count on that. French toast?"

"Love it." Mike sat at the table.

Gram whisked an egg mixture in a bowl and dipped a piece of bread in it. The bread sizzled when she placed it in the frying pan. She talked while she worked.

"What's on your agenda today?"

"I was going to work on the barn but I'm feeling tired

now. Gramps had me run to the barn about a thousand times. How do you keep the bread from breaking? Mom always breaks the bread."

"She probably leaves it to soak too long. The secret is to just coat the bread, not make it sopping."

"You sure are smart Gramma."

Gram smiled. "Oh, I don't know about that. I've done this a lot. Bert, Gramps, likes French toast on Saturdays."

"Maybe I'll just go to town today. Look around. Maybe have a swim."

"Sure, take a day off. You've been working hard these past few days and this is supposed to be your summer holidays."

* * *

Mike headed into town carrying his towel and trunks. He checked out some of the stores and bought himself a backpack. He stopped into the Chuckwagon and had a glass of root beer. It was cold and thick, served in a frozen beer mug. Then it was time for a swim.

Just before he reached the pool, he heard his name.

"Hey." Mike approached Jack and Alan.

"Hey." Jeannie stepped out from behind Jack. Mike smiled.

"We missed you yesterday." Jack said, his voice flat.

"I told you he'd chicken out." Alan spoke for the first time then turned to Mike. "You missed out on some small-town fun."

"What's up?" Mike offered.

"We've got a road trip planned." Jack smiled. "You got a bike?"

"Bike?" Mike felt a bit deflated, "Not here."

"Hmmm," Jack looked at him. "No, never mind. You can double on mine. We're not going far."

They headed toward the ball fields. Mike followed. The

three teens chatted as they walked across the grass toward a set of steps that led up to street level. Mike tried to follow their conversation, looking for a way to join in but didn't find one. It was as though they were speaking just ahead of his comprehension, not letting him catch up. He wondered if it was on purpose.

At the top of the stairs Mike saw three bikes chained to a signpost. Alan pulled a key from his pocket.

"Helmets?" Mike asked. The other three just looked at him. "Oh, they're mandatory in Kingston." He added in a quieter tone.

Each straddled their bike. Jack turned to Mike, "hop on." Mike moved in close and sat on the seat of Jack's bike. Jeannie and Alan were already riding off the curb and across the road. "Hold on." Jack pushed on one pedal, then the other. The bike wobbled a moment then, as it picked up speed, it straightened. They thumped off the curb. A car horn blared. "Yeah, yeah." Jack intoned. He pumped harder and the bike accelerated. Mike had to hold his feet up and out. He held onto the back of the seat but felt like he was going to fall backward.

"Hold on to my shoulders," Jack offered, "you're swaying all over back there." Mike felt steadier then but uncomfortable. He wondered if he had made a good choice to come along. He wondered where they were going, he hadn't been in this part of town before.

"Where we going?"

"Not far. You'll like it." Jack continued pumping.

The road they were on was one of two main ones that crisscrossed at Aylmer's midpoint, John and Talbot Streets, but they were moving away from that intersection, heading north on John. It was wide but only one lane in each direction with parking space against the curb. Soon the curb and paved parking fell away and then it was just a two-lane highway. Mike grew a bit worried.

"You said it's not far."

"It's not. Just up ahead." Jack was breathing heavier;

Mike could feel sweat seeping through his shirt. His legs were heavy, and he wished he could rest them. He thought about seeing if he could put them on the rear wheel axle nuts, even for a minute, but was afraid he might get his toes in the spokes.

Soon the houses that lined each side of the street gave way to industrial buildings. One was a large white warehouse looking building. On the other side of the street was a compound of several red brick buildings surrounded by a chain link fence.

"That used to be the Carnation Milk plant." Jack pointed his chin at the white building. "Bet you didn't know the contented cows came from Aylmer. That there's the tobacco plant." Mike pointed with one hand. The bike wobbled and he returned his hand to the handlebar. "All the leaves come here to be made into smokes. You did know Aylmer is in tobacco country?"

"I had heard."

"Lots of people work here in harvest. Me and Alan have jobs but they don't start until August when the tobacco is ripe. We'll make a ton of cash. Until then it's party time."

About a mile past the tobacco plant, a county road crossed the highway. Jack had taken the lead and turned onto the smaller road.

"Almost there."

Mike was happy for that, his thighs were burning.

Another mile and Jack turned into a gravel driveway. Tall bushes grew along the road and the driveway cut through them and turned at the bottom of a small incline into a wide parking area. Across the parking lot stood a grey, cinderblock building that looked long abandoned. Jack glided to a stop at the start of the driveway.

"What's this place?" Mike asked.

"Fucker's Heaven." Alan and Jeannie skidded their bikes to a halt beside Jack's.

"Trucker's Haven," Jeannie gave Jack a disgusted look. "Used to be a kind of hotel and restaurant."

Mike looked around. Tall grass grew between the

parking lot and building. He could hear bugs humming and chittering in the grass and bushes that surrounded the area. The sun cast shadows across the gravel. After the drone of the tires on asphalt and Jack's laboured breathing, everything seemed quiet.

"Now it's just a target." Jack bent down, picked up a rock and threw it at the building. Glass smashed and the rock clattered on the floor inside. Alan and Jeannie also threw stones at the building.

Mike was surprised. This wasn't what he expected their adventure to be, was certain he didn't want to be part of it. What was he to do? He was stuck out here, not certain where 'here' was and he didn't want to not fit in, after all, Jeannie was here. Anyways, it was an old building, obviously no one cared about it. Many of the windows had already been busted out, only shards of glass remained in some of the panes. He stooped and picked up a rock.

The others looked at him before throwing more stones. Mike felt they were waiting for him to do something, gauging his reaction. He bounced his stone in his fingers a moment then pulled back his arm and launched the rock. Everyone laughed until they heard tires crunch on gravel behind them.

Mike turned to look. He heard his rock clatter against the cinder block wall, he had missed hitting a window. He saw the black and white of a police cruiser sitting at the top of the driveway. O.P.P., the moniker of the Ontario Provincial Police gleamed in gold on the car's door. Mike was all too familiar with them from some of the issues he had been involved with back home, what he was trying to get away from.

"The cops." Jack called out. 'Scram."

Jack, Alan and Jeannie picked up their bikes and ran toward the building. Mike just stood there, not certain what to do. The police car began rolling down the driveway, a voice blasted from it. "Stay where you are." Mike felt his scrotum crawl into his body, he felt tingly all over. His heart raced.

Looking toward the bushes, Mike measured his chances of getting away. He thought he could make his way through them but then what? He would have to follow the road back to town, he didn't know any other way and he would be easy pickings for the police. And, after all, he hadn't really done anything wrong, hadn't even busted a broken window. What was criminal about throwing a rock against a brick wall? Surely running from the cops was much worse than that. He chose to just stand there, feeling small.

As Jack and the others disappeared around the corner of Trucker's Haven, the cop car sped up, leaping forward. It slewed around the bend, tires spitting up gravel. Mike thought now might be a good time to head the other way but realized he would still have the same problem...no way home except the obvious. He decided to just sit down and await the return of the cruiser.

He listened to the sounds coming from behind the building, mostly confusion and racing engine. At one point he thought he heard Jack laugh but it may have only been a bird screeching. After a few minutes the police car drove out and stopped a few feet from Mike. The officer shut off the motor and climbed out. Mike could hear the engine ticking away its heat. The sudden silence closed in as though it had weight.

"I was pretty sure you kids would be back." The cop said as he approached Mike. He was fidgeting with something on his belt. Mike looked at him. *Back?* "Hooligans cannot resist returning to the scene of the crime."

"I was just..." Mike started.

"Shut up unless I speak to you."

Mike didn't offer that the cop had spoken to him.

"Stand up. Turn around." The cop held a pair of handcuffs.

Mike did as he was told, putting his hands behind his back. This wasn't his first time. "That's not neces..."

"Shut up. The only thing I want you to say are the names of your friends." Mike felt strong hands on his shoulders, his feet kicked apart. He almost fell forward, but the cop held him.

"Who?"

"Don't play stupid with me. I know that was Jack Braxton and Alan Carmen. Am I right? Who was the other one?" Hands patted him down, chest, stomach, crotch both legs. Mike was spun around, face to face with the officer.

He was young, Mike realized. Couldn't be more than twenty-two or three. Mike glanced at the name tape on his chest, CAMPBELL. Mike didn't say anything.

"You are in a lot of trouble. Cooperating will go in your favour." Officer Campbell gave his arm a little shake.

"All I did was throw a rock against the wall. I admit that." Campbell opened Mike's backpack and rummaged inside. He tossed it toward the cruiser as though disappointed it didn't hold anything more than a towel and bathing suit.

"You were here yesterday, broke in the back, smashed up everything inside. Will you admit that?" The cop led Mike to the cruiser, opened the back door, put his hand on Mike's head, pushed him in then reached across and buckled his seat belt.

* * *

"Well, I hope you are proud of yourself. You've been here four days and already in trouble with the police." Gramps shook his head. He had been pacing the kitchen for five minutes, his cane tap, tap, tapping. HIs foot clomp, clomp, clomping. "Can't wait to let your parents know what you've been up to, how well we've done by you."

Mike sat at the table, head down. He had tried a couple of times to defend himself, let them know he wasn't as guilty as he seemed. Grumps hadn't let him get a word in, told him to shut up, they would let his actions speak for him. Mike struggled not to cry, he was too old for that but he couldn't forget the look on Grandma's face when the officer took him out of the cruiser; removed the handcuffs. If he had never known what disappointment looked like, he did now. He wanted to explain but knew now was not the time.

"Go to your room. I can't stand looking at you."

Grumps pointed.

Mike skittered away from the table trying to make himself as small as possible; as small as he felt.

"Bert," Mike heard his Grandmother, "don't you think..."

"He should think!" Grumps cut her off. Mike didn't hear any more as he ducked past the curtain, dove onto his bed. He'd really messed things up yet he really hadn't done anything wrong, except not telling the police who he had been with. They knew anyway. And why had he bothered to protect them? Cripes, they took off, leaving him there to be caught. He wasn't a rat, that's why.

The cop had worked on him all the way home, threatening him, trying to get him to tell on the others. And he almost had, just to shut the cop up but then he got angry and when he got angry he knew he had to keep his mouth closed. Too much trouble when he hadn't in the past. And that was part of the reason his parents needed time to themselves. The things he did when he was angry were complicating their relationship. Again, this whole situation was his own fault. Today didn't seem fair. He had been trying to do the right thing. Find some friends, keep busy doing things that wouldn't land him in trouble. He was jinxed.

At supper Mike just picked at his food. Grumps was still angry even though he didn't say anything. Gramma tried a couple of times to start some light conversation, but her words simply hung over the table. She did smile at Mike and that lightened his mood a bit, she still loved him, but even that made him sorrier for being brought home by the cops. He wanted so bad to talk to her but he couldn't with **HIM** there.

After a bit Mike offered to clear the table, do the dishes but Grumps cut him off.

"Back to your room. You'll probably throw the dishes at the sink."

"Bert." Gramma started but was silenced by the look he cast at her.

Mike hunkered out of the room. He had seen this same

behaviour in his parents too many times and knew if he stayed it would only make things worse, end up with them fighting. He decided he would let his parents know his side before they got anyone else's. He took his cell phone from the bedside table drawer.

Hi Mom and Dad. You are going to hear that I got in trouble today. I didn't know what the kids I was with were planning and I got caught up with them throwing stones at an abandoned building. The police caught us, me, and brought me back to Grandma's. Grandpa's really mad and won't listen. I'm sorry I threw a rock. I know it was wrong and I am willing to take my punishment, but the cops think I smashed up the inside of the building yesterday, but I was working here all day. Everyone's mad I won't tell who I was with...I just met them. I wanted you to hear it from me first. I'm sorry I screwed up again.

He felt tears well up, blurring his vision. He wiped at his eyes, refusing to give in and start bawling. Mike read through the email twice, corrected a couple of spelling mistakes then pressed *Send*. He checked his emails to see if any of his friends had written, they hadn't, then he checked Facebook to see what was happening back home without him; not much.

Mike heard raised voices, not yelling but definitely two people not seeing eye to eye. Then a door banged. A moment later Mike heard the distinct sound of the hasp that held the outer door of the back-porch clap open then clump closed. After a brief pause, a car door opened, slammed, then the motor started. After another few moments, the sound of tires on gravel then the engine noise, growing louder, then quieter as the car passed the house and headed up the road. It was unusual for Grumps to go out in the evening. He knew it was Grumps.

A few minutes later he heard Grandma outside the curtain of his room.

"Mike?" The curtain moved just a bit.

"It's ok Gramma, you can come in." Mike sat up on the bed as the curtain was pulled back and Gramma came into the room. She looked older than Mike remembered. His heart burned and he felt tears build in his eyes. He resisted.

"I'm sorry," She started to speak as she sat on the edge of the bed.

"No, I'm sorry." Mike sat up straighter. "This is my fault, I know that. I didn't mean it but I did it. I don't know why I always seem to get myself into trouble, but I have really been trying to be good, to do the right things." Mike felt his voice cracking, the tears threatening to spill out. He paused to let himself settle down, get a grip, then he reached out to her and took her hand. "You do believe me don't you?"

"Michael," it was the first time she had called him that and Mike felt himself grow smaller inside, "I have seen a lot of things in my days, learned from trying to see both sides of a situation. I don't always get it right, sometimes I get it completely wrong despite being slow to form opinions." She paused and looked him in the eyes. Then she smiled. "Mike," she patted his hand, "I have seen you display some pretty incredible tolerance and judgement as you have tried to figure out how to deal with Bert, uh Grampa. I have tried to only offer you advice in that matter, leaving you to figure the rest out and you've done a wonderful job. You haven't got there yet but you're well on your way. You are a smart kid and you've shown me you are not afraid of hard work. These are the things that tell me I can trust you. It's not the words that come out of your mouth, anyone can say things, and it's the showing that speaks loudest. I don't know what really happened at that Trucker Haven place, but I think you are telling as much of the truth as you feel you can. I'm not certain why you feel you need to protect those other kids, but I trust your judgement in the placement of your loyalties."

"Thank you, Grandma." Mike hugged the woman, tucked his head against her breast. She flopped her hands in her lap then hugged him as best she could with her arms pinned to her sides as they were. "Thank you. Somehow I will make up for this."

"Don't worry too much. A muffin can never be just flour again but what it has become can be a wonderful thing in itself."

"How am I ever going to fix this with Grumps....er Gramps." Mike sat back releasing her from his bear hug.

"Is that what you've taken to calling him?" The old woman raised a hand to the bun she had pulled her hair into that morning. "Guess he's earned it." She looked at him with a stern look in her eye, her lips pursed. "But don't ever say that where he might hear you. He's your grandfather and he deserves respect. If you knew..." She waggled a finger at him then smiled. Mike saw the age fall away from her face when she smiled, and he saw her as the young woman who crossed a dance floor to lay claim to the man who had caught her fancy. In that moment he knew why Grandpa had fallen in love with her. She was beautiful. Inside and out, she was beautiful.

"What's going to happen to me with the police?" Mike turned his attention to the dark question that had been picking at his mind.

"I don't really know. I haven't ever been this close to something like this, but I do recall a long time ago when Bert, Grumps," Gram smiled and looked at her hands. "Gramps borrowed a rake from his Uncle Silas. Silas had a farm not too far away, just a tobacco field now. Anyway, Gramps had borrowed a rake to do some haying. We had a small hay field for the cow we had then. Not big enough to need a tractor, could be all done by hand. About a week later Silas came by and asked Bert to give him a drive into town. Of course Bert did, that's what you do for family. Dropped him at the four corners then came home. About twenty minutes later Silas drives in with the constable, didn't have any Provincial Police in those days, just a local sheriff. Anyway, seems that Silas wanted Bert arrested for stealing the rake. Bert explained to the sheriff that he had borrowed the rake, not stolen it. Silas piped up saying 'you should have returned it by now, hay was off the field.' Bert asked him if he needed it? Silas said no, but it had been borrowed out long enough. Bert told him if he wanted it back, he should have just asked. Silas said he shouldn't have had to."

Mike smiled at the story. "So Gramps has a criminal past."

"The point is, everything is in its perspective. Sometimes everyone can be right and sometimes everyone can be wrong and sometimes right is somewhere in-between it all. Anyway, that's the closest I've been to those kinds of activities so I'm not sure what will happen. Gramps didn't do no hard time for that." Gram stood up. "You're young, that'll probably be taken into consideration. Likely what you do from here on out will be looked at too." Gram moved to the curtain then turned back to Mike, "Whatever happens I will still love you just the same Mike. Don't you ever worry about that."

"I know Gramma. I'll try to do better."

"No try. Do." She replied in a decidedly Yoda-like voice. She was smiling when she left the room.

Mike couldn't believe his Grandmother had just quoted Star Wars. Who knew? He sat back on the bed, moved himself so his back was against the headboard, padded by the pillows. He reached for his book, opened it, began reading. Five minutes later he realized he was still reading the first paragraph and had no idea what it said, his mind was mulling over his conversation with his grandmother.

She had said "he deserves respect. If you knew..." That was the second time she had alluded to Grumps that way, the first being when she had related about the dance. Who was he really? And what had the war done to shape him into the muffin he was now? What could Mike do to learn more about his grandfather?

Grounded

The next morning Mike ate breakfast in relative silence. Grumps sat chewing his toast over and over and over before swallowing. He hadn't said anything more about yesterday but the silence in the kitchen was heavy. Finally, after managing to finish the last piece of toast, Grumps stood up, scraping his chair on the floor, and said, "Consider yourself grounded anyway for your shenanigans yesterday. I think its best you stick around here for the next little while. Keep you away from temptations you can't resist."

Grounded? Mike felt lead in his guts. That would keep him even closer to Grumps. Great. He wanted to retort, to defend himself but he knew it wouldn't do any good so he simply replied, "Yes sir. Is it ok if I go in the barn today?"

"What do you want in there? I thought you were going to sweep it out?"

He simply said, "I got distracted, I'm going to do that today and anyway, I like it in there. It smells like yesteryear."

The old man cocked one eyebrow at him and stared for a moment then grunted. Gram turned from the sink where she was washing up the breakfast dishes. Heading into the living room Grumps said, "If you had done it yesterday, you wouldn't have got in trouble. Alright, but don't get into anything. And stay out of the loft, it's filthy up there."

Gram came to the table to pick up Gramp's plate and Mike's cereal bowl. "What are you up to young man?" She asked quietly, a mischievous smile on her face.

"He doesn't know about the barn?" Mike whispered back.

"He peeked inside yesterday but only downstairs."

"Nothing bad," Mike responded to her earlier question. "I need to finish up in there and check out some stuff."

"Ok, have fun."

"Can I help you finish up the dishes?"

"No, this is easy work. You go do your checking out."

Mike stepped up behind the woman and kissed her on the cheek. "You are the best Grandma."

"I know." She smiled and returned to washing the dishes.

***

"My word." Mike turned, startled by the words behind him. Grandma stood just inside the doorway. "You are doing an incredible job Mikey. I've never seen this place look so good."

Mike had finished brushing down the ceiling and between the rafters, cleaned out three of the stalls and was just heading toward the last one, the one in the furthest corner when Grandma spoke.

"Just this last stall and then I'll finish up with the floor, put things away."

A look crossed Grandma's face, it drew firm, tight. "Oh, that one." She strode across the barn getting between Mike and the stall. The space was dim, the fluorescent light above it was dark, Mike hadn't been able to find a switch for it so had figured the neon tube was burned out. In the stall was a large object covered by an old, dirty, stained tarp. Grandma touched the tarp with her toe. "You should just leave this one as it is. Just finish up the floor."

"How come Grandma?" Mike stepped toward it. He had seen the tarp earlier, been curious about what the odd shaped object was underneath it but hadn't ventured in there yet. "What is it?"

"It's Bert's, Grandpa's." She corrected herself. "Best just to leave it be."

"OK," Mike looked at his watch, "I'll finish up the floor. I should still have time for a swim at the pool." Then he remembered he was grounded. "Crap, guess no swim."

"Nice work." Grandma walked across the barn. She touched a few of the stall panels then looked at her fingers.

"Thanks Sergeant." Mike smiled at her.

She smiled back. "I wasn't..."

"I know."

Then Mike was alone again in the barn. With the tarp draped shape.

As he swept the floor he couldn't keep from casting glances toward the fourth stall. The old cover had an odd shape and Mike tried to imagine what could be under there. It was kind of diamond shaped at the front, wide at top and floppy down the sides. When he swept near the stall, he accidentally on purpose bumped the tarp with the head of the broom. The object shuddered a bit. The bump had felt soft, not like something hard, solid. Mike stopped, wanted to just lift that tarp and satisfy his curiosity but Grandma's words bounced in his head 'Best just to leave it be.' Mike resisted, finished up, and then headed to the workbench.

While tidying up the workbench area, Mike arranged the tools on the pegboard. He could tell where most of them went because someone had painted the shapes around them. He had wiped the dusty pegboard with a cloth. Most were already hanging but a couple were in disarray on the bench. Mike thought that was a bit odd with how meticulous Grumps had been with his car. Beneath the bench were a series of drawers and cupboards containing all sorts of containers with nails, screws, oils, some old cans of paint, a bag with brushes, and cans of solvents.

In one drawer he found a stack of magazines. 'Ho, ho, ho,' Mike thought to himself, 'Gramp's porno stash.' But on investigation they turned out to be old Legion magazines. The bawdiest thing he saw when he flipped the pages of a couple was a stripped-down Bren gun in an article about field care of weapons. He simply restacked the magazines into a neat pile and closed the drawer. 'Figures.' He thought.

In a grey metal locker that had a few rust blisters bubbling through the paint, Mike found a golf bag with two woods and four irons. All were covered in a layer of dust and decorated with spider webs. Rust spotted the heads and shafts. Mike was intrigued, he had always wanted to try golfing. He took out the nine iron and gave a couple of slow practice swings. He wondered how it would feel to knock a few balls with that. Then he thought of Grump's frown and put the club away. He wondered if he could ever get his relationship with Grumps to the point where he could ask if he could use the clubs? He wiped the clubs with the rag, and then he wiped the bag. He put a bit of oil on the rag and wiped the clubs again to keep them from rusting any more. He closed the locker door with a metal clang that sounded like a jail cell slamming shut.

That evening they had tea on the porch again. Although it seemed a bit hokey to Mike, he kind of liked it too. He felt relaxed and he enjoyed listening to Gram's voice as she spoke. There was a soothing quality to the lilt of her words.

"It's too bad you are grounded; I think you would have enjoyed the Sales Barn."

"Sales Barn, what's that?" Mike asked.

"It's kind of like a huge rummage sale but better. Vendors come to the market from all over, set up their booths and sell stuff."

"Like a mall?"

"Kind of but better. Most of the stuff isn't new, lots of good used things. Lots of junk too, but you know what they say about one man's trash. It's kind of like a carnival too, lots of people, music, aromas, cotton candy."

"Food too?"

"Yes. There are butchers and bakers..."

"Candlestick makers?"

Gram laughed. "Sometimes there are those who make candles. It's never the same, but lots is the same too. I go when I need fresh vegetables or sometimes when I want a foot-long hot dog." She turned and smiled at Mike. He smiled back seeing the little girl that still lived in this woman.

"When is it?"

"Every Tuesday."

Mike thought about that. "It sounds like fun. Maybe when I'm not grounded, we can go."

Snooping

The next morning Mike waited for Grumps to leave. He had been thinking of how he might get to know the man better. After the car drove out of the driveway, he headed out the back door. As soon as he was inside the barn, he went straight to the workbench and opened the drawer full of Legion magazines. He had looked at a few of the covers as he had straightened up the pile the other day but now he opened the top one and began reading. After a few minutes he took a folding lawn chair from the hook he had hung it on yesterday, opened it, sat and continued reading.

By the time Gram called him for lunch he had worked his way through more than a dozen magazines.

"You've been quiet out there." Gram said when Mike came into the kitchen.

"Wow, this place smells wonderful. Cookies?"

"Go wash up and maybe you can have some after lunch."

"I'll wash twice." Mike said and the old lady laughed. "Can we eat on the porch again?"

"Don't see why not."

Mike washed then helped take the food to the porch.

"What have you been up to out there all morning? Not cleaning again?"

"No, reading. There's a pile of magazines in the workbench."

Grandma raised an eyebrow. "Magazines?"

Mike looked at her then laughed. "Legion magazines." Grandma's face relaxed. "They are all about stuff about the war and what veterans are doing now and about how the Legion is doing things in towns all across the country."

"And you like that stuff?"

"I do now. Hadn't thought about it much before but it's pretty interesting."

"Interesting?"

"Yeah, war is really complicated. All different kinds of weapons and vehicles and people from all over the world. Different terrain, strategies, just feeding the soldiers was a huge deal. And there is stuff in there about Afghanistan and Iraq and Bosnia; stuff that's going on now. Different places, different weapons, different tactics, same challenges. And the stuff the politicians did and do. It's pretty complicated."

"Well I'm glad it's over."

"But it's still going on. It's in the news a lot, but I like the Second World War stuff. That's what Gramps went to right?"

"Yes. He went at the start and was gone for five years."

"What did he do there?"

"Oh, I don't know too much. He doesn't talk about it. When he came home, he just said 'I'm back, that's done, let's get on with things.' and that's about that."

"Is there a Legion here?"

"Yes, it's on John St."

"Is that where Gramps goes"

"He still has friends there but fewer every year."

"Friends eh?"

They finished eating but the talk changed to the weather and about how the crops in the nearby fields were growing well.

"Gramma, do you still have the card the police officer gave you yesterday?"

"It's in the junk drawer. Why?"

"I think I'd like to speak with him again if that's ok."

"I guess so. And Mike," Grandma paused until Mike looked at her, "that stuff we were talking about, the war and all? I think it would be better if you didn't mention it to Grampa. Some beasts are best left sleeping."

Mike found the business card in the drawer, retrieved his cell phone and headed back out to the barn. He had an important phone call to make and more reading to do.

That night at dinner Mike asked if it was ok if he went to the library tomorrow.

"You're grounded." Gramps said, speaking around a mouthful of mashed potatoes and gravy.

"Oh yeah." Mike said, "How long?"

"Rest of your life."

"Bert!" Grandma exclaimed. "Be fair."

"Did you see what him and his hooligan friends did to that place? They smashed it all up inside. Looked like a war zone."

"Grampa," Mike started, "I didn't do that. I was here when that happened. I was only ever there once, and I only threw one rock. It didn't even hit anything, except the wall."

"Don't try to minimize what you did."

"I'm not. I'm owning up to my actions. I don't think it's fair for me to be blamed for stuff I didn't do."

"You're protecting those other ones. Those hoods."

"Now boys. We are trying to have a nice meal here." Grandma remained calm despite the voices of the others being raised. "What's at the library Mike?"

Mike sulked over his food for a minute. He had been perfectly calm, had been thinking about how to ask what he wanted without upsetting Grumps and it had flared up faster than a match on gasoline. "I want to do some research."

"Huh," Gramps chuffed, poking some sausage into his mouth with his fingers. Gramma smacked his arm gently. "Probably wants to learn how to make explosives. Do a better job on Truckers Heaven."

"Haven, Gramps. It's Truckers Haven and no, I don't want that, I just want to learn more about some stuff I heard about. I want to use their computers. They have internet there."

"I think that might be ok," Grandma kept her voice calm and turned to Grumps, "As long as he stays away from those other kids. I don't think they're good for him." She stood and began clearing her dishes from the table.

"Don't be giving into him so easy. What's he done to show us we can trust him."

"Oh, Bert, go a little easier on the boy. Didn't you

make some mistakes when you were his age?" She turned on the taps to fill the sink with water.

"When I was his age, I was working the farm, getting ready for harvest, not running around smashing up other people's stuff."

Mike felt the pressure building up inside himself. He had felt this before, mostly at school when teachers, bullies, and even the principal were all riding his case. He wanted to just explode, let loose with his words, push back, protect himself. But then he thought about how Grandma might react to that, judge him by his actions regardless of what set him off. She was remaining calm, but Mike was certain she was angry inside too. And wasn't she coming to his defense but doing it in a way that wouldn't ignite Grumps? Maybe he could do that too. He felt the bubble of anger move down a bit. He chewed his food a few more times, forcing that bubble to shrink, gathering himself to say the right things.

"Grandpa, can I show you what I did in the barn? I cleaned up out there."

"You better have left everything where it was. I don't want you messing in my things."

"I didn't do any messing."

"I'm going to watch my show." Grandpa pushed himself away from the table and headed into the living room.

After he was gone Mike stood then took the dishes to the sink. He picked up a towel and began drying the dishes Grandma had washed.

The sound of the TV came from the living room and Mike could see the flicker from the screen reflected on the wall.

"I'm sorry Grandma. I didn't mean to start all that."

"You didn't do anything; he's just being nasty. I actually thought you did quite well staying calm and reasonable. And he didn't say no to the library so let's leave it at that." After a minute she added, "I am a bit curious about what you are up to."

"Nothing bad Grandma. I promise." He wasn't certain

why he couldn't share his ideas with her, he just knew that now wasn't the right time.

When the dishes were done and the floor swept, Mike got his cell phone and went and sat in the living room. Grumps was watching a show, talking to the characters on the television. Mike had been hoping for Breaking Bad, he liked to watch that on Mondays, but it was a detective show. "Look in the closet," Grumps called out as though the actors could hear him, "not under the bed, that's where he wants you to look." Mike could sense the frustration in Grumps voice that no one seemed to be listening to him. He decided to go on the porch and check his phone.

There was an email from his parents.

> *Hi Mike. We were disappointed to hear about the trouble you got into but owning up to it is a good thing. Try to learn from the experience. We don't imagine it has helped with Grandpa. How is Grandma? Hope you two are getting along. Dad's busy here, his days are long. He is trying to get the project back on track but doing things here in Mexico is a lot different than at home. You would think that fewer construction standards would make things easier but trying to fix things takes a lot longer than doing them right in the first place. We love you and know you will figure things out. Love Mom and Dad.*

He read the message three times. The late evening sun was still at least an hour from dipping below the horizon, but the heat was rushing out of the day. A light breeze made Mike wish he had brought his jacket out with him. He didn't want to have to walk past Grumps again, so he just huddled himself. After a few more minutes he began to type.

Hi Mom and Dad, sorry to hear things are tougher than expected. The days must be hot there, they sure are here. I do like the long days. It's 8:30 and the sun is still up. Gram sure is a good cook and she likes to bake, I like that. She likes to feed me too. I will try to not be too fat when you get home. They have a cool barn here. Cool as in a nice place to be but it's cool inside too as in not hot. Love you both a lot...A LOT. Love Mike.

    Mike stayed on the porch until he heard the TV turn off. The sun was fully gone, and he was shivering. He could hear the floorboards creak as Grumps headed to bed. After sending the email to his parents he had read through the rest of his emails. There were messages from his best friends, Uwe and Chuck. Mostly they were razzing him about being away, but they also caught him up on some of the things he was missing back home. He fired off a couple of emails, telling them how great it was here and how much they were missing but he was pretty sure they would know he was lying. He didn't mention the police thing or Grumps. And there was a message from Janice.

    He knew Janice from school but they had never really hung out so he was surprised she even had his email address. In her email she said she had heard he was spending the summer in Aylmer and she had cousins in a nearby town and wondered if maybe Mike might run into them. She talked about getting ready for next year at school and some movies she had seen. Mike found it an odd email but, she was kind of cute, so it made him feel better.

    He replied to Janice, just a quick message letting her know he hadn't met her cousins yet but would try to look out for them. He mentioned that he wasn't watching any TV here, hoping she would write back to at least keep him posted on that kind of stuff. He thought it would be ok if she just continued writing.

After that he had tucked his phone away and just sat watching the shadows creep across the grass, listening to the crickets begin their evening orchestra. He stayed huddled there, just watching and thinking. How could he fix things with Grumps? The man seemed impossible to deal with, always turning things black. Was it even worth it? Then he thought about Gram and how kind she was, always thinking about him. And it was obvious she loved the man, despite himself. Mike nodded his head as though he had been speaking out loud. If Gram could love him, Mike could love him, would figure out a way to do that. If he never managed to get Gramps to see him for who he really is, that will be Gramp's loss. Mike realized he had no control over Gramp's view of the world, only how he presented himself in it. He mulled over how he could accomplish this resolution until the latch on the front door clicked open. Gram stuck her head out, but Mike didn't wait for her to speak.

"I'll be right in Gram. It sure is nice out here. The city is never quiet like this."

"The bugs are in full concert tonight." She looked across the lawn.

"Doesn't seem like noise to me, not like traffic and sirens and crowd sounds back home."

"We like it here." With that she closed the door. Mike thought that maybe this was what Gram thought about to keep herself calm, quiet evenings on this porch. After a few more minutes Mike unwound himself from the chair and headed into bed.

Harvest Dance

The next morning Mike woke to the aroma of frying bacon and pancakes. He loved pancakes. He got up, dressed and headed into the kitchen.

"Smells like heaven in here." He said. Mike could hear bacon sizzling in a pan on the stove. There was a large aluminum skillet on the back burner with four pancakes in it. Mike could see the bubbles breaking on the tops, so he knew they were ready to be turned.

"Hmmph." Grumps was sitting at the table reading the paper. A cup of coffee with a spoon sticking out sat near him. Gramma was at the counter.

"Pancakes?" She asked.

"Oh yeah, absolutely."

"How many can you eat?"

"How many can you make?"

"I can make them all day."

"I can eat 'em all day. Can I help?"

"You can get the juice and syrup from the fridge. Anything else you like on them?"

"Jam?"

"In the fridge."

Mike gathered the containers and set them on the table. Then he walked over to his grandmother and gave her a hug. As he walked past Grumps he said "Good morning Grandpa. Isn't this a wonderful day?"

"We'll see." Was all he said as he flicked the newspaper making it rattle.

Mike managed to eat eight pancakes and two rashers of bacon. He watched as Grumps nibbled his bacon, holding it in his fingers. Grandma had cooked it until it was so crisp it didn't bend when he picked it up. Mike could hear it crunch as the man chewed it.

Mealtime here was a lot different here than at home. At home they all talked, planned their day, recapped what had gone on that day or talked about what was in the news, goings on at school. Mike had to admit that lately, that had started to change, meals had been quieter, a sign of his parent's declining relationship but even then, they were still noisy and busy compared to here where it was mostly silence. He tried to initiate some conversation but was afraid he might say something and set Grumps off. He really didn't seem to have much in common with these people who were so much older than himself.

After Grumps left the table, Mike began clearing the dishes to the sink.

"Really shouldn't be doing that." Grumps had come back and was standing in the kitchen doorway. Mike looked at him.

"What?"

"Woman's work." Grumps continued to stand there, hands in his pockets. He wasn't smiling so Mike was certain he wasn't trying to be funny. Could Gramps be funny?

"I always help out at home." Mike responded trying to be light.

Grumps turned and walked away without saying anything else.

"You go on," Gram gave Mike a gentle push. "I can finish these up."

Mike headed outside. He didn't have anything particular to do but he was waiting for Grumps to head into work so he could go to the library. He was certain if Grumps knew he was going to go he would forbid it so he was content to bide his time. Mike wandered into the small garden and began pulling some weeds. He heard the backdoor bang open and closed.

"What are you doing in there?" Gramps called.

"A little weeding."

"You better not pull any of the vegetables. You know the weeds?"

"Grandpa."

"Friggin kids." Grampa muttered just loud enough for

Mike to hear. Then the car door slammed.

Mike's face burned. Why was this man so ungrateful? After the sound of the motor died away, the car passing beyond the curve in the driveway, Mike brushed his hands together and headed toward the house.

"Gram," he called, heading into the bathroom to wash his hands. "I'm heading into the library."

"Alright, you know where it is?"

"I Googled it last night."

"You what?"

"I looked it up on the internet. It's on John St." Mike had been amazed when he learned that the Legion and library were that close together. Visiting the Legion was in his plan, but maybe not today. He realized Jack must have peddled him right past it on their way to Trucker's Haven. He knew he was pushing it, being grounded and still going to the library, but he was working toward making things as right as he could.

"When you go, walk to Talbot street and then to John. If you go down South street, you will go right past Gramp's school. I don't think that would be wise."

"Thanks Gram. I'm taking my cell phone with me if you need to get hold of me."

"Ok. I have your number on the wall by the phone."

That was another thing Mike wondered about. Their phone was mounted to the wall and the handset was connected by a curly cord. Not even a cordless. There was a cluster of papers and business cards stuck to a cork board by the phone and jammed between the phone and the wall. A pencil hung on a string. It all seemed so archaic. He grabbed his stuff and headed out.

Mike was walking along Talbot Street, the main street that ran east and west, John was the other main street, running north and south, when he heard the squeal of bike brakes behind him.

"Hey, Mikey. How'd you get away from the cops?" Mike turned toward Jack and Alan.

"I didn't. You guys left me hanging there."

"You got nabbed?" Allan asked.

"Cops didn't visit us. Guess you didn't rat us out." Jack added.

"Look, I'm in a lot of trouble right now. The cops are pretty sure it was you who was with me. It would be better if we weren't seen together."

"Trouble? For throwing some rocks?"

"For busting the place up inside. I'm getting blamed for that and I think it was you, so you'll understand if I'm not all that thrilled to see you right now." Mike turned and started walking again. He heard shoes scuff on the sidewalk and creaks from the bikes and guessed they were following him. In a moment Jack spoke again.

"We don't know nothin' about that place being smashed up inside." He looked at Allen, then back at Mike. "We just go there sometimes."

"I'm not hearing you." Mike spoke without turning. He had heard Allan giggle after Jack's last statement so he was certain it was a lie.

"Well, thanks for not ratting us out. Later loser." Jack sped by Mike.

"Yeah, later loser." Allan rode by on Mike's other side. The two teens sped ahead, side by side, their bikes wavering a bit as they pumped the pedals hard to pick up speed. They turned right at the next street and disappeared beyond the houses there.

At John Street, Mike turned right. The library was a block that way. A little further past that he could see the school where Grumps worked. He headed inside the library, hoping they had computers with internet. They did.

Mike noticed a sign taped to one of the windows that bordered the door. It was advertising a pre-harvest dance being held at the arena. Wow, he was amazed that a small town like this even had an arena. He guessed it really wasn't so small, just small compared to Kingston. He wasn't much of a dancer, but he might be willing to try if Jeannie was there. She was part of the group that got him in trouble but, she was a girl too. And a pretty one. He wondered if she would be interested in going.

He opened the door and stepped into the cool interior. He stopped and spoke with the librarian at the front counter then headed to the bank of computers. They had twelve, four were only for accessing the library's database of books. The others were for the internet. None of them were being used.

Mike checked his emails then his Facebook account. He spent about an hour getting better caught up with everyone now that he wasn't using up his data on his cell phone. He realized he wasn't missing out on too much back home, just the time with his friends.

Then he got to his real reason for being here. Into the Google search bar he typed "Canadians in World War II" and began reading.

At noon he went to a restaurant for a burger and fries. He had some money in his bank account and he had his debit card. After lunch he wanted to get a look at the Legion, maybe go inside and speak to the Manager. When he had called Officer Campbell yesterday, he had explained that he was sorry for being involved in the Trucker's Haven thing and was anxious to make amends. When he had asked what was probably going to happen, Campbell told him he would likely get a fine, might have to pay for the damages, and probably get community work. The damages thing worried Mike because from what Campbell had said, they were extensive. Campbell told him that if he was innocent, he needed to give up the others. Mike wasn't about to do that and was certain he could convince the judge, with Gram giving him an alibi for the day the place was smashed, that he was innocent of that. The community service thing was why he needed the Legion. If he could volunteer there, he could get that done and maybe have a chance to speak to some of the veterans there who might know more about Grumps, or the war at least.

On the way he passed the swimming pool. From John street he was looking down and across the baseball fields, so he could see the whole pool deck. There were a lot of people splashing and laughing. There were no ball games going on so

Mike thought he would have a peek through the fence, maybe Jeannie was there without Jack. Maybe he could ask if she was going to the pre-harvest dance.

After heading down the stairs to the ball field and crossing the outfield, he hooked his fingers into the chain-link fence that surrounded the pool and searched the crowd for her hair.

The fence rattled. "Hey, missed you yesterday." Suzie had banged on the chain link. "Hardly recognize you with your clothes on."

Mike felt his face warm as he blushed. "Hi, uh, Suzie," Mike dug for her name and she smiled when he said it. Mike noticed that she was quite pretty when she smiled, a sparkle in her eye. "I was just seeing who was here."

"Oh, you mean Jack and them?" Suzie glanced around the pool deck then back at Mike. "I haven't seen them since the other day."

So, Mike thought to himself, she had been watching them...him?

"Not just them."

"Coming for a swim?" Suzie raised her hand to shade her eyes. "Not a great day for lengths but the water would be a break from the heat."

"Not today. I have to get back to the library."

"Oh well, maybe tomorrow." Suzie gave the chain-link a little shake.

"Maybe." Mike said then turned away.

"Hey Mike," he turned back to Suzie, "You heard about the dance?"

"Saw a sign."

"Going?"

"Don't know. Not much of a dancer."

"At one point you couldn't swim either I bet."

Mike waved, turned and headed across the ball fields. Two teams had begun to gather near home plate. Mike thought about Suzie's mention of the dance. Was she asking him to ask her to go? He climbed the steps returning to John street. He paused and looked back toward the pool. He could see Suzie walking around the pool, whistle in her mouth. He watched her for a few moments then headed toward the Legion, one block up.

He was walking up the sidewalk to the entrance when he noticed Grump's car in the parking lot. What was Grumps doing at the Legion? He was supposed to be at work. Mike turned away and headed back to the library.

As he entered, he had another look at the sign and noted the date of the dance. August 1, three weeks away. He wondered if he would be done his grounding by then. He would have to ask. He spent the afternoon reading more about Canada's involvement in World War 2.

At three o'clock the librarian came by his computer. "When people are waiting for the computers, we ask that you limit yourself to one hour."

"Oh sure, Mike said, "didn't mean to hog it."

"Doesn't get busy too often."

Mike signed off and gathered his stuff.

At supper Mike suggested they have tea on the front porch that evening. He knew Grumps liked his tea but usually had it while watching TV. He wanted to know about the limit of his grounding so he needed the best setting to get the best answer. The best answer would be a short period. He also wanted to ask Gramma about the dance. He knew Grumps would head to bed before her and maybe he could speak with her then.

"Jeopardy's on." Grumps stated.

"Oh Bert, you can miss an episode of Jeopardy. It would be nice to enjoy the evening." She turned to Mike. "What a wonderful suggestion."

Mike wiggled a bit in his seat. He saw a line cross Grump's forehead. "Maybe after Jeopardy." Mike wanted Grumps in as good a mood as possible so he just nodded in agreement. Grumps looked at him and gave a little grunt. Mike didn't know if that meant yes or no or what, but the line across the man's forehead disappeared.

Turns out it meant yes. Mike and Gram sat on the porch while Grumps called out answers to the TV. Mike was surprised by how many he got right. While the game show played, he asked Gramma about the dance.

"Did you want to go?" She asked.

"I thought about it. I don't really know much about country music?"

"Oh, they don't just play country, although there is a lot of that. They do big band and jazz and rock. Last year they even did some rap."

"You know rap?"

"I know about it. Don't know that I like it much. Seems pretty angry mostly. Hip-hop sounds nicer but I still can't dance to it. But lots of kids like it and this is a whole family dance."

"Do you and Gramps ever go?"

"Never miss it. Takes me back to the day." She paused and stared across the lawn. "The lights, the music, the laughter. Burgers and fried onions; smells so good. Sometimes it feels like time moves backwards when the music starts." She sighed; her hands clasped in her lap. "Bert, Gramps always goes too. It's a big thing in town. Sometimes the only time we get to see some people. They come from the farms all around too."

Inside they could hear the lilting song that indicated Final Jeopardy was underway. Grumps would be out soon. Gram poured the tea that had been steeping while they talked. "Hope it isn't too strong now. Gramps doesn't like it too strong."

A few minutes later the porch door clicked open then clunked closed. Gramps clomped across the porch, his cane thumping. Mike moved from his chair to the porch swing so Gramps could sit by Gram. Gram set the pot down then added cream from a small pitcher shaped like a cow. Grumps took the cup and stirred, clinking the sides with the spoon. Mike wondered if he was trying to churn the cream into butter he kept stirring so long.

"Gram says you and her always go to the big dance."

Mike spoke as light as he could.

The old man cocked an eye at Mike, pursed his lips and sucked some tea from his cup. Mike didn't see any curds floating in the light brown liquid, so he guessed Grumps hadn't stirred it THAT long. "She did, did she? Used to be better before all that rat music."

"Bert." Gram started then looked at Mike. "The first time we heard that music was at a sidewalk café in London. Bert asked the waiter to change it to something else and the waiter responded that rap was the only music they played there. With his hearing, Gramps thought he said rat and it's been that to him ever since."

"God damn rat crap spoils the air."

"Bert." Gram admonished.

"I was thinking I might like to go." Mike ventured.

"So, what's stopping ya?"

"You said I was grounded, but not how long."

"Rest of your life I'd say," Gramps looked a Mike, pegged him right to the chair with that hard stare, "but I guess if you keep your nose clean until then it would be alright."

Gram reached over and touched Bert's hand.

"What?" He exclaimed, glancing at her, "Oh, I know. You think I'm getting soft," he paused a moment, "but I'm not. Keep the kid grounded and he'll always be underfoot."

Mike sat back and smiled at his grandmother behind Grump's back. Grumps took another slurpy sip of his tea and stared at the sun as it grew wider and softer in its trip toward the horizon, a blazing ball of orange.

Mike Finds Work

The next morning Mike snuck off to the library again. He went by South street to see if Grump's car was at the school. It was. At lunch, he headed up to the Legion, checking for Grump's car in the parking lot. It wasn't. He had to press a buzzer at the door since it was locked. After a moment, there was a buzz and the door latch unlocked. Mike headed inside.

"No kids." A man behind the bar said, pointing out the way Mike had come in.

"I'm here to speak to the Manager." Mike stated. "Is he here?"

"She." The bartender shook his head then pointed with his chin toward a door. "In her office."

Mike knocked and entered when he heard "Come in."

"Nope, sorry." Sheila said after Mike outlined his proposal, "I would like to help you out but you're too young to work here."

"But I checked the laws." Mike countered. "As an employee I can be here, I am just not allowed to handle any alcohol. I can clean, clear tables, work in the kitchen. I can't serve alcohol, restock the booze, or even clear glasses that aren't empty, but I'll do anything else."

"I don't know." Mike liked Sheila, she seemed like a straight shooter, spoke her mind. "I'll check with Dominion." Mike wasn't sure what that was but he was hopeful it would be a yes.

"My grandpa is a veteran if that helps."

"Who's he?"

"Bert. Bert Weinstein"

"Who?"

"Weinstein."

"Hmm, Weinstein?"

"He was in World War II. Walks with a cane."

"You mean DR?"

"DR?"

"Sure, he comes here most days for a bit. So, his real name is Bert? Only ever known him as DR."

"DR?"

"Sure, he was a despatch rider in the war. Delivered messages and stuff by motorcycle. Everyone here calls him DR."

"Please don't tell him I was here."

"Why?"

"It would just be better if he didn't know. If I get to work here, it would be better if he didn't know."

"You'd have to dodge his schedule. Secrets can be hard things to keep, especially in a small town."

"If I get to work here."

Mike thanked Sheila for her time then headed back to the library. He really wanted to learn more about despatch riders. And he thought about the tarp covered object in the dark stall in the barn. Something about the shape.

Mike's buzzing phone roused him from his reading. He had been fully immersed in stories and information about despatch riders. He was both excited and a bit scared when he saw the caller ID RC Legion. It had to be Sheila. It was.

"Dominion says it's ok with them if it's ok with me so it's ok Mike. You seem like a nice young man. And your price is right."

"That's great." Mike sat up straighter in his chair thinking 'if only you knew about my past'. He had been wondering how to keep Gramps from knowing he was working there if he got the job and had come up with a plan. "Can you call me Doug? That's my middle name."

"Doug eh. That's how you'll hide yourself from DR? Sure Doug, we can do that."

"When should I start?"

"Tomorrow? The Ladies Auxiliary is having a tea at 10. Can you be here at 9? Ask for Donna, I'll let her know you're coming to help."

"Sure. I'll be there."

Mike hung up. He hadn't really wanted to work at

something like that, he wanted to get to talk to some of the men who might know his Gramps, but he was willing to do what it took to get what he wanted. He finished reading the article he had been roused from then headed home.

Along the way he thought about what to do, how to honour his grounding and do the volunteer work at the Legion. By the time he got back to his grandparent's house he had decided he would come clean with Grandma.

At supper Mike mentioned about having tea on the porch again. He knew gramps wouldn't join them until after Jeopardy. He could talk with Gram then.

"I looked in the barn today." Grumps frowned at his plate. "You were supposed to just sweep the floor. You did more than that, poking into other people's stuff."

Mike felt the heat rising in his neck again. He wanted to tell Grumps that he should appreciate what people did for him but that wouldn't help him accomplish what he was trying to do. Instead he said, "I saw some straw poking out of some holes in the rafters. When I looked, I saw they were bird nests. I figured you didn't want pigeons crapping over everything, so I cleaned them out too." It wasn't the whole truth, but it wasn't a lie either.

"Don't say crap. Birds turd."

"Sure Gramps, turd. I didn't want the birds turding in your clean barn."

"Hmph."

"Bert, you could say thanks for the work Mike did out there."

"Took him long enough to get it done and he should be thanking me for letting him do penance for throwing rocks."

"Oh Bert," Mike could hear the frustration and anger in Gram's voice, "the boy is trying to help you, trying to reach out to you and you keep shutting him down. Sometimes I think you just want to be miserable and you want everyone around you the same way.

"Hush woman," Grumps banged his hand on the table just hard enough get everyone's attention, "you mollycoddle him and he will never grow up."

Mike started to open his mouth to protect his grandmother and himself but caught himself before angry words could spill out. He reminded himself about some of the things he had read about the war, things Gramps had likely lived through, how he had put his life on the line for years and how, as Gram had said, the man deserved respect for that. Just how much respected Mike wasn't certain yet but until he figured that out, he wasn't going to dishonour him. He bit his tongue but tried to give his Grandmother a look that would let her know everything was ok.

Mike tried to distract the conversation. "What's under that tarp in the barn Grandpa?"

Grumps spun and stared at Mike. "You stay the hell away from that. It's none of your business."

The words felt like a smack. Mike's stomach burned and he felt the muscles in his face sag. "I'm sorry, I was just curious."

"Curiosity killed the scout." Grumps snapped.

"Cat." Mike couldn't stop himself from responding although he wondered how a Boy Scout would be killed by curiosity.

"That's what I said." Grumps pushed his chair away from the table. Mike let the comments go and Gram seemed quite unwilling to wade into the little argument. "I'm going to watch Jeopardy." Grumps tapped his way into the living room. Gram sat with her head down, hands in her lap, her supper not fully finished. Mike got up and moved around the table to stand behind her. The TV blared to life in the living room.

Mike put his hands on his grandmother's shoulders. "I'm sorry. I didn't mean to set him off."

"I know you didn't. Sometimes I wish I understood that man better."

"Let's do these dishes up then have tea on the porch. There is something I need to share with you. Maybe it will help."

Gram looked toward the living room then said, "Might

be better if I clean these up myself." Mike knew she was referring to Grumps' comment regarding woman's work. "You go do your phone thing. These won't take me long."

"I love you Gramma." Mike hugged her from behind and she patted his hands.

Slouched in the porch chair, he had remembered to bring his jacket with him but it wasn't quite cool enough yet for it, Mike read through his messages. There was one from his mom, not much had changed there but her choice of words seemed a bit lighter. He sure hoped they were fixing their marriage. He dreaded the thought of them splitting up, him having to choose between them, all the anger and emotion that would go along with that. Wasn't the thought of that enough to make people work hard to keep their relationships? He knew even from his experiences with his friends that you don't always get along, that you need to find some sort of compromise when there is disagreement. You don't always have to have your way, and you don't always have to give up your way. Sometimes you do it their way, sometimes your way, sometimes both modify what they want so everyone still gets enough of a win to feel important. Cripes him, Uwe and Chuck did that sort of stuff all the time. They were just kids and had it figured out. Chuck always wanted to go fishing but Mike really didn't like it much. They would still go but not all the time, and even when they did go, Mike wouldn't always fish. Sometimes he would bring a book and just read. Sometimes he would drive the boat, he loved that, and sometimes he fished so they would all have common stories to talk about later. Mike had found that that made it all worthwhile. He couldn't imagine how hard that could be when you were living with someone all the time, he got lots of breaks from his friends, but if you really want to be with the person, you have to work hard at it, only give up when one person is unwilling to bend on any issues under any circumstances. Mike wondered if that is the kind of man Grumps is? Did it rub off on his daughter, causing her some of the trouble in her own marriage? It did seem most of their arguments were over Dad not doing everything the way she wanted it done. At least where the fights seemed to start. But there was his own behaviour too.

He wanted to encourage his parents, so he made his response light. He didn't lie to them, but led them to believe that he was making headway in his relationship with Gramps...he honestly hoped he was, but it was so hard to tell. He had started an email to Uwe when Gram brought out the tea pot and cups on a tray, so he put his phone away. He could finish that later.

He stood to help her place the tray on the table. Gramps was still calling out answers at the TV. Mike had been so lost in his thoughts that he didn't know how often the man had been correct today but he expected it was often. He certainly knew a lot.

"Gram," Mike spoke soft after she had settled into her chair. He leaned toward her, leaning one elbow on his knee. She took the hint and leaned toward him. Mike noticed a mischievous glint in her eye, she knew they were about to have a clandestine conversation and she was looking forward to it. Mike marveled that she must have been quite adventurous in her youth.

"I got myself a job at the Legion today."

Her mouth formed into an oh but, before she could say anything, Mike continued.

"It's to begin making up for the Trucker's Haven thing. The cops said I would likely have to do some community service, so I am getting at it. It's volunteer."

"I'm surprised you can work there."

"As long as I never touch anything with booze in it it's ok. Lots of other work that I can do. I wanted you to know what I have been up to because I know I am grounded, and I am not trying to get out of that. I have been going to the library like I said but I made a couple of trips to the Legion to make arrangements."

"You know your grandfather goes there most days."

"Yeah and I want to keep this secret from him. They

are going to call me by my middle name and my shifts are going to be when he generally isn't there. If he shows up unexpectedly I can leave or work in another part of the building."

"Why the Legion if it makes it so complicated."

"So I can talk to the veterans there. I want to get to know Gramps better, maybe understand him. He doesn't seem to be willing to share but maybe he has with some of his war buddies. Maybe they will share with me."

"Well now, aren't you the clever one."

"Do you know his schedule at the school?"

"Some of it anyway. He's a handyman there so it changes if there are emergencies and stuff. Mostly he works mornings."

"And the Legion doesn't open until noon but sometimes they have morning activities. That's the Women's Auxiliary though, not much chance to speak with the Vets there.

"Well, many of those ladies were in the war too you know. Not just the men who pushed the Germans back you know. And some of them were war brides, English girls married the fighting men and then came back to Canada with them. You never know where you might find interesting pieces of information."

"I'll keep that in mind." And then Mike heard the final Jeopardy song and knew they had to change the subject. "I'm sorry I got myself grounded. I would like to go swimming."

"Girls, huh?"

"Gram!" But Mike knew the old lady was right. He had been thinking of Jeannie and the dance. "Well there's something going on tomorrow morning that I'm going to help with. I will see what happens."

Then the door banged open and Grumps clumped and tapped his way across the porch.

Grumps the Sportsman

The next morning Mike was anxious to get going but Gramps didn't seem in much of a hurry to head to work. By 8:30 Mike was worried he wouldn't be at the Legion on time. He didn't want to be late for his first assignment there.

"What's up with you." Grumps looked at him, that crease across his forehead said he wasn't in a good mood. Was he ever, Mike wondered?

"Nothing." Mike said but inside he was screaming 'Go to work.'

"You're fidgeting like a duck on a live wire." Grumps words didn't make much sense to Mike but he realized he was all keyed up inside.

"He's looking for something to do. A young man needs a mission." Gram stated from the sink.

"Well he can concentrate on not busting things up."

"Grampa," Mike started, "how many times do I have to say sorry?"

"I'm going to work."

Mike felt the breath whoosh out of him: 'finally.'

"And your sighs don't help none." Gramps misinterpreted Mikes breathing. He slammed the door on the way out.

After the sound of the car faded, Mike kissed his grandmother on the cheek and headed out. He would have to run to make it to the Legion on time now.

By the time he got there, he was out of breath and sweating. He went to the door but it was locked. He rang the buzzer but there was no response He went around back to that door and it was locked too. He noticed there were no cars in the parking lot. Maybe he wasn't the only one getting off to a late start. He sat down to wait.

About five minutes later a small grey car pulled in and a white-haired lady climbed out. Mike stood as she walked toward the building, digging in her purse and finally pulling out a large key ring. She looked at him.

"You must be Doug. I'm Donna." Mike almost corrected her but then remembered his Legion name. He smiled and reached out his hand. "Sheila said you'd be here. Can you get the stuff from the back of my car?"

Mike carried in three boxes and by the time he had done that, two other ladies, Pearl and Gertrude, had arrived.

Donna introduced him as a nice young man who wanted to help out.

"Well, we'll certainly put you to good work." Gertrude gave him a wink.

They all got busy preparing the food for the tea and they chattered amongst themselves all the while. Mike tried to follow along and ask relevant questions, but they spoke a lot about people Mike didn't know. He wanted to ask questions about the war, his grandfather, even the other vets but never found an opportunity to broach the topics.

Mike was given the task of setting up folding tables in the small basement hall and adding chairs. Pearl expressed how happy they were that he was there to do that work since it involved a lot of lifting. Mike was pleased to do it but it left him working mostly alone.

By the time ten o'clock came, the hall was full of elderly ladies, all engaged in frantic conversations. Then his grandmother came in. Mike was surprised and almost called out to her but remembered he was trying to keep is real identity a secret. He heard someone say, "Oh look, it's Lana, what a special day." Several ladies gathered around her and all chatted with intensity. His grandmother only gave him a quick nod and smile.

At eleven, the ladies started leaving. Mike began cleaning cups and plates and silverware from the tables and taking them into the kitchen. Pearl and Gertrude. 'call me Gertie', began loading the dishes into the dishwasher. Another lady, who had come as a guest but stayed to help and whose name Mike didn't know was also clearing tables.

"I'm Helen," she said when they began working on the

same table.

Mike took her offered hand and said, "I'm Mi.....Doug," remembering himself at the last moment.

"Midoug," that's a different name."

"No, it's just Doug. I'm a bit nervous."

"You seem a little out of place with all these old ladies but it sure is nice to see some young blood here. No need to be nervous, we hardly bite at all." She gave him a mischievous smile, "Most of the young people in town never come here."

"Everyone is so nice. I want to help out." Mike was a bit cautious in how much he was going to share with people he didn't know very well.

"Well, you are most welcome." Helen looked over Mike's shoulder and raised a hand with a finger that was half pointing, "Oh, there's Sheila. I better go say hi."

Mike looked over and Sheila smiled when she saw him, gave him a little wave. Mike waved back then went back to work.

After the hall was back to how it had been when they started, Sheila approached Mike.

"Glad you showed up. Pearl says you worked like a dog. Thanks."

"Actually, it was fun. I am kind of sorry it's over."

"If you are up to it, there are a lot of little socials like this."

"I'm up to it. I'm up to helping up in the lounge too."

"I like your enthusiasm. Let's go up and I will introduce you to whoever is tending bar today, I don't remember off-hand. Most of our bartenders are volunteers. We save the paid help for the busy evenings."

"Everyone works for free? You don't see that much."

"We see it a lot. It's how we support each other. Everyone pitches in and the work isn't so hard. Gives more visiting time too. Come on." Sheila headed up the stairs at the end of the hall.

"You survived downstairs with all the cougars?" Vic the bartender stated with a smile. Mike had noticed a real change in atmosphere as he came up the stairs. Where the hall downstairs had felt open and clean, there was a closed-in, heavy air feeling here in the lounge. The smell of old beer mixed with lingering tobacco was prevalent. Although it was likely no one had smoked in this room since before Mike was born, the walls and furniture had absorbed the smell for so many years and were only leaking it back out with reluctance. It wasn't altogether unpleasant, just noticeable.

"Behave yourself." Sheila admonished him. "Doug is young, may not understand your humour."

Sheila explained how Mike was able to help and what he was not allowed to do.

"Things will be a bit boring then, there won't be much business until after supper. Even then there won't be too many people I expect."

"That'll give you lots of time then to teach Doug what he needs to know." Sheila headed into her office.

"This ain't no rocket science." Vic called after her.

After working with Vic for a bit, Mike took a liking to him. He was quite willing to speak his mind and peppered his speech with profanities after which he always said, "pardon my French." Mike found himself standing around a lot, not knowing what to do. It seemed he spent more time getting out of Vic's way than he did doing anything else.

The downstairs hall had been bright and open, upstairs was darker, dark wood walls covered in memorabilia and plaques and flags. Up here there were few windows and those were small. There was a distinct change in mood in this room. After a bit Mike realized this was an area designed by men, the downstairs showed the tastes of women.

After a bit, a few older gentlemen came in and ordered drinks. Mike watched them from behind the bar. Now that he was where he had wanted to be, he wasn't sure how to get to the next part of his plan. It wasn't as though he could just walk up to those guys and say "hey, tell me about the war." Too, now that it was after lunch, he had to watch for Grumps coming in.

Mike watched as the men drank their beers, waiting for the moment when their glasses were empty, so he could go clear their table, bus the table as Vic had said. Actually, Vic had put in an extra word before 'table', adding "pardon my French." Mike had smiled wide at that.

Finally, one of the men set down an empty glass. Mike approached the table and reached for it even though the man's hand was still holding it. The man looked at Mike and cocked an eyebrow.

"You're glass." Mike said hesitantly.

"Don't worry kid. I'm not going to steal it." The man didn't smile. "Vic, there's a kid in here. No kids."

"He's working." Vic responded, "Let him clear your glass."

The man gave the glass a bit of a push toward Mike. "What'll they think of next. Vic, pour me another, maybe the kid can bring it to me."

"Come get it Andy, still self-serve here." Vic filled another glass and set it on the bar.

Mike brought the empty back to the bar and set it in the glass washer. "Sorry about that." He said to Vic.

"They'll get used to you kid. Don't worry. Try not to pounce on them. They are used to bringing their empties to the bar themselves."

Mike nodded, looked around, picked up a bar rag and wiped the tables he had already wiped twice.

At two thirty Mike saw Grumps come in the front door. He scooted over to Vic and said, "Guess I've been here long enough for today. I think I will go. Thanks for showing me things."

"Sure kid." But Mike had already slipped out the back door.

During the walk home Mike thought about the day and the people he had met. He could understand why Gramps liked going there, it felt comfortable even if it was a bit dim. Not everyone was nice but most people seemed to be.

Then he thought about the golf clubs he had seen in the

garage. He thought it might be fun to knock a few balls around. He wondered how he could raise that topic with Grumps. He knew he could ask Gram but since the barn seemed to be Grump's territory, she would probably just tell him he had to ask Gramps anyway. He practiced several conversations but none of them ended with him being allowed to use the golf clubs...one even ended up with him being grounded longer for poking into places he had no right to.

* * *

That evening on the front porch, while Jeopardy played on the TV, Mike shared his day with his Grandmother.

"Try not to be too anxious." She advised him, "The men will get used to you. Just be yourself, you are a very likable young man. Be yourself and you will do fine."

"But I need to know now, before summer is over."

"Patience."

Mike sat back in his chair. It was hard to be patient. He didn't want to spend the whole summer with Grumps mad at him, having to carry the burden of that every day. He wanted their relationship to be like the ones he had seen on TV and in the movies with grandpa and grandson going fishing or building things or just talking without someone being in trouble.

Gramps clunked his way to his chair and sat down with a wheeze. Mike wondered if he should bring up the golf clubs. Then an idea came to him.

"Grampa, did you ever play sports?"

Gramps sputtered a bit, gripped the arms of his chair as though it was going to throw him out, then looked at Mike.

"Sports? What the hell do you want to know that for?" Grumps didn't smile.

"I was just curious. You work at the school and I guess I kind of thought you might be doing some coaching there."

"I work there. Not play games."

Realizing the conversation wasn't going the way he had hoped, Mike tried to get it back on track.

"I play a little basketball at school. Our coach is one of the player's fathers. He works pretty hard at it, runs the drills with us and everything."

"Yeah," Grumps shook his cane, "I'd be running drills with this."

"Yeah, I guess," Mike continued to struggle to turn the conversation positive, "but before? You have a pretty good set of shoulders on you," Mike smiled, "I thought you might have played football or something."

Grumps looked at him, that crease forming on his forehead. Did he think Mike was kidding him...baiting him?

"Nope, worked. That's what I did."

"Come on Grampa," Mike was feeling a little frustrated. Didn't this man ever have fun? "No one works all the time. Everyone needs a little recreation...like watching Jeopardy. Or hockey. Or something."

"Hockey, shmockey. Just a bunch of millionaire brats playing games and calling it a career." Mike grew concerned he had touched a nerve but then something changed in Grump's voice, "Back in England we got introduced to rugby. Them Limey's sure know how to put together a game. And no one got paid to play, in fact we had to kick in a few pounds to buy the equipment. That's their money in case your internet never told you."

Mike felt excited. Grumps, Gramps, if he was going to have a nice conversation Mike was willing to call him Gramps, was actually talking about his time in the war.

"Rugby?" Mike asked.

"Yeah rugby." Gramps looked right at Mike. He wasn't smiling but he wasn't frowning either. "Ever heard of it?"

"Sure. We played a little in P.E. class. Scrums and all that."

"Hmph." Gramps sat back in his chair. "Guess they do teach something in school."

Grumps sure had a way with turning conversations

bleak, Mike thought but then forged ahead.

"When you were in England, did you get to visit Scotland?" Mike felt clever turning the conversation back toward golf, since golf was invented in Scotland.

"Hmph. Didn't have no time for visiting. Played a little rugby after training is all."

Mike felt the conversation slipping away again. Was there something about the golf clubs? "I don't know much about that time, but I'd like to." If he couldn't turn their talk to the golf clubs, maybe he could get Gramps to talk about his war experience. That would save a lot of time at the Legion.

"Thought you were going to the library? Ain't you learning nothing there with all those books and the internet thing too?"

"I am but that really mostly just says what happened. It would be better to know what it was like, really like there."

Grumps just looked at him then looked away as he said, "Too long ago. Days under the bridge."

Mike started to say something else but he noticed Gram in the corner of his eye. She shook her head 'no' a bit. He changed his tactic mid-thought. "Gramps, I saw some old golf clubs in the barn when I was looking for a broom."

Gramps didn't acknowledge Mike's words. Just stared at the porch floor as though there was something interesting there. Mike thought it was probably better to just leave Gramps in his thoughts. He sat back and sipped the last of his tea.

After a bit Gramma told Gramps he should drink his tea before it cooled. He sipped at it but didn't say anything. Mike excused himself and went to his room.

He checked his phone for emails and there was one from Janice.

*Hi Mike, I hope you are having as good weather as we are. Went to the beach today. Was glad to cool off...*the email continued with descriptions of movies and TV shows she had seen lately and some chit chat about her girlfriends and shopping.

Mike wrote back letting her know that he hadn't

watched any TV and that Aylmer didn't even have a movie theatre anymore. The building was still there but the box office was papered up, tufts of grass growing in the doorway. The closest theatre now was in St Thomas about twenty kilometers away. He told her about working at the Legion and going to the pool, but he didn't mention the lifeguard there or Jeannie. He thanked her for writing and said he looked forward to more from her. He really did.

That night Mike was woken by shouting from his grandparent's room. Were they fighting? Mike listened and realized it was Gramp's voice that was loud, Gram's was calm. She said something about 'just a dream' and Mike guessed Gramps had had a nightmare.

Work at the Legion

Gramps was already gone by the time Mike got out of bed.

"Good morning Gram." Mike scratched his head as he walked into the kitchen.

"Ready for some breakfast?"

"Cereal will be fine." Mike noted the aroma of bacon in the air. His stomach grumbled but it seemed most of Gramma's day was spent preparing food. He wanted to give her a break. "Maybe one day I can make you breakfast."

"Well," she turned from the sink for a moment, "that would be a nice treat."

"Gramps got an early start." Mike waited a moment but when he didn't get a response he continued. "I heard him last night. Sounded like he had a nightmare."

"We all have those at times."

"Does he have them often?"

"Oh, not too often." Something about how she spoke made Mike think she wasn't being completely honest.

"Do you know what he dreams about?"

"No," again her tone said she wasn't telling the truth, "mostly just grunts. Sometimes he calls out 'No'."

"About the war?" Mike thought that if he was direct, it might help.

"Perhaps. Sometimes he says his brother's name."

"His brother?"

"Yeah, Wenner."

"I've never heard of him. Does he live around here?"

"No," then Gram sighed, "he passed a while ago."

Mike thought about that for a moment then realized she was saying he had died. "Oh, what happened?"

"I don't want to talk about it and please don't talk to Gramps about him either." She placed a bowl of cereal on the table and turned back to the sink. Mike was certain now was not the time to ask more questions.

Mike headed to the library and did some research on rugby during the war. There wasn't a lot of information, mostly around the various rules, Rugby League and Rugby Union. He went back to despatch riders.

He decided to Google 'Wenner Weinstein' which earned him a hit on the Canadian Virtual War Memorial site that listed his date of death as April 27, 1945 and that he served with the Royal Corps of Signal Soldiers. A few more searches and Mike learned that was the group that many Despatch Riders were associated with and that, although the war officially ended on September 2, 1945, Germany had surrendered on May 7, 1945 ending the campaign in Europe. His grandfather's brother had also been a Despatch Rider and had died less than 2 weeks before peace was declared. He was buried in France; he never made it home. No wonder Gramps didn't want to talk about the war.

When he got to the Legion, he saw Vic was working again. Mike was surprised when Vic gave him an envelope that rattled. Mike opened it. There were some bills and coins inside.

"You got some tips." Vic said.

"Tips?" Mike wasn't expecting this.

"Sure, we share the tips. That's your share."

"But I'm volunteering. This doesn't seem right."

"Customers still give us tips and you're entitled to a share."

"Well OK. If you say so. Thanks." Mike tucked the envelope into his pocket, still feeling funny about it.

"There's a private function going on tomorrow night," Vic said, "a wedding. If you talk to Sheila you might be able to work it. We could use a swamper. It'll be busy."

"Ok, thanks. What's a swamper? Wrestling 'gators?" Mike felt good that Vic wanted him to be there.

"You a funny boy." Which really had to be followed by "Pardon my French" then Vic added "That's what you do here, clear tables and stuff, swamping. In the meantime, get a bucket of water and scrub out under the bar. Gets pretty sticky around the mix hoses."

Later that day Mike spoke with Sheila.

"Here," Mike handed her the envelope Vic had given him. "I don't feel right keeping this. Vic said it was tip money and I was entitled to it."

"Guess you are." Sheila didn't reach for the envelope. "Why don't you keep it?"

"I'd be happier if it stayed here. Maybe you can use it for something to help the vets or something."

"Well, the coffers never have enough in them but a young man like you must have use for a little pocket money too."

"I'm ok."

"Well, alright then." Sheila took the envelope and put it in her desk drawer. "We'll just keep it here for the time being."

"Vic said there was a wedding here tomorrow and that maybe I could work it."

Sheila smiled, "He's taken a bit of a shine to you. Not bad for only working here one day."

"Really?"

"Yeah, once you get to know him, you'll know what I mean. As for tomorrow, we'll start setting up around two. They want to decorate at four and we need everything in place by then."

"Ok, two."

A bit later Vic introduced Mike to Eliza.

"Eliza's another bartender. He's going to cover for me this afternoon, I got an appointment." What Vic actually said had to be followed by 'pardon my French' to which Mike smiled and Eliza scowled. And, while Mike tried to shake Eliza's hand, Vic stood behind Eliza, shaking his head and making a scrunched-up face. Mike thought he was indicating that Eliza wasn't too friendly as though that wasn't already obvious.

"I heard of you." Was all Eliza said before turning his attention to the bar and his back to Mike.

"Are you going to be working the wedding tomorrow?" Mike tried to strike up a conversation after Vic left. The only response was a brief glance. It appeared Eliza had found a stubborn stain that required his full attention. With nothing else to do, the lounge was almost empty, Mike simply browsed the memorabilia on the walls.

Knowing that many of the vets who came to the Legion had seen front line action, Mike still found it difficult to picture them doing that. When he tried, he saw old, grey-haired men in uniforms, not the young, strong, brave men he saw in the photos. It was difficult believing all the things the photographs showed had really happened. It was even harder to believe that every one of the men and women who participated did so voluntarily. Mike had learned that, unlike many countries, Canada hadn't used conscription to fill its ranks except for a brief period near the end of the war. Mike didn't know if he could volunteer like that. Doing this work at the Legion was what he considered volunteer even though he never would have thought to do this if he hadn't got himself into trouble. Mike thought about that for a few minutes. He was enjoying doing this but would have missed out if he hadn't been mixed up in the Trucker's Haven mess.

At that moment, a hand gripped his shoulder and, after Mike looked at whose hand it was, he felt the irony of his previous thoughts. It was Officer Campbell.

"I heard you were working here."

"Hi," Mike said, "It's legal. Even though I'm underage." At the same time Mike thought 'small town news travels faster than Facebook.'

"That's not why I'm here."

Yeah? I thought I would get a head start on my community service.

"That hasn't been decided yet."

"Probably though."

"Actually, when I heard what you were doing, I was impressed. Most kids would wait until they had to."

Mike looked at the police officer, noting the sharp

creases in his uniform, the shine on the brim of his hat which was tucked under one arm, the gleaming polish on his boots.

"I don't know," Mike said, "I kind of like it here." He didn't mention that he had other motives.

"Amongst the old guys? I can't imagine they much like you being here."

"I don't know, they are mostly nice."

"Anyway, I'm thinking maybe you were telling the truth when you said you hadn't been at Trucker's Haven before that day."

"You talked to my Grandma, hey?"

Campbell rubbed the back of his neck, "Yeah, she said you were working in their barn, had lunch on their porch. Gives you a pretty good alibi." After a pause Campbell continued, "It would help a lot if you would confirm who was with you that day, who took you there. I might even decide to drop any charges against you."

Mike felt a flare in the back of his brain. He thought about the faces in the photos on the walls. Undoubtedly some of those faces belonged to men who were captured during the war, thrown into POW camps, pumped for information, maybe even tortured. Would they have given up secrets that might get their comrades killed? Help the enemy win the war? Get a bit easier life behind the wire fences? Maybe save their own lives? Some did, but Mike imagined that most resisted, kept their knowledge to themselves and endured whatever fate that resulted in. He knew what he was facing didn't compare to that, but the basis was the same. You don't rat out your friends.

Then he thought more, were Jack and Alan even his friends? They had abandoned him after all, taken him there without letting him know what they were up to until it was happening all around him. Why would he protect them? Why didn't he just give their names to Campbell and be done with it? Campbell wasn't really the enemy after all, he was just doing his job, protecting the community. And he was being reasonable, almost friendly. Mike almost gave in but then he remembered that Jeannie had been there too and he was pretty sure that even if he left her name out, Jack and Alan would give her up in a moment. Then he realized that Campbell was using this tactic on him the same way interrogators use tactics on their subjects to gain their confidence, minimize the value of the information they wanted, soften them up to make them more compliant. And that did make Campbell the enemy.

"Can't do that. Sorry. I need to get back to work."

"Alright Mike. Have it your way. If you change your mind..." Campbell turned and headed toward the door. On the way, he stopped by one table and spoke to the men there briefly. After a moment, they all laughed, then Campbell left. Mike stared after him wondering if he really was doing the right thing or if he was following a stupid rule put in place by people who were often in need of other's silence to protect them.

And then he wondered how Campbell knew to find him here. Could Gramps find out so easy?

On the way home, he stopped by the swimming pool looking for Jeanie's curly hair. She wasn't there. Mike looked for Suzie, he felt he could use a little of her cajoling today, maybe lift the mood his conversation with Campbell had resulted in, but she wasn't there either. He headed for home.

As he passed the Andrew house, Mike studied the old faded yellow building that squatted in perpetual shadow. It seemed to be sad, sagging toward the middle. With one window on each side of the door and the rotting porch across the front, it looked like a face in distress. The lawn was unkept, tufts of grass amid the bare spots and patches of fallen leaves. Mike looked for any sign of occupancy but everything was dim, dingy, dusty, forgotten, dead. He felt sorry for the house. It reminded him of the men in the photos on the Legion wall and how they were so different from the men now. He tried to imagine how the house had been when it was new, the family who had lived there; the dreams they had held on to; the laughter they might have shared; but the dying house kept pulling him out of his imagination. Then he was past it, the tidy red and green farm with the long greenhouse that came next, brightening the day.

That evening as he sipped his tea Mike told Gramma that he would be working late at the Legion tomorrow.

"I'm not sure how we can let Gramps know without telling him what you are doing."

"Maybe he won't notice?" Mike was surprised at her confession, he thought she knew everything.

"That is highly unlikely."

"Sometimes it is easier to seek forgiveness than permission."

"Whoever told you that never knew your grandfather."

The two fell to silence while the final strains of Jeopardy drifted through the screen door.

"I'll tell him I never told you. No point in both of us being in trouble."

"No." Her tone was sharp bringing Mike's head around to look at her. "No lies. You must have learned that by now."

Mike felt the colour rise in his face. He was angry with himself for disappointing her again. "Yes, you are right. No lies," Mike paused then continued, "but I don't have to tell him the whole truth if he doesn't ask."

"I'm not afraid of him you know. He's not a monster." Gramma whispered.

"I don't think he is. I just want things to be good, happy."

Then the door banged open and the clumping on the porch stole any further conversation they might have had. Mike decided he would just keep his mouth shut, let things play out as they may.

The Wedding Kiss

When Mike arrived at the Legion, he was disappointed to see Eliza was there. He certainly hadn't felt any positive vibes from him the day before.

"I didn't know you were working the wedding." Mike said.

Eliza just looked at him then went back to wiping the bar.

"I guess I'll go downstairs and start setting up." Mike felt desperate to escape the wave of negativity emanating from Eliza. He certainly wouldn't want someone like that working a happy event, he thought as he trudged down the stairs. He had been feeling quite positive but now he was feeling like he had when he passed the Andrews house yesterday.

In the downstairs hall Mike saw Vic and Sheila talking. When Sheila saw him, she raised one finger to Vic then turned to Mike.

"I'm glad you're here Mike. Can you start setting up the tables?"

"Sure."

"Head table there," she pointed, "Put three tables together, it's a big group. Then set up fifteen separate tables, six chairs at each."

"Sure thing." Mike headed toward the pile of folded tables.

"Oh, one more thing." Mike stopped and looked at Sheila, "The band will be setting up there." She pointed to one corner. "Leave lots of space."

Mike got to work.

A few hours later Mike stood at one end of the hall and looked over the transformation of the room. White balloons, streamers, tablecloths, all had been melded into a cohesive theme for the bride and groom. Glitter and table centrepieces with frond-like stems and silver sparkly stars caused the light to reflect and refract into a melody of colour. It seemed a little frilly to Mike but overall, he liked how it looked. He was proud to have been a part of it.

When the guests started to arrive, Mike tried to stay out of their way while staying available. He welcomed those who came near them, smiled and responded to questions. The happiness of the day worked on him and he found himself feeling the positive energy of the occasion.

A teenager came up to him, she looked quite pretty in her pink dress. She spoke quietly, "Where are the restrooms?" Mike pointed to the doors across the room and down a little hallway. "Thanks." She smiled at him. Mike smiled back. Then she looked at one of the tables and giggled. Mike looked too and saw another teenager, maybe a few years older, sitting there wearing a similar chiffon dress but it was blue. Both girls had blond hair, curly, and Mike guessed they were sisters. The girl sitting looked at the one who had asked directions then at Mike and she brought one hand to her mouth. Mike thought she was giggling too.

He wondered if they were giggling at him. He looked down to make sure his fly wasn't open, it wasn't, then he touched his hair, but every strand felt in the proper place. He smiled back at her and she turned away, averting her eyes as though caught doing something wrong.

"Doug," Vic called from the bar. The bar was an opening in the wall from another small room. There was a shutter that had always been closed whenever Mike had been in the hall, that covered the opening. Mike looked at Vic. "Can you bring more ice from upstairs?"

"Oh sure." Mike directed his mind back to the job at hand. Just before he headed upstairs with the plastic ice bucket, Mike glanced at the girl's table again. The older one was looking at him but this time, instead of turning away she bit her lower lip, looked down a bit and smiled.

Between Vic and the ladies in the kitchen, Mike was kept too busy to think about the two girls in the chiffon dresses. The kitchen was steamy and thick with the aroma of the roast beef in the ovens and potatoes boiling on the stove tops. Knives clattered, pots and dishes banged and the steady conversation between the ladies filled the room with activity. The tables had already been set with cutlery, glasses and napkins but the food would be delivered 'plated' which Mike understood to mean with the food on them. He was to be one of the servers and then 'bus' the tables afterward. When he asked about that it turned out bussing meant the same as swamping except in a dining room. Why didn't people just say 'clear the tables'? Every different group seemed to feel the need for their own code words. It all seemed overly complicated.

Mike was a bit nervous about serving. Gertrude had told him that he needed to make sure he served from the right and when he cleared the plates, to clear them from the left. However, Pearl had said, serve from the left, clear from the right. Again, it all seemed so complicated. He was mostly afraid he would drop a plate or spill something on someone. By the time he was to serve, he was a jittery mess. The plates in his hands shook a bit.

He decided to do what Gertrude had said. Everything from the right was easier to remember. He concentrated on what he was doing but cast glances at the ladies serving once he had delivered his plates. No one seemed to care if they got their food from the left or the right.

Then he found himself at the table of the two girls in the chiffon dresses.

"Your dinner." He said to the girl in blue so she would move her shoulder a bit allowing him to set the plate in front of her.

"Thank you." She said and reached out and touched his hand. An electric current buzzed from his hand up his arm. It was a light tingling and felt nice but was unexpected and Mike pulled his hand away involuntarily. "Mmmm," she seemed to not notice he had jerked away a bit and smiled up at him, "smells delicious. Thanks Mike."

Again, Mike couldn't control his reaction as his head

snapped toward her. How did she know his name? Everyone here called him Doug. Just then Helen passed by "Don't dilly dally Doug, more plates to deliver before they get cold."

Mike gave the girl one more look then headed back to the kitchen. Her smile went with him.

As Mike continued his duties attending to the celebrants, he couldn't help but cast quick glances at the table with the two girls. It seemed every time he did, one or the other were looking at him. Then they would avert their eyes and giggle or smile or give the other a quick flick of a hand or foot. Mike didn't miss these actions.

"Mike," Vic spoke from his bar cave, as Mike had started calling it, "give the washrooms a quick check. See if they need a mop or anything."

'Gross.' Mike thought but headed down the hallway anyway. He peeked in the men's, not bad but maybe the floor could use a little attention. He knocked on the lady's door then opened it a bit. "Hello." He called. There was no answer, so Mike stepped inside. There was water all over the sink counter, toilet paper on the floor and one of the toilets hadn't been flushed. He worked the handle with his foot. He sighed. This room needed some attention big time. He headed out to get the mop and bucket.

When he opened the door, the older of the two girls was standing there.

"Oops." Mike said, startled and a bit embarrassed. "I was just...."

The girl glanced once toward the hall where another round of toasts was being delivered, then she turned back to Mike, gave him a little push backward against the privacy wall that shielded the washroom from the hallway when the door was open, stepped in close and kissed Mike full on the lips.

Mike's first reaction was to push her away, but he was delayed by the shock of her action. By the time he gathered himself enough to do anything, he realised how nice what she was doing felt. Then she pushed her tongue into his mouth. Feeling like he was going to smother, Mike did give her a little push but not too much. As surprised as he was, he was rather enjoying the moment too. She started to pull back but then Mike reached up, cupped her head in his hands and pulled her close again. The feelings and tingles that raced through his body took over his mind.

Then she pulled back and both teens gasped in a few breaths. Mike's mind was still muddled but realization seeped in. "Wow," he said, "what was that for?" Mike became aware that his whole body was reacting to the stimulation it had just received. It wasn't unpleasant but if she looked down it would be obvious. He leaned forward just a bit.

"I wanted to know how it felt." She smiled at him, holding his eyes with her.

"Kissing?"

"Kissing you." Her tongue danced on her upper lip. "I saw you watching me."

"You were watching me."

"Maybe," she stepped back and took a quick look toward the hall again. The coast must have been clear because she stepped forward and said, "Would you like to do that again?"

"Sure," Mike responded. He was anxious to experience again what that first kiss had set off.

She moved closer and raised her mouth to his. This time Mike was ready and pressed his lips against hers. He tilted his head a bit and she tipped hers the other way. Their mouths joined and the burning in his stomach flared to a super nova. Mike raised his hands behind her back and pulled her closer. She pressed her tongue against his teeth. Never having experienced this before, Mike was uncertain what to do. She pressed a bit more and he let his mouth relax. When her tongue rasped against his, he thought he was going to explode. He moved his mouth and pressed back with his tongue. He could feel her breath hot on his cheek while he gasped for air. After a moment, she began to pull back. Mike held her and she pushed harder. Their mouths parted.

"Whoa, slow down there tiger." She said.

"Sorry," Mike realized he had gotten a bit carried away. "it's just that...." She smiled at him, "that was great."

"You never kissed a girl before?" Her eyes were wide.

"Sure I have," now Mike was feeling a bit embarrassed because it really was the first time he had kissed a girl. "but not like that." He was still trying to catch his breath.

"For a newbie, you're not bad." And then she disappeared down the hall, toward the festivities.

Mike gave himself a moment to settle down then stepped into the hallway. He wondered who this girl was and why she had done that. Then he wondered if she would do it again. Then he thought about Jeannie and then about Suzie. As he stepped into the hallway a man walked by, giving him a strange look, then turned into the men's room. Mike hardly noticed.

While he was mopping out the two rooms he kept wondering if she was coming back in, hoping she would. But she didn't. When he went back to the hall, he looked at the table where she had been sitting but both girl's chairs were empty. There were other empty chairs too. Mike checked the dance floor, but they weren't there either. Had they left? How was he going to find out who they were? Who she was?

No matter how much he hoped, every time he checked their table, they were still gone.

After the party ended and everyone went home, Mike stayed and helped clean up. Sheila told him he had done enough but he insisted he stay. He wanted to know that he had done the whole project and he didn't feel right about leaving with work unfinished. Work that would be done by those who had already done so much, given so much.

"Can I give you a ride home?" Sheila asked as she locked and checked the door. It was dark and cool, Mike was feeling tired but good. The scent of the kissing girl, the pressure of her body against his, the taste of her lips, her tongue, were all so fresh and vivid in his mind.

"Thanks," Mike looked around in a dramatic way, ensuring Sheila couldn't miss his actions, "it's a nice night. I think the walk will be good after all the noise and commotion of the wedding."

"But it's so late." Sheila looked at her watch. Mike pulled out his phone, 1:30.

"It's not far. Thanks Sheila and," Mike moved his head toward the Legion, "thanks for this. It was fun."

"Ha. That was a lot of work. We sure appreciate your help and enthusiasm." Sheila turned toward the parking lot. "Last chance."

"I'll be fine. Goodnight."

During the walk home Mike tried to get the image, the sensations, the reactions to the kissing girl out of his head but he wasn't successful. It wasn't that he didn't like them, he was uncomfortable with how they were making him feel, the thoughts they brought on. Mike knew about sex and everything, it was hard to get out of public school without having to sit through hours of Healthy Living lectures which were nothing more than warnings about STDs, the consequence of teen pregnancy, and fodder for school yard jokes. He had laughed behind his hands so many times when teachers, obviously uncomfortable with the subject, gave names to the body parts: penis, vagina, breasts. He and his friends had their own names, used them frequently and chided each other about this or that they knew about the whole sex thing, or thought they knew.

He remembered a comment Uwe had made when they were seven or eight, 'Wouldn't it be embarrassing if you were doing it with a girl and you popped a boner?' They had all laughed because at that time, popping a boner was flat out embarrassing and they didn't understand as much about it all as they thought they did. But that was a long time ago and now Mike was thinking more and more about the sex thing. What was wrong with him?

And then he was at the Anderson house. The streetlights had ended a half block before and now the house seemed be absorbing the light around it, a mini black hole. The cool evening became cold, goosebumps stood out on

Mike's arms. He glanced toward the house, unable to look fully at it. There was no mistaking the face look of the windows and porch. The darkness making the features evil looking. Mike decided it would be better to walk on the other side of the street for a bit.

Then he was home. The house was dark, quiet. Mike's footsteps disturbed the silence, scraped across the stillness. He had never heard such noisy walking. Then a creek from the front porch.

"Mike." His name whispered from the darkness.

"Yes, Gram." Mike whispered back.

"You are so late."

"Sorry. I stayed to the end to help clean up."

"Gramps is sleeping. Come in the front way."

"Is everything ok?" The porch steps creaked as Mike climbed them.

"He was upset that you were out. You know, the grounding and all. I told him you were working."

"Did you tell him about…"

"The Legion?" Mike was close enough to see the shape of his grandmother. She was wearing her housecoat, standing with one hand on the door handle." No. I didn't say too much. Didn't want to lie."

"Thanks. Sorry you were in that position."

"Sometimes he can get so…" Then her voice trailed off. She opened the door, stood there holding it for him. "It's late. Get into bed."

"Good night Gram. I love you."

"You too sweetie."

Cure for a Hangover

Mike was in a long line, waiting to get to a kissing booth. When he finally got there, it was the kissing girl from the wedding. She puckered her lips and Mike puckered his, closed his eyes, leaned in close and she said, "UP and at 'em." Gramps' voice and the thumping of his cane yanked Mike from his dream. As the shreds of the booth fell away, Mike rolled over and picked up his phone.

"What time is it?" He said as the numbers on the screen came into focus. 7:03.

"Time to get up. Want to play like a man, work like a man. Get out of that bed. We have a day ahead of us." Mike wondered why Gramps was talking so loud. 'Play like a man?' What was he talking about?

Mike sat up, rubbed his eyes and tried to shake off the ache that rested in his joints.

"Come on, daylight's burning." Gramps pulled the curtain to the room back with his cane. He was dressed in jeans and a checked shirt, sleeves rolled above the elbows. Jeans? Mike had only ever seen the man in his green pants and shirt; sleeves rolled down and collar buttoned.

"What's going on?" Mike tried to make sense. Why was Gramps waking him when he knew he was working late last night?

"Get dressed. Breakfast is on the table. Let's go, no time to waste." Gramps clapped his hands twice.

Pulling his pants on, Mike tried to figure out what Gramps was doing. He sounded more like a drill instructor than anything. Why was he making Mike get up at this ungodly hour?

Yawning and pulling his shirt on, Mike stepped into the kitchen. Gramma wasn't at the sink, that was odd. There was a bowl and spoon on the table with a box of cereal, Corn Flakes, Mike flinched, the pitcher of milk and two pieces of bread on a plate.

"If you want toast you'll have to do it yourself." Gramps took his cap from the hook by the door. He reached for the doorknob, "Eat then come outside. Don't dilly-dally." Then the door closed with a wall-shaking bang.

Mike stood looking at the table, scratching his head. He still didn't feel fully awake. He dropped the bread slices into the toaster then put the cereal in the cupboard and took down the box of frosted flakes. Nothing like a sugar rush to get the body moving. He thought about his favorite comic character who ate Sugar Bombs for breakfast in the company of his stuffed tiger.

Mike looked at the coffee pot. He didn't drink it very often, but this morning felt like a good day to try it. He lifted the pot. Not enough for a full cup but there was some. Bless Grandpa and his aversion to doing 'women's work'. Mike poured the remainder into a cup, tasted it. Only warm. If there was a microwave, he would have nuked it but nothing so modern in this house. It would have to do.

A motor started up outside. It revved and revved and revved. Mike felt it was Gramps urging him to action, so he gulped down his breakfast and coffee then headed outside. The motor was still revving.

"Bout time," Grumps called from the small orchard in the side yard. "Thought I was going to have to send a search party." He continued to rev the motor, which Mike could now see was attached to a hedge trimmer, while he spoke, making it difficult for Mike to hear what was being said. "Go get the ladder from the barn."

'Nothing like getting right to it. Bossing me around.' Mike muttered to himself as he headed toward the barn.

"Get a move on." Grumps shouted and emphasized his command with another rev of the motor. "We ain't got all day you know."

'Wonder what we got then.' Mike opened the barn door, 'will the day implode at noon?'

"What are we doing?" Mike asked as he set up the ladder. He had decided he was going to try to put a positive spin on the day despite Gramps' best efforts.

Grumps shook the trimmer, "Trimming." He said it as though he thought Mike was mentally deficient and Mike felt his anger flare.

'Trim yer ass' flashed through his mind but he clamped his tongue before it got away from him. Instead he reached for the trimmer.

"Not on your life. You'd probably cut fingers off." Gramps stared at Mike as though defying him to try to grab the machine. "Your job is popping suckers."

"Popping suckers?"

Grumps gave him a 'holy cow, don't you know anything' look and twist of his head. "Yea, suckers."

Lollipops and hard candies on sticks flashed through Mike's mind but he knew there wasn't going to be anything sweet about what Grumps was talking about. And he was right.

"There," Grumps pointed into the branches of the tree, "in the crook of the branch. See that little thing growing there?"

Mike peered into the tree, following Grump's finger. Where a branch joined the main trunk, there was a little branch growing. It had what looked like a tightly rolled leaf at its end. "Yeah, I think so."

"Pull it off."

Mike reached in and grabbed the little growth. He pulled but it didn't break off. He twisted it and it started to split but still didn't break off.

"Cripes, not like that." Grumps stepped in close to Mike, reaching toward the sucker. "Use your thumb. Pop it off like this." Grumps flicked the sucker with his thumb, and it came right off.

Mike looked for another one. Found one. Did what Grumps did, but it still didn't come off, just bent and split.

"No, no. Not like that. Pop it against its growth line."

Mike wondered what a growth line was but decided now wasn't the right time to ask that question. With Gramps' tone this morning he felt like the adage 'there are no dumb questions' might be right but there are questions with push-ups attached to them. He remembered Gram's 'white glove inspection' swipe in the barn and knew where she had gotten that from. Then he noticed that the sucker had a bit of a curve to it. He had pulled across and with the curve, now he pushed against the curve with his thumb and the sucker popped right off.

"Get them all." Gramps said then climbed the ladder and began trimming the tree branches. "And don't forget the ones further out on the branches.

Mike looked along the branch and saw that there were suckers growing out of the crooks of the smaller branches too. Further out it became impossible to tell if the growth was a branch, a leaf, or a sucker. Recalling the comments Grumps had made the day he was doing the weeding, Mike decided he would only pull what he was certain was a sucker. Something told him that no matter what he did, Grumps was going to find something wrong with it.

Ten minutes later his thumb was getting sore so he tried doing the popping with his fingers. It didn't work as well but it gave his thumb a break. All the while the trimmer blasted in his ear. It seemed that Grumps could only find branches to trim that were near Mikes head. When Mike looked at the ground, there was not a lot of trimmings. Was Grumps just making noise? Why would he do that? Was he trying to punish Mike for something?

Every time Mike moved around the tree to get to a new branch, Gramps followed. Ten minutes later Mike had had enough.

"That thing is hurting my ears. Do you have to work so close to me?" He tried to make his voice light, but he was feeling frustrated by this time.

"What?" Grumps revved the motor again, "This little thing?"

"When it's right in my ears." Mike heard the whine in his voice. He didn't want to be on the defensive, but he didn't want to make Gramps any angrier than he might already be.

"Is your head hurting?"

"No." Mike was confused.

"Maybe you shouldn't have been partying so late. You might feel better now."

Then it blossomed in his brain. Gramps thought he was hung over, had been out partying last night.

"I feel fine. Just a little tired."

Grumps revved the motor again.

"Please stop doing that." Mikes words were clipped. The constant noise had set up a buzzing in his head. "I'm not hung over you know."

"Oh really? You were pretty late getting in last night and your clothes reek of booze." Another rev of the motor.

"I was working." Mike felt the conversation going in a direction he didn't want. He didn't want to admit he was working at the Legion.

"You are supposed to be grounded."

"Well, I thought it would be ok since it was work." Mike only cast half a glance at Grumps. "It's not like I was having fun." He smiled inside because the kissing thing had been quite fun, but Grumps didn't need to know about that.

"You didn't ask permission."

"Sorry, I'm not used to being treated like a kid."

"Then maybe you should stop acting like one."

Mike felt the anger flare again. He turned to Grumps intending to scream, "What the fuck do you think I have been doing?" but he caught himself. That would only reinforce what Grumps had just said. He was stuck with him all day and he didn't want the whole day to be shit. Instead he asked, "Are we doing all the trees?" He looked at the four other trees that lined the driveway.

"You got something else to do?"

Again, his anger flared. Instead of lashing out like he normally would, Mike snapped off a few more suckers. When he felt he had himself under control again he said, "Look Grampa, I can do this all day if you want but I get the feeling you really don't want to be doing anything with me. If you're punishing me because I was out late last night I get it, but tell me. It would be really nice if we could have a grandpa grandson kind of day. You know, where you pass on some of your wisdom and I get to keep some happy memories that I can look back on later." Mike felt tears building, pressure in his neck and chest. He didn't want to start bawling but he knew he was on the edge of it. Why did things always seem to go from such great feelings like last night to such crap like right this minute?

He took a deep breath then continued, "But instead it seems you are going to just keep on me and not give me any idea on what to do to make things right. I don't know how to make you happy. I kind of get the idea that you don't want to be happy, that you feel your lot in life is to spread your misery to all those around you. I don't know what makes me want to try to please you when you act like that but for some friggin reason I still do." He snapped off another sucker. "But if nothing else, please stop running that trimmer right in my ear."

"Don't say friggin." He revved the engine again, moving it a bit closer to Mike.

Mike stomped his foot. "I'll go work on that tree there." He pointed to the next tree in the line. "When you're done with this one, I'll come back and finish it." Mike strode to the next tree, waded into its branches and began picking at the suckers. His movements were quick, harsh, he hardly thought about what he was doing, his mind was fumbling and stumbling over the rage that burned in his chest.

Gramps revved the engine and went back to work.

About ten minutes later Gramps asked, "Do you know what kind of trees these are?"

Mike was still thinking over what he had said and what had led to his tirade. "Huh?"

"These trees," Grumps pointed at the tree he was working on and then the rest of them. Mike was surprised by the tone of his voice. It was as though their recent exchange had never happened. "do you know what kind they are."

Mike looked at each tree, they all looked the same.

"Crabapple?"

"You're not sure?"

"They look like crabapple." Mike wondered where this conversation was going.

Gramps flicked a switch on the trimmer and the engine died. Blessed silence to Mike. "They are. Malus pumila to be exact." He set the trimmer on the ground and took a few steps toward Mike. "They come from Europe. My father brought them over."

"He brought trees from Europe?"

Gramps laughed a short chuff, "Seeds. When he came to Canada, he brought seeds. I think he was worried there would be nothing familiar to him in this new country and he wanted to bring a bit of the home country with him."

Mike watched Gramps. They didn't make eye contact and Mike thought the man was wandering in his memories, remembering his youth.

"He planted them and grew them into trees. When I got this place after the war, I took some branches from his trees and planted these ones."

"Really?" Mike marveled at the tone of Gramps' revelation. This was a Gramps moment that he had been hoping for. He felt the knot in his stomach loosen.

"Yup. Your Gramma has made a lot of jars of jelly from the fruit of these trees." Gramps smiled and patted the trunk of the tree. Mike was amazed at the change in his face, how the years peeled off. He almost glowed.

"Crabapple jelly. I didn't know you could make jam from crabapples."

"Course you can. Had to back in the day. Didn't have money to just run to the store to buy everything. Had to do for yourself." Mike heard the edge coming back into Gramps voice. He wanted to get him back to where he had been.

"I guess I'll pay more attention at breakfast tomorrow. Really taste the jam. Crabapple jam." Mike smiled.

"Pears too. And cherries."

"Where are those trees?" Mike had only seen apple

trees on the property.

"Right here." Again, the edge in Gramps' voice. He pointed at the tree he had been trimming.

"But that's an apple tree."

"That's what's wrong with you kids. Never pay attention. Always running off to the next great thing." By the time he was finished talking Gramps was spitting his words. The lines were deep in his face again, across his brow.

Mike wondered what Gramps was talking about. What was making him so angry? Not really wanting to, he stepped closer, looking into the tree where gramps was pointing.

"What?" Then he saw it. Some of the leaves were different, the branches were a different colour, one smoother, two others darker and rough. The leaves different shapes. "I think I see but I'm not sure what."

"Pear branch." Gramps gripped the branch and gave it a little shake. He reached toward another branch, "cherry."

"On the same tree?" Mike couldn't believe what he was looking at. "Three fruits from one tree? How did you do that?"

"Spliced 'em." Gramps stared into the tree and Mike could sense the years peeling away again. "Split the branch, work in a seedling of a pear tree and two from a cherry. Wrap 'em in sphagnum and water 'em" Gramps made an exploding motion with his hands, a magician's flurry, " Whamo, away they grow." The man was smiling, remembering.

"And you did that?" Mike knew his mouth was open, but he didn't care. This was amazing.

Gramps brow furled and his smile faded. "Course I did. Think I've always been an old man?" He was spitting his words again.

"I didn't mean..." Mike couldn't believe he had blown it again. They were having a moment and then he opened his mouth and now it was shit again. "I mean. I just didn't know what else to say." He wanted to follow that with 'I think this is the coolest thing I've ever seen,' But Gramps cut him off.

"Well maybe you ought to shut up then." Gramps

waved his hand in a dismissive motion. "There's lots of suckers on that tree to pop."

And with that Mike was discharged. What had been building between them was smashed and Mike was left in its rubble and he had no idea how to fix it. He decided the best thing at this moment was to just do as he was told.

He worked in silence until Gramma drove the car into the driveway just before lunch.

"Have you boy's been having fun?" She walked from the car pulling white gloves from her hands. She wore a round pillbox hat and was wearing a knee length pink skirt. Mike thought it looked old fashioned, but he didn't say anything.

"Go get the rake and pick those things up." Grumps snarled toward Mike, waving a hand at the ground where the suckers had collected.

"Can you help me with the groceries in the car?" Gramma asked.

"Sure Gram, then I'll rake the lawn."

"Get the rake I said." Anger emanated from Grumps. "Don't you try to override me." He had turned to Gram.

"Now Dear," She started.

"Don't you talk to her like that." The words were out of Mike's mouth before he realized he was speaking. Then a bit quieter, "I can do the groceries and the raking. It'll only take a few minutes."

"Oh, so now you're running the show are ya?"

Mike felt the whole situation getting out of control. Gram had stopped walking, just stood there. There was a question in her features and Mike had the feeling she too was wondering what to do to diffuse the building tension.

"I'll go make lunch." She turned toward the house.

"I'm not running anything," Mike struggled to keep his tone light. He could feel the rage building in him though. "There's probably stuff that needs to get in the fridge or freezer."

Gramps stood in the shade of the tree looking at the ground. Mike was surprised he hadn't come back with some sort of angry comment but right now he was looking a little lost. Mike had never seen him with such a blank look in his eyes, on his face. He reached into the trunk and grabbed two bags of groceries.

"How was your morning with Gramps?" Gram asked as the two of them sat on the front porch after lunch. She poured a bit of tea into her cup, seemed satisfied it had steeped long enough and filled both.

"It had its moments." Mike poured a little cream into his tea and then stirred it. He was careful not to clink his spoon on the cup like Grumps did, that he found so annoying.

"We all have our struggles." She took a sip, holding the cup with both hands.

"I know." Mike set his cup down and leaned forward. "Sometimes we were having a great time. He was telling me about grafting branches from different trees onto the crabapple tree and it was feeling like a real special moment. Like he actually cared about me. Then all of a sudden, he's climbing down my throat and I have no idea what I did wrong. "Mike sat back with a sigh. "It's pretty frustrating."

"He'll be better after his nap. He was probably just a bit tired and that made him cranky."

"Gram, you don't need to make excuses for him." Mike looked at her while he judged the words that he wanted to speak. The last thing he wanted to do was have her angry at him, but he needed to speak his mind, get his feelings out in the open. "It wasn't like he was just cranky; it was like he was two different people. One minute he's describing how to splice a branch onto a tree and the next he's all snarly and then he's right back to being nice." Mike paused, chewed his lower lip while he looked at the boards of the porch floor, noticing how dried out and worn they looked. "I think there's maybe something wrong with him."

"Wrong?" Gram sat back and raised her chin. "Like what?"

"I don't know. Like maybe a stroke or something."

"Oh, pshaw." Gram sipped her tea. "He's always like

that. I think we all are. We just react to the moment."

Mike sat back. He was certain Gram knew there was something wrong with Gramps but didn't want to admit it. Maybe she just didn't know what to do either.

"I have to head back out." Gramma sat forward then stood up. "So many errands sometimes." She sounded tired to Mike.

"Can I go with you?" He asked.

"I think it would be better if you stayed. Show Grampa you are honouring your punishment."

Mike slumped back in his chair, his arms between his legs, head down. "OK, but you might need someone to carry stuff."

"I think I will be just fine young man." She smiled at him. "Keep working on Gramps. Don't give up."

Then she disappeared into the house. A few minutes later Mike heard the back-door bang, then the car start. He heard it shift into reverse, then into forward, then it drove past in a cloud of dust. He waved but couldn't see if she waved back.

Not wanting to be around Grumps when he got up, Mike went to the barn and got some Legion magazines. Then he went into the stand of sumacs behind the garden plot and found a shaded spot and sat down to read. After a few minutes, he thought about his situation and laughed to himself. Here he was hiding from his grandfather and he was reading magazines to try to better understand him. It seemed so ironic. Then he read an article on post-traumatic stress disorder and the difficulties young veterans were having getting support for it.

Later he went and finished suckering the trees.

That evening Mike read an email from Janice. She said her cousins thought he was a nice guy. He wondered how they might know that. Then it occurred to him, perhaps they were the girls at the wedding. That would explain how they knew his name. He wrote back and asked what their names were. It would be nice to know who had kissed him. He didn't mention the kiss.

War Stories

Mike busied himself dusting the pictures and plaques and other memorabilia that decorated the lounge walls at the Legion. He wasn't in a hurry and took time to study the artifacts, read the dates, the places, look at the faces. Some had placards explaining what the photo was of, some even had names of the people in them. Some were just photos. Mike came across one of a man on a motorcycle, kind of a funny looking motorcycle compared to ones now. The handlebars were wide, the seat on springs. He wondered if the man might be Grumps. It was impossible to tell; he was too far away to make out his features, but he was young. Mike looked at the motorcycle, there was something a bit familiar about it, about its shape. In a moment, it dawned on him and he couldn't wait to get home.

"You like that stuff?" Mike looked around and saw the only customer in the lounge looking at him.

"Huh?" He wasn't certain he had heard correctly.

"That stuff on the wall, you like it?" It was Andy, thin, lanky, a couple days growth of white whiskers on his chin. He took a sip from his glass of beer. Vic had introduced them on the first day but Andy hadn't seemed too interested. In fact, it had been Andy who Mike had taken his first empty beer glass from.

"I don't know if I like it, but it's interesting."

"Think it's cool?" Andy's eyebrows raised, "Romantic?"

"No, well, kind of cool but not romantic. It must have been scary. I wonder what these guys were thinking when the photo was taken."

"Can't help you there, but there," Andy pointed toward the opposite wall, "I can tell you what one of the chaps in that photo with the airplane was thinking."

"Really?" Mike walked across the room looking for a photo with a plane. He saw it, a wide one. "Which one?" Mike squinted at the men sitting on the wings and in front of a large plane with four propellers.

"That one right in front of you." Andy snapped.

Mike looked at him, "I mean which one is you?"

"Can't ya tell?" Andy sipped his beer again. Mike wasn't certain if the man was kidding or not and looked toward the bartender, Dan was working today, for a clue. Dan just smiled and shrugged.

"That plane's a Lancaster, MK-X. Best damn plane ever built. But she was a bitch to keep in the air. German's kept shooting hell out of them."

"Andy," Dan spoke and pointed to a sign above the bar 'Profanity Not Tolerated'.

"Yeah, yeah. Pardon my French." Andy flicked his hand at Dan. "Shot the heck up every mission." Andy turned and gave Dan a wry grin.

"You flew one of these?" Mike asked. He couldn't believe he was actually talking with a real war veteran about the war.

"No, not me but I helped keep her in the air."

"Mechanic?"

"Mechanic, welder, loader, fueler, miracle worker, whatever it took to keep those birds flying."

"Which one are you?" Mike peered at the faces staring into the camera. "Here, on the wing, between the engines, the tall guy?"

"No, that was Gus, Gus the Gunner. Twice we had to cut him out of the tail. Third time only part of him was still in there." Andy looked down at his table. "That's me holding onto the landing gear."

Mike looked at the young man who had one hand braced against the wheel strut, leaning, one leg crossed over the other. He was smiling. There was a rag in the hand on his hip or maybe it was hanging from the pocket of his coveralls. The coveralls had been rolled down to his waist, the arms tied in front. He wasn't wearing a shirt. He looked dirty but his smile looked as though he was enjoying the moment.

"Where was this taken?"

"England, Waddington. Near the end."

"How old were you."

Andy looked toward the ceiling, his chin moving a bit as though he was chewing something small. "Twenty, twenty-one. Something like that."

"What was it like?"

"What?"

"Being there. In the war and everything."

"Like nothing you can ever know. I remember…"

Then the lounge door opened and two voices broke the spell that had been building between Mike and Andy. Andy stopped talking and looked at his table. Mike looked at the men who walked in, ready to make a break for the back if one was Grumps. None were, they were much younger. They called to the bartender, got their drinks and sat at a table. Mike went about his duties but took a moment to pause by Andy, "Thanks for sharing."

An hour later, Mike saw Grumps pull into the Legion parking lot so he headed downstairs into the hall to see if there was something he could do down there. He let Dan know he would be leaving soon. Everything had been put away, so he settled for pushing the broom around the floor for a bit. After that he left by the basement door. He expected Grumps would stay for at least an hour, so he had time to get home and check something out.

During the walk, Mike thought about his conversation with Andy. He wondered about the story that the man had been about to share before they had been interrupted. He hoped they could get back to it again. He thought about stopping by the pool, maybe talk with Suzie but then he remembered his grounding and he didn't want to press that. He redirected himself back to the library where he could look up more information on Lancaster bombers.

By the time Mike was almost home the urge to look under the tarp in the barn was burning within him. He decided he would just do it. Then he rounded the driveway and saw Gramps' car in the driveway. A cloud passed in front of the sun and the wind kicked up a bit, raising goosebumps on Mike's arms. Thoughts of the tarp fell out of his mind.

"Where have you been?" Grumps stood inside the kitchen, blocking the doorway when Mike opened it to enter.

"At the library."

"I was at the library. You weren't there."

"Maybe I was at lunch?"

"What time did you go for lunch?"

Mike was silent. He was caught because he had no idea what time Grumps had been there. He took a guess, "About one or one thirty, I don't remember. What's the issue Grandpa?"

"You are grounded. Did you forget about that whole smash up you did?"

"No," Mike felt his world growing smaller, his vision narrowing, a buzz started in the back of his head, "I didn't forget that."

"Think you can just do whatever you want?"

"Gramps," Mike wasn't certain what he should say, if he should say anything. It seemed every time he spoke with Grumps, he was defending himself.

"Why don't you try doing some good?" Gramps banged his cane on the floor then stomped out of the room leaving Mike standing there looking at the floor.

"Mike..." Gramma started. There was a pained look on her face.

"It's ok." Mike was seething inside, his anger boiling. This was his worst time, the point at which he would make a very bad decision. He wanted to scream, rant, stomp and smash; use Hulk-like reactions to try to control a world in which he had very little control.

"Mollycoddling the little hooligan isn't going to help him." Grumps called from the other room.

Mike bubbled more, felt his fingernails biting into his palms, realizing his hands had transformed to fists. Mike was ready to unleash. Then the face of the young man, smiling as he held onto the landing gear of a heavy bomber, floated in front of him. Compared to what Andy had faced in those war days, what Mike was facing right now was calm seas. Andy's situation was not of his own making, Mike had certainly had a hand in his own fate; he had picked up that rock and thrown it of his own free will. He might have been succumbing to peer pressure, but it was still his own choice. And Andy could smile even though he was living in mortal danger every day, when his choice had only been to serve his country, protect innocents. Mike chose to accept the fact that how he was feeling was entirely his own fault. The fact that Grumps was unwilling to look at any aspect of him except one single action was out of his control, that was Grumps' responsibility. At that moment Mike felt his anger flush out of him leaving him feeling…free.

He smiled at his Grandmother, stepped toward her, embraced her and said, "It's ok Gramma. It's all ok." He hugged her tight and whispered, "I still love him, and I can handle this."

Mike went and stood by his Grandfather who had turned on the TV.

"You are right," Mike confessed, "I wasn't at the library this afternoon." Grumps turned from the TV to Mike. "I thought that if I could get a job it might show you that I am not what you think I am, that I can be responsible. That's what I was doing. That's why I wasn't at the library this afternoon. I'm sorry I broke my grounding."

"Really?" Grumps had a look on his face that Mike could only interpret as gloating. "So not only a smasher, you're a liar too. You just finished telling me that you were at the library and now you're admitting you weren't. That makes you a liar."

Mike felt the ball of anger rushing back into him again. Was there no way to get this man to be reasonable? "I can't control how you see me, but I wish you would see all of me, see me very well. If you only want to see what I can do wrong, I guess you might miss out on the best parts of me." Mike saw the sneery smile fall from Grumps' face, but he felt no accomplishment in that. "Can I work if I get the opportunity?"

"That might help keep you out of trouble." Grumps said after a pause, "but know this, this is a small town and eventually everything gets around. I might as well lift the grounding; you are going to get what's coming to you for the rock thing anyway and I obviously can't control you. If you're going to hang yourself, I'll give you the rope."

Mike wasn't certain how he should respond. On the one hand, he was now free to work toward his goal without the need to deceive his grandfather, but he certainly couldn't say 'thank you' to the offer of the rope to hang himself so he settled for, "OK."

With that he headed back into the kitchen which now smelled like a wonderful supper in the oven. He knew he had crafted his words to his grandfather carefully, so he wasn't really lying but he wasn't giving out all the details either. He didn't really feel good about that but felt it was justified.

"We'll chat after supper on the porch." Gramma said. Mike understood. He knew it would be too easy for their conversation to be overheard here and he didn't want her supporting him to be perceived by Grumps as dishonouring him. Sometimes life could be so complicated.

That night he wrote to his parents.

Dear Mom and Dad. I hope things are going well for you there, that Dad can figure out the issues at the dam and that you two are able to work on the other issues together. I am learning how important it is to be respectful of other people's opinions and feelings even when you don't agree with them. Gramma has taught me that it is important to compromise on issues even when it can be very difficult. I guess that is why their marriage has lasted, they (mostly she from what I've seen so far but I'm sure there is good in Grampa too) struggle to fix things, not throw them away and replace them with something else. I want you both to know that I love you and need you as my parents. I know I haven't shown this very well in the past but I will do better in the future. I know there is good in me but I need to be better at showing this to everyone else. This is something that Gramps has taught me. I know I've done a lot of complaining about having to be here but I think this is actually going to be my best summer ever. At least I am going to do everything I can to make it that way. I wish I hadn't messed up the start of it so bad...that hasn't helped. Love Michael

And there was an email from Janice.

Dear Mike. There isn't a lot of new news to pass on. I have been busy with soccer and dance. I think I told you that I am in jazz and ballet classes. They are fun but a lot of work too. I like them. Haven't seen any new movies but have started a new book. It is called Love Under Two Stars. It is science fiction but a love story in case you couldn't figure that out from the title. It's about a human girl who falls in love with a guy (sort of) from another galaxy. Guess what? The galaxy has two suns...duh.

My cousin told me about the kiss. She said you are a good kisser. Maybe I can find out for myself. Janice

'Whoa!' Mike thought and read the last sentence again, and again. He felt tingly all over. Suddenly in his memory she seemed even prettier. He tried to write back to her but couldn't come up with any words so he put his phone away, leaving her email unanswered but in his mind, he was pretty sure he would like her to find out too.

Under the Tarp

The next morning when Mike headed into town, he felt like he had been released from prison. He didn't have to worry about being seen someplace he shouldn't be, didn't have to hide from Grumps. He wasn't certain he wanted Grumps to know he was working at the Legion yet, so it was more like he was on parole, but at least now he could go back to the pool when he wanted. And he wanted. He had tucked his trunks and towel under his arm as he was leaving the house. All that and there was a girl who wanted to kiss him.

"Kid," Mike heard as he was walking past the Andrews house. He looked around for the voice but didn't see anyone. Then it came again, "Kid."

Mike continued to look around but still couldn't see who was calling but there was something familiar about the voice.

"Here. Ya blind?"

Mike turned toward the Andrews house, peering into the perpetual gloom that was the front yard. A form shuffled from the porch.

"Mr. Andrews?" Mike squinted at the man.

"Just Andy and of course it's me. Who were you expecting? Ghandi?"

Mike swallowed, trying to judge if the whitehaired man was joking or not. He wasn't certain so he just smiled.

"You DR's kid?"

"DR?" Mike said then remembered his conversation with Sheila.

Before he could answer Andy said, "I seen you walking along this road a few times. You living here?"

Mike looked up and down the street then back at Andy, "I'm staying with my grandparents. At the end of the road."

"Oh, so you're DR's GRANDkid."

"Yes, but I only know him as Bert...I mean I don't call him Bert, I call him Gramps."

"Bert, so that's his name. Everyone knows him as DR, everyone from before anyway."

Mike took a few moments to process what Andy had said. "They still call him DR?"

"That's his name. At least at the Legion."

"I know they call him that. Sheila told me."

Andy interrupted, "All the riders got called that. Medics got called Doc." Mike was curious what aircraft mechanics might be nicknamed. The old man shuffled beyond the shadows and Mike was able to see him in the sunlight. He really looked old, his chin stubbled with grey and greyer growth.

"Didn't he tell you? That he was a rider in the war, zipping around on his motor bike delivering all kinds of stuff for the brass?"

"He never talks about that."

"Yeah, DR, Despatch Rider," Andy spoke as though he hadn't heard Mike's last statement, "you're not daft, are you?"

"No, I don't think so. He just never talks about it. What did they call you?"

Andy gave Mike a strange look, his head tilted a little, eyebrows knitted. "Andy."

"Oh, I just thought..."

"Don't they teach you kids anything in school anymore?" Andy squinted at Mike; one eye completely closed.

Mike tried to catch up with Andy's conversation, "Not much about the war but I've been studying it at the library."

"Ah, that's why you're hanging at the hall with all us old farts, studying the walls and crap."

"Do you know much about Gramps? When he was in the war I mean."

"Some. Doesn't talk about it much but we've shared words a time or two. My toast must be done and I'm out here jawing with you." Andy turned back to his house.

"If you see him, please don't tell him I'm working at the Legion. I don't think he would like that."

Andy turned back to Mike and looked at him for a

moment then raised his chin and turned back to the house, fading into the shadows. Mike watched him climb the steps. It seemed to take a long time. 'Wow,' Mike thought, 'someone does live in this old house.'

As he walked toward the library Mike thought about Andy's words. He wondered what Gramps had shared with Andy and why. When he had spoken about the Andrews house, he hadn't sounded like he liked it very much. Mike tried to picture Grumps on a motorcycle, leather helmet and goggles but the image wouldn't take shape in his mind.

At the library, he looked up more information on despatch riders. He became absorbed. He was startled when someone grabbed his chair from behind, giving it a hard shake. Jack and Alan laughed.

"Hey bookworm, heard you were hanging out here at the library." Jack said, giving Mike a slap on the shoulder.

"Don't get enough of this at school?" Alan said, looking around as though he was unfamiliar with the library.

"Just reading up on some stuff I'm interested in." Mike did his best to be casual.

"What kind of porn they let you cruise in the library?" Jack leaned over Mike's shoulder and adjusted his screen so he could see it.

"Not porn," Mike started.

"What's this shit?" Jack asked. "War? You a war monger Mikey?"

"No," Mike bristled at the Mikey, turned his screen back. He didn't want to share any of this with these guys. He had no reason to trust them so he had no reason to share with them. "Just getting ready for history next semester. I heard there is a segment on the war.

Then the alarm on his cell phone went off reminding him of a Ladies Auxiliary event he had agreed to help with. He didn't want these guys to know he was working there.

"I gotta go." He said, signing out of the computer and gathering his stuff.

"What ya up to now, Mikey?" Jack asked.

"Look, it's Mike, ok? I just got something to do." Mike headed to the door.

"Whoa, chill man." Jack held up his hands.

"Going for a swim?" Alan pointed at his towel.

"Maybe later."

"Secret mission?" Jack asked.

"No, just something." Mike really wanted them to leave him alone. He was certain if they found out he was helping at the Legion; it would just become a source of ridicule from them. They would tease him about chasing old ladies or something. He didn't want them to taint what he was doing, knowing that he was enjoying the experience.

Jack and Alan gathered their bikes and followed him.

"You can tell us; we won't give you up."

"You wouldn't be interested."

"Let us decide that."

Mike headed to the drug store. He knew it had both a back entrance as well as a front. Maybe he could ditch these guys there; they wouldn't be able to bring their bikes in the store. He had to get rid of them quick or he would be late.

They left their bikes outside.

Mike rushed through the store, not running but keeping up a good pace. They followed him out the front door. Mike hadn't expected that. He turned right, heading away from the Legion. What could he do now?

"Come on Mike, we just want to hang."

"Maybe later."

"Just tell us what you're doing."

Mike stopped and turned to face them. "Look, I am doing something. OK? You're not invited. OK? Maybe we can hang later. OK?"

"Whoa, bitey Mikey." Jack held his hands up again. "If you don't want us along just tell us. Don't need to chew our heads off."

"Yeah," Alan intoned, "If you want to go play with yourself, just let us know."

Mike just looked at them.

"Ok, ok, we can take a hint. You're doing something private," Jack elbowed Alan and both teens laughed.

"With your privates." Alan finished.

Jack whispered something to Alan who nodded. They turned and took off at a run back toward their bikes. Mike was certain their plan was to follow him so he turned and ran the opposite direction. At the next corner he turned right again, circling back toward the back of the drug store. By the time Jack and Alan got their bikes and returned, he would be long gone.

With them out of his way he headed to the Legion at a trot. He was going to be late.

"Thought you went AWOL." Sheila smiled at Mike ten minutes later.

"Sorry," Mike went to the stack of folding tables and dragged the top one off. He knew how the room needed to be set up. "Got way laid." He carried the table to where it needed to be set up.

"We are happy to have your muscles helping us out."

Mike felt the blood rush to his face. He continued with the set up as he pondered how to ask Sheila about the war. More ladies came in and Mike recognized Pearl and Helen and was introduced to others. He tried to remember all their names but there were too many.

"Sheila, what did you do when the war was on?"

"Which war?"

"World War Two"

Some of the other ladies snickered.

"How old do you think I am?" Sheila stood with her hands on her hips.

Mike felt the colour rising in his neck again. He really hadn't thought about that, he just figured everyone in the Legion was around at that time. He didn't know how to answer her question or if he was really expected to.

"You might want to talk to Pearl or Gertie, they had husbands in the war." Sheila raised a hand to her hair, "Guess I need to have words with my hairdresser."

Mike thought it was best that he kept his mouth shut for a bit. He thought about what she had said though. He knew the war ended in 1945, that meant that anyone who was alive then had to be over sixty. Anyone who had been in the war or working in the war effort had to be in their eighties now. Sheila seemed old to him but not that old. He would have to be more sensitive.

When he was working in the lounge later that day, he asked Dan the bartender about Legion members.

"I thought everyone here had been in the war."

"World War 2?" Dan gave a little laugh. "Sometimes it seems like it but anyone who ever served in the military can be a member here. Even their spouse or kids or grandkids can join. Most of our members have never been to war. Lots of peacekeepers, a few Korea vets, even some who were in Vietnam. We're kind of running out of war vets though. The buggers have a bad habit of dying on us." Dan smiled at that so Mike figured it was a dark joke.

"I guess that's a good thing. There being fewer war vets, not them dying."

"I would agree with that. Still seems a shame though, the number of young men and women Canada still sends into war zones and them coming home broken."

"At least it's not like how it was in Europe. I've been doing some reading and there were thousands and thousands killed and wounded."

"Thankfully."

"I asked Sheila what she did during the war." Dan stopped wiping the glass he had just taken from the dishwasher and looked at Mike, his eyes wide, "I think I insulted her."

"You think? She probably wasn't even born then. She's younger than me and I was just a kid when my dad enlisted."

"You're not a vet?"

"Nope. Son of a vet. I don't remember when he left but I remember when he came home. That's how young I was."

"I hope she's not mad at me."

"She'll get over it. Why are you so interested in all this?

Most kids are into video games and stuff."

"Well, if you promise not to tell," Mike looked at Dan and waited until Dan nodded, "I want to know more about my Grandpa. I know he was in the war."

"Why don't you just ask him? He's still alive?"

"Yeah, but he's hard to talk to."

"Who is he?"

"He doesn't know I'm working here. I think he would be mad."

Dan leaned toward Mike, "I'm a bartender. We know how to keep secrets."

"Bert Weinstein but I think everyone calls him..."

"DR." Dan finished. "The old guys call him DR."

Mike laughed. Not because Dan knew him by his real name but because he called the vets 'the old guys' and Dan was almost as old as they were.

"You know him then?"

"Hard not to, he comes in here most days. He's pretty quiet though. Doesn't talk much to me."

"I know that feeling. Seems he only talks to me when it's to give me trouble."

"Makes you mad at him?"

"No, not mad. I want him to understand me though, like me. I think if I get to know him it might get better that way."

"So, you're hoping to talk to the other vets, learn about him that way?"

"Something like that. Even just more about the war. I've been studying it at the library but that mostly just says what happened. I think there's a lot missing. Like what it was really like to live through that."

"The personal aspect."

"Yeah. Most the them who went weren't much older than me. I couldn't imagine doing that."

"I'll see if I can soften up a few of the members for you. The ones who were in WWII are getting pretty thin. That was a long time ago."

"That'd be great. Thanks Dan. I better get to work."

"Yeah, I can see it piling up here." Dan looked around the mostly empty lounge.

Mike wandered around the Legion looking at the memorabilia on the walls. He had seen most of it already but now he was studying the artifacts, especially the photos. He was trying to picture the old men in the lounge as the young men in the photographs. One thing he did notice was how the young men all seemed to be smiling. Mike wondered how they could do that knowing they could be killed at any time.

Then he saw the motorcycle photo again and remembered he wanted to look under the tarp. How had he forgotten his earlier mission? He decided that if things didn't get busier here, he would cut out early. He would head home and look under that damn tarp, pardon his French.

While he was working someone mentioned the Sales Barn. Mike recalled Gram speaking about it too. He enquired, "Excuse me, I heard you mention the Sales Barn. It's on Tuesdays, isn't it?"

"Yes," the man of about fifty said.

"Where is it?"

"At the sales arena."

"Where's that?"

"Not far from here. Just up the road on Murray Street. On the right."

"Is it still open?"

"Pretty sure." The man paused a moment then looked at his friend on the other side of the table, "It closes at four, doesn't it?" His friend nodded in agreement.

"Thanks." Mike turned and let Vic Dan know he was leaving.

"Oh sure, abandon me to all this work." Dan waved his are arms indicating the still mostly empty lounge.

Mike smiled, hung his apron on the hook at the bar, washed his hands, then headed out. It was just after two so if it wasn't too far, he would still have a good chance to check it out.

It turned out to only be three blocks away. Mike was really getting to like small towns, easy to get around with everything so close. He had been expecting old rickety booths with a few people picking over tables with stuff heaped on them, he wasn't prepared for the crowded parking lot and the number of people milling around. The sales arena was more like a rustic barn, but more modern, with regular doors, garage-style roll-up doors and a constant parade of people moving in and out of the building. There were also booths set up around the entrance and along the walk leading up to it. Mike could feel the increase in energy generated by the people. It seemed that everyone in Aylmer must be here. Then Mike remembered that Gram had said people come from all over the county. He waded in.

Mike spent the next hour bumping his way through the booths both outside and inside the building. The noise level inside was high as people talked, laughed and negotiated deals. He was jostled a lot, bumped into, spoken to. He found it difficult watching where he was going and looking at things at the same time. No one seemed to be upset if they got bumped a bit so he figured everyone was feeling the same way. Every time he stopped to look over a table, the owner would speak to him. Everyone looking to sell something and there seemed to be everything for sale. Skates, luggage, books, Mike even saw a sign pointing to cars for sale in the parking lot. Old stuff, new stuff, ancient stuff, rusty stuff, dented and bent stuff and stuff to eat. Grandma had been right in her observation that it was like a carnival. Mike found it entertaining just to see the variety of wares and the efforts of the owners to sell them.

Then he saw something that made him stop. Behind a table full of used things, Mike saw a blue and white dirt bike. A helmet hung from the handlebar.

"What size is the motor?" Mike pointed at the bike.

"90 cc." The man behind the table was raw-boned, scrawny, wearing a sleeveless t-shirt and dirty jeans.

"How much?"

The man looked Mike up and down, not even trying to

be discreet. "Hundred and twenty-five."

Mike wasn't sure what other questions to ask. He thought it would be cool to have a motorcycle like that, give him something to do besides the library and Legion. But that much, it would take all his savings and then some. And what would his parents think? And how would he get it home to Kingston? And what about Grumps? But, to be able to twist that throttle, hear the engine rev, feel the vibration, the power waiting to kick him over bumps and jumps. Mike felt his heart speed up. But then there was Grumps.

"Ok, thanks." He said and turned away.

"Don't' be too hasty there Slick." The grizzled man called after him. "You know it won't last long at a price like that."

Mike turned back. "I'll be back." As he walked away, he really wanted his words to be true.

"I got parts too." The man wasn't giving up too easy. Mike waved at him

As he continued to explore the Sales Barn, Mike kept thinking about the bike. When he saw something that caught his eye, he would think about how much further away from the motorcycle the purchase would put him, and he resisted. Except for a jumbo dog. The smell of food was everywhere and he just could not deny himself everything. With a healthy dollop of spicy mustard and horseradish, he couldn't resist. When he bit into the hot delicacy, he felt steam blast from his eyes and knew it was a worthwhile expense.

Soon the vendors were packing up their wares. Mike couldn't resist one more pass near the table that had the motorcycle. He hoped it was still there. The man was pushing it toward one of the big doors.

"Didn't manage to sell it?" Mike asked.

"Had lots of people looking at it."

Mike smiled. This guy was a true salesman, always applying pressure, urgency, encouraging you to buy now. And sure, there would have been lots of people looking at it, everyone who walked past the table couldn't miss it. That didn't mean they were interested in it.

Mike headed toward home.

He thought he might stop by the pool, see if Suzie was working but then he remembered about Jack and Alan. They had seen his towel and might be waiting for him there. They were too nosey about what he was doing so he decided to skip it today. Besides, he wanted to make sure he got home before Grumps.

When he got home, he went straight to the barn, straight to the back stall and lifted the tarp. He had been right. Hidden in this dark corner was an old motorcycle. It could have been the same one as in the photograph on the Legion wall. From his reading at the library he knew it was a Scout, made by Indian Motorcycles and it had been a favorite of despatch riders. He wondered how Grumps had gotten it home and why it was secluded like this.

Mike pulled the tarp all the way off and dropped it in a heap. Clouds of dust puffed up from the floor. It hadn't been moved in a long time. He still couldn't see the bike very well since the stall was dim, the fluorescent light above it, dark. Mike reached up, gave the tube a twist. The light flickered then blazed bright pushing the shadows into the corners. Someone had simply undone the bulb to keep the stall in shadow. Mike stood back and looked at the motorcycle. It was a mess.

It was covered in dust despite the tarp, but also mud and other stuff stuck to the metal. There was old straw and what looked like black rice on the seat and pedals. And cobwebs. Spiders had been busy all over. The handlebars, wheel spokes, wires and cables all festooned with white, wispy threads. Mike stepped forward, reached to touch the hand grips but heard gravel crunch in the driveway.

With a start, he grabbed the tarp and dragged it back over the motorcycle. He rushed to get it back into the same position it had been in before. He had noted a dark stain in the area that formed a V between the handlebars and front fender and got that back in the same place. It mostly looked right but now there was a lot less dust on it. He hoped Grumps wouldn't notice.

He heard Grumps walking on the gravel. It sounded like he was coming to the barn. Mike realized he had left the door open a bit. Grumps must have seen. He looked at the bike and thought it looked like it had. Then he remembered the light, the fluorescent tube bright over the crime scene.

Mike reached up and twisted the tube. Darkness enveloped the stall as Grumps pushed the door open.

"What are you doing?" The old man asked him.

"Um," Mike scrambled to come up with something to say, "The light here was out so I was checking it." He twisted the tube and it flickered to life. "Must just have moved a bit. Lost its connection."

"Turn that thing off. I told you don't be messing with stuff. Don't be wasting 'lectricity back there." Grumps looked around the barn. "Hmmm." He walked across to the work bench and opened some of the cupboards.

"I straightened things up a bit." Mike offered.

"Thought you were just sweeping."

"Mostly."

"Stay out of things." Then Grumps left.

"OK." Mike called after him. He felt totally deflated. He was happy Grumps hadn't taken the time to see that he had been messing with the motorcycle, but he had put so much work into cleaning the barn up and all Grumps could say was 'stay out of things'? Didn't the man have a sensitive bone in his body? 'Oh well,' Mike thought, 'at least I'm not in more trouble.'

He got the broom and swept up the evidence from the tarp that had fallen onto the floor where he had swept before.

That evening, as they sat on the porch having tea, Jeopardy and Grumps sounding off in the background, Mike said, "Gramps saw the barn but didn't say anything about the work I did there."

"You were in the barn today?"

"Yeah," Mike paused. He didn't want to say anything about peeking under the tarp, but he didn't want to lie to his

Grandmother either. "He looked in and only told me not to get in trouble."

"Sounds like good advice." Grandma's tone was light, and Mike wondered if she was kidding him or making a point.

"I mean, couldn't he even say 'good job' or something? At least acknowledge that I worked hard out there?"

"Is that why you did it?"

"Well no." Mike looked into his teacup as though there were leaves arranged in the bottom that might foretell his future. There weren't, the leaves were in a teabag in the pot.

"So then, why does it bother you so much?"

"I guess because I want things to be better between us. It would be nice if he wasn't angry with me all the time."

"Is he?"

"I think so. At least it feels like he is."

"And your feelings have always been correct?"

Mike thought about that for a minute. He looked out across the grass of the backyard, seeing the shadows creeping away from the house as the sun went down, hearing the crickets chirping in the long grass where the lawn ended, and the fields began. He had to confess that he really didn't understand Grumps.

"Try to remember," Gramma broke the silence, "he is not used to having to deal with anyone but me and he's been doing that for so long he's comfortable with it. I wonder how he really feels about you."

"Why don't you ask him?"

"Why don't you?"

And there it was, back in his lap. Mike looked at his grandmother, studying the lines in her face, the set of her jaw, the shape of her nose, the look in her eyes. He wondered about all the things she had faced and gotten through in her life, gathering her knowledge, wisdom, insights, thoughts and feelings just so she could share them with him on this night. He had kind of felt like she was a timid woman, dominated and controlled by her husband but Mike realized she was strong enough to bear what she had to, do what she had to, plan how she had to, in order to make her world work best for herself and her family. Sometimes storming the beaches is not the best approach. Sometimes you have to move covertly behind the lines, stealthy, making tiny little victories until everything sits as needed before striking. Much as his grandfather had done in the war; riding his motorcycle to deliver messages, enemy positions, strengths, weaknesses, movements so his higher headquarters knew the right time to strike. Even though each despatch rider was just one man, their cumulative effect could be devastating. Mike wondered if the war would have ended sooner if the Allies had employed a few grandmothers as despatch riders, or Generals.

"You're pretty smart Gramma." Mike said.

"Smart enough to have a wonderful grandson like you." She reached over and gave Mike a big hug. He hugged her back. Then Grumps banged open the door and thumped to his chair.

"What you two caterwauling about out here?" He dropped himself into his chair.

Gramma poured him some tea. "Life and all that's in it." She said simply.

Lying in bed, Mike thought about the motorcycle and his relationship with Grampa. Then it dawned on him how he could get everything in good with Grumps. He would restore the motorcycle, clean it up and get it running. There was no way that plan could fail. Feeling lighter than he had since he arrived here, Mike drifted off to sleep.

Closer Inspection

After Gramps headed to work, Mike headed to the barn to get a good look at the motorcycle and the scope of the work he had committed himself to. He raised the tarp, turned the light above it on and took a slow walk around the machine. It was a mess, worse than he remembered from his first look.

There was straw, mud, spider webs, rust and corrosion everywhere. The green paint was bubbled on the fuel tank and frame. One of the hand grip handles was broken, the tires were cracked and flat. This was going to be a big job. Mike decided the first thing he needed to do was clean it up. He retrieved the bucket he had found when he cleaned the barn, filled it at the tap by the workbench and got to work.

An hour later he replaced the tarp, spread straw and dirt around the floor of the stall so it wouldn't be obvious that anyone had disturbed it, and turned the bulb, leaving the stall in deep shadows. From the barn door it looked like everything was as it had been for...how long? Forty years? Too it didn't escape him how his actions must be like those of POWs hiding their efforts to escape from their captors.

"Gramma," Mike called into the house from the back-porch door. She answered him from somewhere in the house, "I'm heading to town. Do you need anything?"

"What are you up to?" She came into the kitchen from the living room. She was carrying a laundry basket.

"Going to the library then the Legion. Got another shift."

"I mean out in the barn. That place is becoming a second home."

"Oh nothing," Mike stumbled for words. He didn't want to lie but he couldn't tell her he was disobeying one of the few rules she had laid down 'leave the tarp alone'. "I just like it out there."

She gave him a funny look then said, "No, I don't need anything but thanks for checking. You need some money?"

While he had been working on the motorcycle Mike had thought about what it might cost to buy the parts he would need to replace and had decided he was going to accept the tips at the Legion. He ha told Sheila to use his tips to help a veteran and wasn't that what he was doing? He had some money in his savings account, but he was supposed to be saving towards college. "No, I'm good. I've been earning tips."

"Have fun."

Mike headed to the library. He needed to find out where he could get parts for the motorcycle. Mr. Google had served him well so far; he didn't think he would disappoint him now.

Later, on his way to the Legion Mike thought about what he had learned. Parts for old Indian's were not only hard to come by, they were expensive. He would need to earn a lot in tips to complete his project. When he asked Sheila about the envelope he had given her with the tips, she smiled, opened the drawer of her desk and brought out the money. "I kept this safe just in case you changed your mind."

"Don't worry, I will be using it to help a veteran." Mike noticed the envelope was heavier now, they had continued to add his tips to it.

"You're a good kid Doug. Even if you aren't too smart about how long ago the war happened."

"Hey, I'm real sorry about that."

"Forget it. I know what you were trying to do and it's ok."

Mike left her office feeling like they had gotten their relationship back on the right track. Now if he could only do that with Grumps.

That evening when Gramps clomped onto the porch for his tea he said, "I heard they got some kid working sometimes at the Legion. Seems you can't go anywhere without a bunch of kids messing things up."

"Oh?" Gramma said. Mike remained quiet not knowing what to say. "What's he like?"

"I don't know. I haven't seen him yet. Heard some of

the other guys talking about him."

"Were they upset?"

Grandpa grew quiet for a moment, "I don't know. I just heard them talking. Some brat named Doug or something. Goddamn kids everywhere."

"Well maybe you will just have to let that kid make his own bed with you." Grandma smiled at Mike and gave him a wink.

"Better just stay out of my way. That's all I can say."

Girls Everywhere

Mike spent most of the morning in the barn going over the motorcycle, it was already looking better. It was amazing what a little soap, water and elbow grease could accomplish. He noted the model and serial number of the bike and made a list of the parts that were broken. He confirmed later at the library that it was a Scout, probably a 1941 model. That would make it a bit easier to get the right parts.

He made a list of the parts he would need:
- Front and rear tires
- Ignition wiring
- Hand grips

He was confident he could fix up the rest of what was wrong, seized cables, torn upholstery, scratched and rusted paint. It wouldn't be perfect, but it would be ridable. He took a photo with his phone so he could find the right colour paint.

Before he left the barn, he replaced the tarp and messed up the floor in the stall. He headed into town.

The smell of the pool washed over him and Mike felt like he was returning home. He hadn't been swimming for days and was looking forward to doing some lengths, letting the cool water drain some of the heat from his body. He saw Jack and Allen and Jeannie's bikes locked up in the rack near the entrance. It had been a while since he had spoken to any of them, maybe it was time to give in a little.

Mike spotted them sitting on some deck chairs by the fence. He waved, smiling, and they waved back. Even Jeanie. Mike felt a flush run through him.

"Come on over." Jack called.

"Yeah." Jeanie offered. Her bikini bathing suit was dark blue with gold and made her legs look long. Slender and long, Mike caught himself gawking and averted his gaze.

He strolled over, trying to act nonchalant, and tossed his towel onto an unoccupied lounger. "I need to get some lengths in. Then I can come over. Cool?"

"Cool." Jack nodded.

"Do a couple for me." Allan flexed his arms, "I'm feeling a bit out of shape."

Everyone laughed.

Mike noticed Suzie in the white lifeguard chair. She was wearing a red, one-piece bathing suit that had a blue stripe with yellow piping down each side. Aviator sunglasses and a white pith helmet hat shaded her eyes. She was speaking to some kids in the shallow end but Mike couldn't hear what she was saying. He tried giving her a little wave, but she didn't notice. He remembered to jump into the pool, not dive.

As the water closed over his head, he relished the coolness that engulfed him. He let himself sink to the bottom drinking in the distorted sounds of kids at play, the pressure of the water, the way his pores seemed to open, letting the fire in his skin leak out. When his head broke the surface a minute later, he was once again surrounded by the laughter, splashes, echoey noises of kids at play, the real world. Picking the clearest path he could, he swam using the breaststroke to get warmed up. Soon enough he would change to the crawl to do his serious lengths.

Water dripped from his body as he approached his small-town friends.

"You trying to become a fish?" Jack asked. "Didn't think you were ever getting out."

"I need to keep in shape." Mike picked up his towel, "Did I tell you I'm on the swim team at school?" Mike glanced at Jeanie. The three just looked at him. "Coach is murder, especially at the start of the year when everyone seems out of shape. Almost killed me last year."

"You have the build of a swimmer." Jeanie said. Jack turned to her and slapped at her leg. "What?" She asked with a mock shocked look on her face that immediately changed to a smile.

"Don't be checking out alien meat." Jack said. His face was set but his eyes were dancing. Mike assumed this was a bit of a game between them but didn't know for certain. He was happy that Jeanie had even noticed he had a body.

"So, what's with you two anyway," Mike felt himself venturing into an area he wasn't certain he wanted to go, but he had to know.

"Whadda ya mean?" Jack looked at him, one eye closed.

"You two a thing?"

Jack, Allen and Jeanie all laughed. Jeanie's mouth opened in a silent scream.

"Us?" Jack waggled a finger between him and Jeanie. "Don't know what you city kids do, but us hicks don't go in for all that incest stuff."

"Oh, you're related?" Mike felt himself jumping inside. Maybe Jeanie wasn't hooked up with anyone. "Brother sister?"

Jeanie expanded her silent scream face and covered her mouth with her hands.

"No," Jack snorted, "my sister's a nerd. Jeanie's my cousin. Her dad's my uncle, my mom's brother.

"Cool." Mike intoned. "And what about you?" He looked at Allan, "You related too?"

"Naw, town's not that small but we've been friends forever."

"Cool." Mike felt a bit like a parrot.

"I'm glad I'm not related to that." Jack pointed with his chin. Mike turned and saw Suzie walking near them on the pool deck. "I could use some of that." Mike turned back to Jack feeling uncomfortable with the tone in his voice.

Jack spoke again, a bit louder and it was obvious he wanted to be heard. "Suzie Lucknow...get me luckynow." Suzie's head turned in their direction.

"Hey Jack," Mike moved a bit, placing himself between Jack and Suzie, "That's not cool."

"Wadda ya mean?" Jack squinted up at him. Jack seemed to be striking a confident pose, leaning back on his arms, legs outstretched. Mike saw his pelvis move in then out. "Suzie makes everyone luckynow." His voice raised a bit more. He licked his lips.

"That's enough." Mike stepped forward.

Jack sat forward. "What's your issue?"

"There's no need to talk like that."

"What?" Jack pointed in Suzie's direction.

"Just shut up. No one deserves to be talked about like that. You wouldn't like it," Mike turned toward Jeanie, "would you?" He wanted to shut this conversation down before Suzie was close enough to hear what was really going on.

Jack stood up, his body tense, face tight, "Just who do you think you're talking to?"

"Oh," so it's ok for you to talk trash about someone but when the talk moves in another direction..." Mike's words were cut off when Jack swung his fist.

Mike caught the motion at the edge of his vision and managed to turn a bit, taking the blow at an angle rather than full on. He staggered to the side, caught himself and lashed back. His punch was low and Jack moved to the side at the same time. Mike's fist landed on the side of Jack's throat and Jack dropped to the concrete deck. Mike stepped forward, readying another hit when Suzie spoke behind him. "Mike."

As though coming from a trance, Mike realized the sight he was presenting. The sounds of laughter, splashing, play had all ceased. He looked around. Everyone was looking at him standing over Jack who was coughing, gasping, holding both hands to his throat.

Suzie pushed past him, knelt by Jack. She looked back at Mike, "How could you do this?"

"I, I, ... he," Mike pointed at Jack a moment then dropped his hand. How was he going to explain? "He was saying nasty things..." Mike knew how weak his words sounded.

"And you punch him for that? In the throat? Do you know how dangerous that is?" She turned back to Jack not hearing the end of Mike's statement "...about you."

"I didn't mean to..." Mike stood staring at the shambles his afternoon had become. Everyone was looking at him as though he was guilty of something more than protecting the honour of a girl, standing up to a bully. Didn't anyone know that he was the innocent one? That Jack was just a strong-arm, insensitive, inconsiderate, ignorant? And he had punched first.

Allan was glaring at Mike, his hands fists, the cords in his neck standing out, his whole posture a sign of warning. Jeanie was squinting at him as though a gross zit had suddenly erupted on his face. Suzie glanced at him again, the same look of disappointment on her face as had been on Gram's when Campbell brought him home from the Trucker's Haven incident. Once again, he was up to his neck in it and it wasn't his fault. No one had seen Jack strike first, except Allan and Jeanie.

Mike felt the blood rising to his head, pounding in his temples, narrowing his vision. He felt a cloudiness creep into his consciousness and thought he was going to pass out. Blackness in the shape of hundreds of tight packed hexagons fell across his sight, a fuzzy buzzing pulsed in his ears. He turned and rushed toward the locker room; afraid he was about to faint. He slipped on the floor, fell to one knee but caught himself on one of the benches, sat down and held his head until his vision cleared. He felt his breathing slow and realized he had been hyperventilating. That must have been what triggered the faint.

After a few moments his head cleared but his body still tingled, felt weak, empty, hollow. Mike changed and left the pool, the whole incident feeling more like a bad dream. He looked at himself in the mirror before he left and noted a red mark on his jaw where Jack had hit him. It was likely going to bruise. Worse though, Suzie thought he was the bad guy.

He felt tears building again and he began running. He didn't know what else to do. Why was it that everything turned to shit for him? He thought he had made some friends, had a chance to get to know Jeanie better, start to enjoy his summer and now it was all crap. How could he go back to the pool? He'd likely be banned now. The place he liked the best. He stopped running, stood with his hands on his knees, breathing in gulps of air. How could he fix this? Maybe he could make Suzie understand.

He decided that was his best option. If he could speak with her, he could give her his side of the story, make her see what really happened. At least then he might be able to rescue the pool. He headed back to wait in the park across the street for Suzie to end her shift.

He watched Jack, Allen and Jeanie leave about thirty minutes later. They didn't see him, too busy laughing, probably at his expense. He was too far away to hear them but could see their animated movements as they unlocked their bikes. Why did he ever think he could be friends with them and what did he really see in Jeanie?

Sure, she was pretty, but she had been mostly cold to him. Except for that one comment about his body, she had hardly acknowledged he existed. But still, something in him wanted to be near her. Mike banged his fist on the bench he was sitting on, why was he focused on her.

Ten minutes later Suzie came out. Mike almost didn't recognize her. She must have curled her hair after her shift. She was wearing denim cutoffs and a white, short sleeved top with puffy shoulders. She looked so different than when wearing a swimsuit. Mike stood up then angled across the street to intercept her.

"Suzie," Mike called. She had set a quick pace and Mike had to jog a bit to catch up.

Suzie glanced at him. For just a moment her face softened, a smile started to curl her mouth up but then her features hardened, lines creased her forehead just like Grumps when he was angry. She looked away from him and quickened her pace.

"Suzie, please." Mike hated the pleading tone of his voice, but he needed to get her to listen to him. "I want to explain."

"I thought you were a nice guy Mike," She stopped and spun toward him. "but nice guys don't go around picking fights."

"I didn't pick that fight." Mike realized how loud his voice was, that he likely sounded angry. He paused a moment getting hold of himself then continued, his voice soft. "Jack swung first." Mike touched his face where the red mark was.

"And why would he do that?" Suzie's eyes were narrowed.

"Because I called him on his crap." Mike kept his head up, looked her in the eyes so she could see he was telling the truth. "He was saying things about you. Nasty things and that wasn't right. When I told him to shut up, that's when he punched me."

"I didn't hear any of that."

"I don't know how you couldn't, he wanted you to hear."

"What did he say?"

"I don't want to repeat it." Mike could feel the blood rushing to his face and looked away.

"Tell me. Tell me what was so bad that you had to fight about it."

"He called you," Mike paused, raised a hand to his mouth, "he said."

"Luckynow?" Suzie said for him.

Mike looked at her and swallowed. "Uh, yeah."

"Cripes, they've been saying that for years." Suzie turned and began walking but her pace wasn't as fast as it had been before.

"Well I don't think it's right." Mike followed a half step behind her.

"Well thank you for defending my honour, but it's really no big deal." Mike heard something in her voice that made him think it was a big deal.

"He's a bully and a creep and someone needs to reign him in. Let him know he can't just go around disrespecting people."

"Can't have people punching it out in my pool either."

"Well, I'm sorry about that but I'm not sorry I knocked him down. I'll do it again if I have to, but maybe I'd wait until we weren't in the pool."

Suzie gave him a quick glance and Mike noted that she was smiling. Not a huge smile but a little shy smile. Relief washed through him; he was certain she believed him.

"I hope you don't believe that." Suzie said.

"Believe what?"

"That luckynow thing. I'm not a slut you know." Suzie looked Mike in the eyes when she spoke.

Her remark shocked him. "I never thought you were. I mean," again Mike's mouth was getting ahead of his brain. He wanted her to know that he wasn't thinking about stuff like that about her, "um," Mike paused, if he said he never thought about sex and her, he might hurt her feelings, make her feel unattractive but if he said he had, he'd look like a creep. It seemed that no matter what he said it would be the wrong thing.

She flicked him another glance. "You mean you hoped I was? Is that why you waited for me?"

"No, no, no. Not that at all. Look Suzie, you seem like a nice girl," again she cast him a quick glance, "young lady. You've been nice to me. All I am trying to say is I am not the kind of guy who goes around picking fights. Well," again he paused because, in his past he certainly had been, "not anymore anyway. I didn't want you being mad at me, thinking I was something I'm not, or at least trying not to be. I wanted you to know the truth." Mike stopped and a moment later she stopped too and turned toward him. "You do believe me, don't you?"

"Yes, I think I do Mike Tuthill." She smiled and looked down a bit, raising a hand to pull some hair away from her face. "Thank you for being honest, and honourable."

"Thanks for listening to me." Mike took a step toward her. "Would it be ok if I walked with you? This is on my way home." It wasn't but he didn't care.

"Sure," Suzie turned and began walking. "that would be nice. But I thought you said you lived on Andrew street?"

"Yeah," Mike felt the blush climbing his neck, "I can get

there from here. Or there." He pointed up the street in the direction they were walking. Needing to change the subject he said, "So, what do you do when you are not lifeguarding?"

As they walked, Mike felt his mood lighten. He maintained a calm composure, at least he hoped he was, but inside he was jumping and leaping and dancing. For the next three blocks they chatted about life and movies and tv and their experiences. After she walked up the steps to her house, Mike headed home. He had had a full conversation with a girl, a pretty girl, and he didn't make an idiot of himself. He had managed to turn a sour situation into a comfortable stroll. Now if he could only do that with Grumps.

He thought how he might have handled this situation just a few weeks ago, before he recognized that his behavior was affecting his parent's relationship and realizing how important his parents were to him. He would have been sulky mad, he would have self-talked himself into a rage, lashed out. And his lashing out would have been at anyone. At school he might be mad at another kid but he would lash out at a teacher or janitor, even the principal, he wouldn't have cared. This time though, he had made himself work it out and he had done good. He was now convinced he could do it with Gramps. After all, he hadn't blown up a single time since getting here even though he had wanted to.

By the time he arrived home he was feeling pretty good but his newly realized talents were about to be tested.

As soon as he walked into his grandparent's house a look crossed his grandmother's face.

"What happened to you?" She crossed the kitchen then brought a hand to Mike's jaw. She turned his face to get a good look.

"Oh, it's nothing." Mike offered.

"It's bruised."

"What's going on in there?" Grumps voice carried from the living room. Mike heard the couch creak and knew the man was standing up. A moment later he heard the cane thump.

"Just a little bang." Mike wanted to downplay the mark. Didn't want them to know he had been in a fight but he didn't want to lie to them either. Lies had caused so many problems in the past.

Grumps stepped into the kitchen. "That's no little bang boy. What have you been up to? I know a punch mark when I see one."

Mike slipped into the bathroom. The mark had not been much when he looked at it at the pool. He looked into the mirror over the sink. He felt a burning in his stomach. Now it was a full on, purple and angry red bruise. How could he explain that? His shoulders slumped, he couldn't.

Mike walked out of the bathroom. "I got in a fight..."

Grumps made a gesture with his hands that said, 'see what I mean?' A look of concern crossed Gram's face. Both started to speak, Mike continued.

"but let me explain." And then he shared the truth with them. As he spoke, he watched Grump's face. The man went from anger, to concern, to understanding but something told Mike he wasn't going to get off that easy so he ended with, "She deserves to be treated with more respect than that, all girls do. What would you have done Grampa if someone spoke like that about Gram?"

Gramps rubbed the back of his neck. "Well I guess I wouldn't let it go either." Then after a moment, "Are these the same boys you were with the other day?"

Before he thought about what he was saying, Mike blurted, "Yeah but," and then he caught himself, but he knew it was too late. Gramps smiled, he had out witted his grandson, then said, "I don't know why you want to protect idiots like them. Why would you want to hang out with them?"

"I didn't know they were like that."

"You're not stupid."

"No, of course not. I kind of thought that but also thought maybe they were not all they appeared. Like me, I've done some things I wish I didn't but that's not me."

"Well," Gramps turned and headed toward the living

room, "I hope this has taught you something."

Mike turned to his Gramma. "Seems I am always telling you sorry."

She stepped forward and hugged him, "I hate the thought of you fighting but I understand. That was a noble thing for you to do…a bit dumb, but noble."

Mike smiled, not because of her words but because this was the first time he had come away from a bad situation with his grandfather somewhat on his side.

That night Mike sent an email to his parents. *Dear Mom and Dad. Hope all is ok with you. Hope Dad is working through his challenges. It seems I always have bad news when I write but I don't want to keep things from you, and I am not going to lie. I know I've done that in the past and it does nothing but mess things up…*then he went on to tell them about getting into the fight, but he finished with how it had turned out, him walking Suzie home. He was happy he could close his message with such positive news.

He had received another email from Janice. He wrote her back but didn't have much to say. He was sure she wasn't interested in his accomplishments with Suzie. There was nothing from Uwe or Chuck, but Mike wasn't surprised. They were not very active that way, hardly posted on Facebook or anything. He put his phone away and went to sleep.

Sweet Temptations

Mike thought that if he could order the parts he needed for the motorcycle today, he might get them before the end of next week. He hoped he wouldn't have to order them through eBay, he wasn't certain he would end up with what he wanted, and he wasn't sure about the whole on-line purchase thing. He didn't have a credit card so would have to set up a PayPal account and that all seemed a bit risky. And he didn't know how he would explain boxes being delivered to the house.

There wasn't a motorcycle shop in town, so he wondered where others got their parts. Maybe in the next town, St Thomas, it was quite a bit larger than Aylmer, but how could he get there without Gramps finding out?

After spending a few hours cleaning up the bike more and starting repairs to the cover on the seat, Mike headed to the library. After a bit on Google he found an ad from someone in Aylmer selling old motorcycle parts. Mike decided to pay the man a visit to see if he knew where to get what he needed.

Walking up the driveway toward a dried-out husk of a mobile home, Mike glanced around the yard cluttered with old appliances, bike frames, cars in various states of disassembly and scrabbles of brown grass amid large patches of dull earth. In the middle of the lawn was a round bare spot. In the centre of that was a scruffy looking dog on a heavy chain. Somehow, he wasn't too surprised when the man who had the motorcycle at the Farmer's Market slammed his way out of the trailer.

"I remember you." The man said, wiping his hands on coveralls that had been rolled down to his waist. "Can't resist the motorcycle eh, so you come to see old Don? Well I got two other people interested..."

"I'm not here for that." Mike cut him off. He wasn't interested in listening to sales pressure. "Can you get parts for old motorcycles?" Mike described what he wanted, showing Don his list.

"A '41 Scout?" Don squeezed one eye shut as he looked at the photos on Mike's phone. He was a thin, grizzled man. Mike had almost kept on walking when he realized this was the place he wanted, but it was the only lead he had for the parts he needed. "Don't see too many of those."

"Any idea where I might be able to get the parts?" Mike asked.

"Now hold on there. I may have what you need. Let me see that list again." He held out a dirty hand and Mike passed the paper he had scrawled the parts onto.

"And you got money?" The man's eyes darted over the paper.

"Well, I got some." Mike was feeling uncomfortable, but he was desperate enough to stay.

"Leave this with me. See what I can do."

Mike took that paper back and wrote his phone number on it. "OK, you can reach me here. How long will this take?"

"Don't rightly know," the man spoke slow, like he was dragging out his words or struggling to push them out of his mouth. Mike thought it was some sort of accent, but he had no idea where from. "Could be a few days, maybe a month."

A month! Mike felt his vision narrow. That wouldn't be any good. He wouldn't be able to hide what he was doing that long. "Well, as quick as possible would be best."

"Sure, sure. I'll call you." The man squinted at the paper then added, "You know, you'd look right smart sitting on the bike." He glanced toward the garage and Mike saw the motorcycle leaning against the wall. "Why don't you see how it fits?"

"Naw," Mike started.

"Come on. No harm in trying it out, getting the feel."

Mike really wanted to, but he didn't want to distract himself either. He knew he could only have one, the parts for Grump's bike or that one. "No thanks." He said.

"I'll let you start her up." Don smiled revealing several missing teeth. "Maybe give her a little run around the yard."

"I've never actually ridden a motorcycle." Mike confessed taking a small step toward Don.

"Nothing to it." Don's smile widened and he turned toward the garage. "Come on, I'll show ya. Just a little clutch, a little throttle and some balance."

"Well," Mike felt an irresistible pull. He'd always wanted to ride a motorcycle. "Maybe just sit on it."

"Sure, sure. Come on." Don coaxed him forward with a beckoning wave of his hand.

Mike took a step toward the bike then paused, he couldn't have both the parts and that motorcycle so why was he bothering? Because he wanted to, he needed to experience sitting on it, maybe understand a bit of how his grandpa and his great uncle could ride one of those things behind enemy lines, into mortal danger. He wanted to know that thrill.

Don lifted the bike from the wall, he gave a bit of a flourish when Mike approached. "Get on." He encouraged.

Mike paused a moment, savoring the experience, then he lifted his leg and straddled the bike.

"Got it?" Don asked still holding onto one handlebar.

Mike felt the weight against his thighs, "Yeah." It felt good, right. He sat, feeling the bike's suspension give a bit under his weight. This felt natural.

Don kicked the start lever out with one foot then stomped down on it, giving the throttle handle a little twist. The motor roared, spitting exhaust in a small white plume. An electric current, similar to the one that had coursed through him during that kiss at the wedding, shot up Mike's back and down his legs. He reached to the throttle and gave it a quick twist. He was lost in the blat of the engine and the thrill tickling every part of his body. Now he understood.

Don gave a little wave indicating, 'take her for a ride.'

Mike looked at him hoping his fear wasn't evident. He so wanted to just go tearing along but he had no idea how. Instead he gave the throttle another little turn. The bike responded.

Don stepped forward and gave Mike a few instructions

on how to work the gear shift, the clutch and the throttle. "Just take it easy, you'll do ok. Stay in the yard and don't dump it."

Mike kicked the bike into first gear, eased off on the clutch. The bike jumped forward then stalled.

"Happens to everyone. Just kick it back over and try again."

This time Mike managed to get the bike moving. It felt wobbly and unsteady and he was confused by the hand controls, but he persevered. After two times around the yard, almost dropping the bike on the turns, he felt a little more confident. Once it was moving it became a lot steadier. After a few more turns he pulled to a stop in front of Don.

Turning the bike off Don said, "You caught on quick. What'd ya think?"

"Pretty sweet." Mike didn't know what else to say. He was excited but still a bit scared too. The vibrations that the bike had sent up his arms, into his thighs were exhilarating. The feeling of power when he twisted the throttle was intoxicating. "That was so sick."

"Sure you want to be buying parts for an old bike?" Don held up the paper with the list. "You could ride her home." He gave a little point at the bike that Mike was still sitting on.

Mike sighed. He was really tempted to do just that, buy the bike and forget the motorcycle he had been told to leave alone. Then he remembered his real reason for fixing the Scout. He wanted that relationship with Gramps. That was something that would last a lifetime. That was something worth sacrificing for.

"I still want the parts but thanks for letting me ride her." Mike set the bike on its kickstand and stepped off it.

"Whoa there kiddo," Don rushed forward, taking the bike from Mike. He leaned the bike against the garage again. Mike looked at the depression the kickstand had pressed into the ground under the bike's weight. If Don hadn't caught it, it would have fallen over.

"I better get going. You'll call me when you know about

the parts?"

"Sure, sure." Don made a phone to his ear sign with his hand using his thumb and little finger.

Hoping he had done the right thing by trusting this odd man, Mike headed toward home.

Swim Lessons

Mike headed out early the next morning. Suzie had invited him to swim class and he thought it couldn't hurt. Couldn't hurt to spend a little more time with Suzie. At the very worst, he would be a bit better prepared for swim team in September. Mike found the cool morning invigorating; the dew was still on the lawns. Birds chirped in the trees. It was a perfect day.

He felt a bit vulnerable and out of place standing on the pool deck surrounded by kids half his age and height. A girl of about six squinted up at Mike and said, "I learnt to swim when I was little." Mike just smiled at her.

Suzie approached from the girl's locker room and, when she saw Mike, she smiled and gave a bit of a laugh.

"You came for lessons?"

"If the offer's still on the table...or the deck." Mike smiled back. "You said you would give me pointers."

"Sure, if you can keep up with these dolphins." Suzie waved at the kids standing around.

"Hey, we're not dolphins." Some of the young girls looked at each other, wrinkling their noses.

"No, but you can swim like them. Everyone in the pool. Swimmers 4, two lengths front crawl, 5, four lengths, 6, ten lengths." groans were heard at this announcement. "Anyone who outswims this guy," Suzie gripped Mike's arm, "gets floater privileges later."

Cheers and excited chatter erupted. Kids streamed into the pool shattering the calm surface of the water.

"Take the middle lane," Mike saw that lane markers had been installed, breaking the pool up into eight swim lanes. "Up and back then stop and wait for me. Start with breaststroke."

Suzie moved off to monitor the kids as they entered the pool and began their lessons.

Mike jumped in then kicked off the end. The water felt

good sliding down his body. He concentrated on his stroke, trying to remember all the pointers his coach had talked about. When he reached the end of the pool, the did a quick summersault, pushed off from the end and glided back toward the shallow end. He stopped at the end. Suzie was waiting.

"Don't let your hips drop. Concentrate on keeping your legs behind you, not below you. Again." Then she moved on calling out instructions and encouragement to the other swimmers.

Mike was disappointed that she didn't think his form was already perfect. He pushed off, thinking about his hip position. After each length Suzie was there to speak to him.

"Relax your shoulders."

"Look down during the glide. Look up only between strokes and for as short as possible."

"Don't anticipate your roll, flow into it."

By the time Mike pulled himself out of the pool an hour later he was feeling pretty defeated. She had picked apart every one of his strokes as though he was a rank beginner.

The rest of the kids had headed to the change room when Suzie met him on the deck.

"You did well. You are a good swimmer."

"Doesn't feel like it with all the criticism."

"That's coaching. Doesn't matter how good a swimmer you are, there's always room for improvement. My intent is help you get there. I was actually pretty impressed."

That made Mike feel better. Maybe he was taking it all too personal.

"Maybe we can swim together sometime." Mike asked.

"Perhaps." Suzie gave him a little smile.

On his way home his phone rang.

"Hey man, it's Don."

"Don?" Mike didn't recognize the voice.

"You know, Don, motorcycle parts?"

Mike wondered how he could have missed that. Maybe too much girls on his mind.

"Hey Don. You got news for me?"

"Yeah, I found the parts you wanted. They are all used but should fit."

"Can I come get them?"

"No, they're not here yet. I wanted to confirm with you. They're a bit pricier than I thought."

Mike groaned inside, 'here comes the screw' he thought. "How much?"

"Two twenty-five plus whatever the shipping is. I can have 'em here Monday if I get your OK."

Mike groaned again. That would pretty much clear out his bank account plus what he had saved in tips from the Legion.

"Look bud. I still got that dirt bike here...I'll knock off five bucks but can't go any lower than that."

Mike closed his eyes. If he took the motorcycle, he would still have lots in his bank. "OK," he started Gramps didn't want him messing with the bike in the barn anyway... "go ahead and order the parts in. It's going to blow my budget, but I really want them."

"You're the boss. See me at the Sales Barn Tuesday. Bring cash, man" Don hung up.

What made him do that? He was going to buy the dirt bike, but he went ahead with the parts anyway. Was Gramps that important to him? "I guess so." Mike said out loud. He changed direction, heading toward the Legion. Maybe he could get in a few extra hours, make some more tips.

* * *

Later that afternoon Mike headed into the lounge. He noted Eliza was tending bar. He saw him roll his eyes when he saw Mike.

"Hi, Eliza." Mike strolled up to the bar. "Anything special you would like me to do today?"

Eliza just put away the glass he had been wiping and turned away.

"Is something wrong?" Mike asked. Eliza had never been friendly, but Mike was feeling icy waves coming off him today.

Eliza spun around, "Don't know why you're even here. Hardly enough business for one person."

Mike stepped back; Eliza's tone was hostile.

"Did I do something wrong?"

"Frigging leaches," Eliza muttered turning away. Then he said some more but it was muffled. All Mike heard was something that sounded like hits.

"Sorry." Mike said, raising his hands and turning away. He felt burning in his cheeks. What had he done to anger Eliza? He had so far been only ok to work with, but this was nasty. Mike decided to speak with Sheila.

"Did I do something wrong?" Mike asked after closing her office door.

"What do you mean?"

"Eliza seems really mad at me. Won't even talk to me. If I did something wrong, I want to make up for it."

"Just Eliza being himself?" Sheila held her hands in front of her, fingers entwined as though praying.

"No, worse than that. I think he said something about hits. Am I causing a problem by being here?"

"Maybe it's the tips thing." Sheila said. "I know some of the bartenders really count on them."

Mike thought about that a moment. Mike remembered the day Vic had given him his first envelope of tips. Vic had seemed almost excited. He hadn't considered how his taking a share of the tips might impact someone else. Was he the leach that Eliza was referring to?

"Well, I think it's his issue to deal with. I like you here and so do the customers. Don't worry about it." Sheila gave Mike a little wave with the back of her hand. He turned to leave but didn't feel right about the situation. This wasn't just Eliza's issue. How could he make this work to everyone's benefit? He avoided Eliza as much as he could for the rest of his shift. No sense in rubbing sand in an open wound.

That evening Mike talked with Gramma as they sipped their tea on the porch. It was a warm evening but not hot. A light breeze rippled the corn stalks in the fields near the house, the tassels bowed and fluttered.

"...so I'm not sure what to do. I need the tips for something I'm working on but if I'm taking that right out of someone's pocket, that doesn't seem fair. Maybe I should find work elsewhere, a real job." Mike had been careful not to mention any names.

"Why did you start working at the Legion?"

"Well," Mike had to think back to what took him through the front doors in the first place. It was funny how circumstances can steer you down a track you had never thought of. "I wanted to get to know Gramps better, maybe learn about his war experience."

"That all?" She gave him a little sideways glance, the one she used when she already knew the answer to the question she was asking.

"Well, there was the Trucker's Haven thing. To do community service to show I'm sorry for what I did there."

"Are those issues resolved?"

"No. I'm still working on them."

"Then I would say you are where you need to be. Do you bring value to the Legion?"

"Huh?" What was she asking him?

"Value. Does your work make the Legion a better place?"

"I think so. I try and work hard; do everything they ask me to, and even things they don't but that I know need doing."

"Do you do all the nice jobs?"

Mike thought about mopping out the bathrooms, crawling under the bar to wash the pop lines. "Not really, most are pretty dirty. Scrubbing toilets doesn't offer much glamour."

"So, you make it so the others don't have to do the jobs he doesn't like?"

"I never thought of it like that." Mike realized the everything Eliza had told him to do had been a nasty job. And

Eliza always told him what to do, Vic and Dan always asked him, gave him a choice.

"Well, maybe you need to think of it like that. It would seem to me that if I had a pleasant young man helping to make my stay better, I might drop a few extra coins in the tip jar."

Mike sat back and contemplated what his grandmother was telling him. He hadn't considered that maybe there was more money in the tip jar because of him being there.

"I'm going to church in the morning. Would you like to go with me?" Gram looked at Mike.

He groaned a bit inside, that certainly wasn't his favorite place to go. Fire and brimstone and a bunch of dusty old singing. He was ready to say no but then thought, 'she cooks and cleans and is always available for me and never asks for anything in return. Maybe this is her asking.' Instead he asked, "What time?"

Gram cocked one eyebrow, "Service is at ten and there's a tea after."

"I don't have anything nice to wear."

"Seems to me that when God sent you into this world, you didn't have anything to wear." Gramma laughed and raised a hand to her mouth. Mike again glimpsed the young woman she had once been. "You just make yourself presentable."

"Sure Gram." It was the least he could do.

Whitewashing Grumps

After church Mike waited for Gramps to head out to do his 'errands' then headed into the barn. He finished polishing up everything he could on the motorcycle, even digging stones out of the tire treads. It wasn't looking like new, but it was looking so much better. Many parts of it sparkled. He had wondered how to deal with the rust spots where the bike was painted. Mr. Google had offered a ton of advice but when it came time to set the sanding block against the bike, he was nervous. He was going to have to sand off the rust, smooth the area to make sure the new paint would blend with the old without leaving any ridges. And then he was going to have to make sure the paint when on smooth, with no drips.

He had never done anything like that before and was afraid he would really mess it up. Using newspaper and masking tape to keep any paint from going where he didn't want it, he worked slow, being as careful as he could. By the time he was stuffing the newspaper mess into a garbage bag, he was feeling a whole lot better. The olive drab spray paint he had bought at Canadian Tire was a perfect match. When he was finished, he couldn't tell that it wasn't original.

All the while he worked, he was afraid Gramps would return home. There was no way he could hide the smell of the paint, and he had to leave the bike uncovered while it dried. He couldn't do any other work because that would raise dust that would mar the paint job. He read some Legion magazines while he waited for the paint to dry.

He heard the crunch of tires on gravel. Gramps was home. Mike realized the open barn door might act like a beacon to the old man, warn him that someone might be messing in his stuff. Mike looked around, he didn't have enough time to cover the motorcycle and what about the paint smell. Then an idea blossomed in his mind, but he would have to move fast.

"What's going on in here?" Gramps stepped through

the door a few minutes later. "What the hell do you think you're doing?" Gramps face was twisted into a snarl.

"Hi Grandpa," Mike turned from where he was brushing paint onto the timbers of the stall. This was a desperate move, he hadn't even had enough time to stir the paint in the can, but he hoped it would be enough to distract Gramp's attention from the back-corner stall. "I thought some fresh paint would help make the barn look even better. I found this while I was cleaning up the other day." Mike pointed at the paint can. He was anticipating that Gramps had been at the Legion and might be affected just enough by a few beers to dim his senses.

"That'll make a mess. Look, you're dripping there." Gramps pointed toward the floor.

"I got that Gramps." Mike used a rag to wipe the drip. "I'll be more careful."

"Who said you could do that?"

"I wanted to surprise you." Mike did want to surprise the man but not with white-washed stalls, the real surprise was sitting fully exposed in the darkened stall. "Do you think this paint is white enough."

"What?" Mike had been correct; Gramps was a bit dimmed by his drinking. "Can't see that. Too dark in here."

Mike stepped toward him, picking up the paint can as he did. "Here, let's go outside where the light is better." Mike turned him toward the door.

Outside Gramps seemed to gather himself. "I didn't say you could do this. You can't just do anything you take a fancy to."

Mike hung his head. "I'm sorry, I thought you would like this. I'm doing it for you." So I can distract you, Mike didn't say.

"I would tell you to stop but now that you've started, you'll have to finish the job. You better do a good one." Gramps was squinting at Mike, looking into the paint can. "You didn't even mix that paint up, you can't do it like that." Gramps reached out, "Here let me…"

Mike didn't want Gramps going back into the barn so he pulled back. "I can do it. You're right, this needs to be stirred. I can do it. I'll do a good job."

Just then Gram opened the back door. "What are you boys doing?" She shaded her eyes with one hand.

"This kid's painting the barn. I never told him he could do that."

"Well maybe it needs it." She said, looking at Mike with a strange look on her face. "Come inside, I have something to show you." Mike sent up some silent thanks for the woman's intuition. She was going to help distract Gramps.

Taking advantage of the window that Gram had opened for him, Mike returned to the barn to get things back in order, and to finish painting the stalls.

Fore

"Good morning Gram." Mike was feeling chipper this morning. Finishing painting the barn had taken a long time, he had even had to go back out after dinner to complete it, but he had kept Gramps from discovering what he was doing with the motorcycle, so the work was worth it.

"Good morning Picasso." The old woman looked up from the bacon she was frying.

Mike felt his stomach rumble when the aroma struck him. "Sure smells great in here."

"I thought you could use something to get the paint smell out of your sinuses." She cast an eye at him, looking over her shoulder. "I don't know what you're up to out in that barn, but I trust it's nothing you shouldn't be." She held him with that one-eyed stare for a moment.

"Thanks for distracting Gramps." Mike lowered his voice.

"Don't worry, he's headed into town already."

Mike was amazed again by just how smart this woman was. He tried to picture his mother as a little girl trying to get one over on her. He didn't think she would have been successful.

"How would you like your eggs?"

"Over-easy?"

"Over-easy it is."

"Gram," Mike waited until she was looking at him again before continuing. "Those golf clubs. Gramps doesn't use them but he won't let me use them either."

"Oh, those clubs." Gram cracked two eggs into the skillet where they sizzled and snapped. "He was never a golfer." She looked up, into the corner of the kitchen but Mike was certain it was the past she was seeing. "He tried so hard." She paused again, a big sigh escaping as she shifted her weight. "He just had to be better than him." Again, she paused. "At everything." She shook her head then turned back to the eggs.

"Do you mean Uncle Wenner?" Mike asked as she took a plate from the cupboard.

She looked at him, her face blank for a moment, then she brightened. "Yes, Wenner. Funny to hear you call him Uncle. He would have been proud to be called that. He was too young when he died." She slid the eggs onto the plate and added a pile of bacon." Now he could golf." She placed the plate in front of Mike then opened the silverware drawer.

Mike took the utensils she handed him. "So, Gramps tried to be better at golf than Wenner?"

"Oh yeah," Gram placed two pieces of toast onto a side plate, buttered and cut them, then carried the plate to the table. "This was after the war. Even with Wenner buried in a French field, that man still had to try to outdo his brother. Just didn't have the knack for it though and that was that. Those clubs went into the barn. I guess he hid them there unwilling to admit that he got bested at something."

"OK," Mike dipped his toast into his egg yolk then spoke around the bite he took, "I guess I won't raise that subject again."

Motorcycle Parts

On the way to the Sales Barn to get the parts for Gramp's motorcycle, Mike stopped at the bank and withdrew most of his money. Combined with what he had been given in tips, he hoped he would have enough to pay for everything. Seeing the small balance remaining on the slip spit out by the ATM gave him a dull feeling in his guts. He knew that what he had in there really wasn't all that much, but it had taken him a long time to accumulate it, a lot of work to earn it.

He had received an email from Uwe last night telling him that Chuck had lost his job at the Tasty Grill. Uwe explained how Chuck had shown up late for work three shifts in a row. There were too many people on the waiting list who were willing to be on time, so he got canned. That was just like Chuck, everything on his own time. Mike took no comfort in the fact that now only one in three of them was gainfully employed. But it did get him thinking about applying for a job at the Chuckwagon. He jammed his wad of cash into his pocket and headed to get his parts.

Mike thought there had been a lot of activity at the Sales Barn the last time he was there, this morning it was even busier. Many of the vendors were still setting up, moving containers of goods and supplies through the crowd of potential buyers. Twice he stopped to help someone struggling with a large load. He took the time to have a look over the tables before making his way to Don's.

Jack and Allen were there, talking to Don. Mike looked around for Jeannie but didn't see her golden curls anywhere. Mike ducked down a bit, held back. He didn't want them to know he was there considering the incident at the pool a few days ago. Then he wondered what they were doing here, at Don't table. Mike moved closer to try to overhear their conversation. He kept his head down, turned away but edged closer, trying to be inconspicuous. He noticed several clear plastic bags with old golf balls in them on Don's table. He pretended he was interested in them.

"Alright then." Don said to the two teens.

Jack's words were muffled but sounded like "bundle buns". They waved at each other, just a quick one-hander. Mike thought they seemed to know each other. Then Jack and Allen melted into the crowd. Mike turned to Don.

"Hey kid," Don greeted him, "glad you made it. I got your stuff right here." Don rummaged under the table. He placed two tires, a ball of wires and the hand grips Mike had asked for, on the table. Mike looked them over. The tires seemed in only slightly better shape than the ones on the bike now. The ignition wires were a thick cable with a couple of strands snaking out from the rest. He hoped he would be able to figure it all out, hoped it was the right part. He peeked in the bag at that the hand grips were in. They were dirty with a few scratches but not broken.

"How much?" Mike asked and cringed inside.

"Two fifteen." Don said, "Would have been cheaper but overnight shipping is expensive and you wanted them fast."

Mike relaxed inside. That wasn't as bad as he had feared but would still use up most of his money. He looked around Don's table.

"Would you throw in that bag of golf balls?" He pointed as though he had just seen them.

"Now kid," Don's eyes narrowed, "you're getting a deal as it is."

"I know, just a good will gesture. I'm still thinking about that motorcycle." Mike pointed with his chin. He smiled inside knowing he was now applying a little sales pressure himself. 'Serves him right.' Flashed through his mind.

Don's face lit up. "Oh yeah, my nephew's bike? Sure, sure, take the balls."

Mike packed the parts into his backpack and slung the tires over his shoulder. "Thanks a lot for getting these for me. I really appreciate it."

Mike held out his hand and Don shook it after staring at it for a moment. 'Maybe he doesn't get too many appreciative customers' Mike thought. 'Or maybe just not too many who want to touch him.' Mike glanced at him again, noting the dirty shirt, greasy black lines on his hands, uncombed hair. Then he turned into the crowd, anxious to get home to reassemble the motorcycle.

Mike called his grandmother. He didn't want to be caught sneaking the parts into the barn. Gramps had still been at home when he left, and he didn't know what his schedule was today. Gram told him that Gramps wasn't working today but would likely go into town after lunch. Mike knew this meant he was going to the Legion. He thanked her and hung up. With a few hours on his hands he decided he would go to the library and look up information on how to rewire a motorcycle.

Mr. Google coughed up diagrams about wiring harnesses. Mike figured it wouldn't be too difficult, the wiring on old Scouts was simple compared to what modern motorcycles needed. He made notes of the suggestions in the articles he read, things like applying electrical grease to all the connections to help waterproof them and using zap straps to secure the wires in place. He decided to stop at the Canadian Tire store to pick up a few supplies before going home. Another hit to his bank account.

The store was across the street from the ball parks by the pool. After shopping, Mike wandered over there to see what was going on. As he crossed the street someone yelled, "Watch it dip-shit." There was a skidding noise.

Mike looked toward the voice, cringing a bit. Jack and Allen had stopped their bikes only inches from Mike. "Idiot. You blind?" Jack's face was a twist of attitude.

Embarrassed that he hadn't seen them, may not have even looked for traffic before crossing the street Mike only stuttered, "Sorry." And that was out before he even realized who he was talking to. 'Shit,' he thought, 'of all the people I could walk in front of, why these morons?'

"Too busy thinking of your privates?" Allan chimed in.

Mike resumed crossing the street, jogging a bit to get out

of there faster. 'First at the sales barn, now here.' Mike thought it was a strange coincidence. He headed to the pool.

"Hey," Suzie approached him at the fence. She was wearing a one-piece, green bathing suit with ribbed, tan coloured side panels. Her aviator glasses hid her eyes, but she was smiling. "What you been up to?"

"Not much," Mike replied, "mostly just summer stuff."

"What's that?" Suzie raised her sunglasses and perched them on top of her head. She pointed to Mike's pack. He had hung the motorcycle tires on it.

"Oh," Mike glanced over his shoulder, trying to be nonchalant, cool, "just something I've been working on. No big deal."

"Really?" She moved the sunglasses back down to her nose.

"Yeah, you know how it is." Mike wasn't certain why he was being evasive; this was more like the Mike he was trying not to be. He realized too; he hadn't even looked for Jeannie's curls. He had come looking for Suzie. Now that she was right in front of him, he was acting like a dork. "I'm doing something for my Grandfather, helping him with a project." Mike wondered why he just couldn't tell her the whole truth. It was as though his efforts to evade Gramps were spilling over into his whole life. Why couldn't he just be himself? 'Because then no one would like you.' Screamed in his mind.

"Well, I hope you are successful." Suzie offered.

"Thanks," Mike said but thought, 'That's really nice. I'm being elusive for some unknown reason and she wishes me well. This is a nice girl.' Now he wanted to say something nice back, but his mind was all muddled up.

"You sure have a lot of bathing suits." The words were out of his mouth before he realized he was going to say anything.

"Oh, thanks." Suzie said taking a step back. "When you work at a pool you kind of have to."

"I mean," Mike stuttered realizing how stupid what he had just said sounded. "I noticed you wear a different one a lot. They're nice."

"Oh, well thank you." Mike saw the colour rise in her cheeks. He hoped he hadn't embarrassed her. He thought that was a nice thing to say but he had a habit of not saying what he was meaning. "I don't think most guys notice."

Mike as feeling a bit anxious, off balance. Still not certain what to say he said, "Well I do." He stood there looking at her and she looked back. Neither spoke and Mike felt uncomfortable with the silence. Had he blown it again? He thought he should get out of there before he did something really dumb. "I gotta go. Get this stuff home." He hitched a thumb toward his backpack. "See ya."

He gave the chain-link fence between them a bit of a shake in what he hoped was a cool move.

"Hope so." Suzie said as he turned away. She had a funny look on her face, had been looking over Mike's shoulder. He glanced in that direction but only saw the branches of a hedge that lined part of the playground. They were moving, had someone been standing there?

The rest of the way home Mike replayed their conversation in his mind. He thought to himself 'Why couldn't you just say something normal like "What did you do last night?" or "You sure look pretty." or "Would you like to go to the dance with me?"' But even as he thought this he knew the answer. He was afraid of rejection, that she would laugh at him. He could picture it, "Go out with you? Little boy? Not in your wildest dream." But he knew too that Suzie wouldn't ever say that, she had only been nice to him so why was he so scared? Now Jeannie, he could see her saying something like that but he was still focussed on her. He didn't think he would have any easier time talking with Jeannie than with Suzie but somehow, it would be almost ok to be laughed at by Jeannie, but not Suzie. 'Oh man,' Mike held his hands to his head, 'girls are so confusing.'

As he had hoped, Gramp's car wasn't in the driveway. Mike stashed the parts under the motorcycle tarp...only he ever looked there anymore.

That night during tea Gram asked Mike about his day.

"And have you thought about asking anyone to the dance? You still plan on going, don't you?"

"Yeah, I'm going to go."

"No one has enamoured your heart?"

Mike wasn't certain what enamoured meant, but he thought it probably meant 'captured' or at least 'caught the eye of'.

"Gramma." Mike felt heat in his face.

"Dances are much more fun when shared with someone." She raised an eyebrow at him. Her smile said she knew she was embarrassing him a bit.

"I really don't know anyone."

"All the time you spend in town and you haven't noticed any girls? Teens must be way different these days."

"I don't hardly speak with anyone." Mike paused a moment, chewing his lower lip, then said, "The only girl I could think of hangs out with the guy I got in a fight with. I don't think she likes me much."

"Gotta be more than one starling in that big sky out there." Gram looked at the knitting her hands were weaving.

"Yeah, maybe." Then Mike thought of Suzie, how nice she always was to him. Then he thought, 'why wouldn't I ask her to the dance?' After a brief pause he admitted, 'Because she might say no!' That was followed by, 'but she might say yes.' Mike sat back in his chair, staring into the sky.

Dance Date

As soon as Gramps left for work Mike headed to the barn. He wanted to tackle the wiring harness while he knew he had a few hours. It gave him an excuse to put off asking Suzie to the dance too. Now that he had committed himself to that, he wasn't sure how he would approach her. He didn't want to sound like an idiot.

Looking over the wiring on the bike and comparing it to what he had found in the Google printout left Mike feeling overwhelmed. How was he going to get all the wires into the right places? They were threaded throughout the frame. The bulk of the wires were stored inside the headlight. He decided he would trace each wire from there.

Once he located the end of a wire, he secured some fishing line to it then pulled it out through the headlamp. Then he fastened the fishing line to the new wire and pulled it back through. It was slow work, he had to stop frequently to work the wire through tight spots. Once the wire was threaded, he dabbed a bit of dielectric grease on the bare end of the connection then hooked it to the connection it was supposed to be fastened to. The grease would help protect the connection from water and corrosion.

Three hours later he was hooking up the last connection. He pulled the tarp back over the bike and tucked the old harness wires into his backpack for disposal later. Then he headed in for lunch, another stall before he headed to the pool.

Mike hoped Suzie would be working. Now that he had his nerve up, he wanted to get the asking done. He smiled when he saw her blowing her whistle and pointing at something in the pool even though his stomach was fluttering. She saw him, waved and headed toward him.

"Hey, Mike," she greeted him through the fence. "You coming in for a swim?"

"No," he shielded his eyes from the glare of the sun,

"After the last public swim I've been a bit hesitant. Also, I have to go to the library. That project with my gramps."

"At least you still come by pretty much every day." She smiled.

"Yeah, I guess I do." Mike had practiced what he was going to say to ask Suzie to the dance but now that she was right in front of him, he found it hard to come up with the words. "What have you been up to?" he asked but found the words strange after they had come out of his mouth.

She looked at him for a moment then answered, "Not much. Mostly working."

"Um, er," Mike searched for better words, "I wanted to ask you about the dance next week."

"What about it?" she took a step closer to him.

"I, uh, I know you're going."

"Yes."

"I was wondering…I mean I meant to ask…um, can you tell me…."

"What Mike? What?"

"Are you going with anyone?" Mike dug a toe into the grass as though drilling for oil, "I mean, is someone taking you?" Mike felt himself flush all over and hoped it didn't show, that she didn't know how nervous he was.

"Are you asking me to the dance?"

"No, um, wait, yes, I guess I am."

"Well, are you, or aren't you?"

"Yes," Mike looked right at her, "Suzie Lucknow, will you go to the dance with me?" Then Mike paused before adding, "I mean, that is, if you aren't going with someone else, like a boyfriend or something."

"Oh, that is nice, but someone else has already said he would take me." Mike felt his heart sink, then Suzie smiled, "but he will just have to settle for taking only my mom."

Mike felt like jumping, he tried to restrain the smile that stretched his face but failed. "You will?" his knees felt weak, "I mean, of course, I mean, that's great."

"I know what you mean Mike Tuthill."

Walking away from the pool Mike couldn't believe how good he felt. He was actually going to have a date, and with an older girl. By the time Mike got back to his grandparent's house, he couldn't remember what he had read at the library that afternoon.

That evening on the porch he told Grandma about his date.

"I hope that's ok," He said, "I know you and Gramps are going, but I said I would pick her up at her house and walk her there. She doesn't live too far."

"That will be just fine." Gramma patted his knee. She had a small, satisfied smile on her face.

The door banged open and Grumps clumped across the porch.

"Grandpa," Mike decided it was time to be direct with Grumps about the golf clubs, "when I was cleaning up the barn, I found some old golf clubs in a locker."

"I thought I told you not to mess in stuff."

"I wasn't messing, I found them while looking for a broom." That was a bit of a lie but just a little one. "They look like they haven't been used in a long time, kind of rusty."

"Hmph."

"I cleaned them up. The bag too. Did you used to play golf?"

"I see what you're up to. Poking around." Gramps wasn't smiling and Mike felt the conversation going in a bad direction.

"I'm just asking because I thought maybe, if you wanted to of course, maybe you could show me how to use them." Mike thought he had figured out a clever to get Gramps to teach him about golf. Maybe that would give them something in common.

"Those clubs haven't seen the light of day in a coon's age."

Mike wondered how long that was but thought it wasn't the right question to ask right now. Instead he didn't say anything, just let Grumps think about what he had said.

Finally, Gramps said, "Frigging things 'd probably break first swing."

"They seemed ok to me." Mike wanted to encourage Gramps.

"And what do you know about it."

Mike was quiet for a moment. This man was a pro at shutting down conversations. "Nothin' I guess." After another brief pause Mike continued, "I just thought it might be something we could do together."

"Together!" Grumps leaned forward on his cane and his shoulders jumped a bit.

"Sounds like a good idea to me." Gramma spoke up. "You always had good form at the tee."

'Thank you', Mike thought as he smiled at his Grandmother.

"I'd probably throw my back out." Gramps sat back, set his cane against the wall then reached for his teacup.

"You wouldn't if you were giving the boy pointers. Let him throw his back out." Grams voice was low, calm.

Gramps laughed and smiled. Mike marveled at how Gram seemed to know just how to speak to him. In fact, he couldn't remember a time when Grumps had been able to shut her conversation down.

"Mike was just telling me he's taking the Lucknow girl to the dance." Gram changed the direction of the conversation.

Grumps looked at Mike. "You can dance?"

"A bit." Mike didn't know what else to say.

"We'll see." Gramps sipped his tea. "Not that jittery crap?" Gramps jerked his hands and arms up and down in a poor imitation of an arm wave. Mike smiled at Gramps' contortions, the way his tongue hung out and his eyes bugged and rolled. Then he stopped and stared at Mike and there wasn't anything to smile about at that. Despite the lingering heat from the day a definite chill settled on the porch.

In a bit Gramps slurped the last of his tea then headed into the house. After the door banged closed Mike said, "Thanks for helping with the golf. I don't think he's convinced though."

"Don't be too quick to give up Mike." She paused a moment then cocked one eyebrow at him and finished, "He didn't say no."

Mike sat back with his own smile, he hadn't at that.

War Stories

Mike was trying to stay busy at the Legion but not doing a very good job of it. There were not a lot of customers and he had already cleaned up everything that he and Vic could think of cleaning. Mike felt good when Sheila came in and commented on how much nicer the whole lounge felt since he had been there. She liked it neat, tidy and smelling fresh.

Then Andy came in and Mike grew a bit excited. He wanted to speak to him about Gramps and the motorcycle.

"Let a man have a sip of his beer." Andy held up one hand when Mike approached him. Feeling a bit like a vulture, Mike took a step back.

"Sorry," he offered.

Andy curled his upper lip over the rim of his glass. The golden liquid rippled and the froth scooted across it and into Andy's mouth.

"Nothing better than the first sip of the day." Amber droplets clung to Andy's upper lip, vibrated when he spoke. "Now, what were you after?"

"I need to know more about Gramps, D.R. Is there anything more he has shared with you?"

Andy was quiet for a few moments. During that time his gaze wandered around the walls of the room, all the history there. "There was one day," Andy paused. Mike wondered if he was doing that on purpose, drawing out the moment. Then Mike wondered why Andy might do that, linger, make Mike wait. Was Andy lonely? Was this how he kept company near him longer? "he had had a few beers. I could tell by the way he was talking, slurring a bit." Andy looked at Mike, "He wasn't drunk, I've never saw ol' D.R. in that state, but he was feeling no pain if you know what I mean."

Mike stepped closer, not wanting to miss any of what Andy was saying.

Andy continued, "He was upset, sad upset, not mad upset. This was a few years ago as I recall."

Mike wanted to shake the man, get the story out of him but he restrained himself.

"I asked him what had him all up in his attic like that and he said..."

> "It's today." D.R. said, his voice unsteady, so low that Andy had to lean in close to hear him.
>
> "What's today?"
>
> "His birthday."
>
> "Whose?"
>
> "His," D.R. paused a moment as though bringing up the name was a feat just beyond his strength. Then in a rush it came out sounding almost like a scowl, "Wenner." D.R. puffed out a breath then sucked it back in quick
>
> "Wenner?" Andy's eyes rolled up as he thought. The name was familiar, then it came to him, "Your brother."
>
> D.R. nodded so deep that his shoulders moved.
>
> "And that got you thinking about him." Andy didn't know what else to say.
>
> "Sure, but too, it's the day..." Then D.R. grew silent.
>
> "What?" Andy asked after a moment, when he realized D.R. wasn't going to finish his sentence.
>
> "it's the day..." Again D.R. grew silent.
>
> Andy squinted at him as though that might squeeze the words out the man. D.R. just looked at Andy, his mouth open a bit, his eyes frantic, darting around Andy's face, searching for something. In that moment Andy was back in Europe. He had seen those same eyes multiple times in the airmen as they climbed into their planes. But not all the men, the men who had been on missions before, bad missions, cut men out of their gun turret missions. Those were fear eyes. D.R. was scared.

"It's the day he died." Andy said what D.R. had not been able to.

D.R. raised a hand to his mouth and his chest hitched. Sweat stood out on his forehead. Andy felt something rise in his own chest as he looked at this man full of grief over something that had happened more than forty years earlier. He had to bite back the words that danced on the edge of his tongue because he was afraid the hitch he felt in his own chest would push tears out of his eyes and there was no way Andy Andrews was ever going to cry, not in front of someone else. Instead he reached a hand across the table and gripped D.R.'s elbow. He sucked in a big breath then said quietly, *"Look, it's ok..."*

Before he could finish D.R. slammed his hand to the table. *"It's not ok."* The darting eyes were gone, had snapped onto Andy's face with the steadiness of a sniper's scope, *"It'll never be ok. He's dead because of me and I can't never fix that."*

"Doug," Mike was pulled out of Andy's memory by Vic's voice. Mike looked toward him, his face slack, still very much in the moment Andy had been sharing. "Don't be bothering the customers."

Andy waved at Vic letting him know it was alright.

"And then what happened?" Mike looked back at Andy.

"Nothing. He got up and left." Andy splayed his hands up on the table showing he was hiding nothing.

"He killed his own brother?" Mike felt his world spinning around him. Could Grumps have done that? Mike didn't really think so but what else could have made him make that confession to Andy?

"I don't know. Doubt it. That's all he shared, and he never spoke of it again. Least not with me."

"Wow." Was all Mike could think to say. This revelation was huge. Mike didn't know what to think of it.

"The times we was in back then, they can distort the truth just as easy as they can distort a man. War brings out the worst in people, but it brings out the best too. I saw lots of guys do things that took real guts. I mean guts beyond just doing what had to be done. I mean guts like putting yourself in real danger to save someone, give it all up sometimes. Sometimes they had to do things that you could never imagine, just to stay alive. Then they got to find a way to live with what they done, twist things or remember them different than they really happened just to keep yourself from going bat shit...pardon my French." Andy looked at Mike and there was something in his look that said Andy wasn't just talking about what he had seen, it was also about things he had done. How he had come to live with his own experiences and actions. "What I'm saying is, I wouldn't put much stock in what he said. Probably just feeling bad about his brother. You know, big brother little brother thing? Maybe feeling guilty that he lived when Wenner didn't. That's all I'm saying. Maybe you want to talk with some other despatch riders. Maybe they'll know more."

On his walk home Mike pondered what Andy had told him. He wished he had the whole story. How could he talk to other despatch riders? Both Andy and Vic had said they didn't know of any others around Aylmer. Maybe he could find some on the internet. He would have to research that.

Then his mind wandered to the upcoming dance. He still couldn't believe he had a date to it. He wondered what he was going to do about the dancing part, he really hadn't danced much; shuffled his feet and waggled his arms at a few school events. Mostly he had hung with Uwe and Chuck and made smart comments about others who were dancing. He wished he had paid a little more attention. And what about if Jeannie was there and saw him with Suzie? Why did he care anyway, she really hadn't shown any interest in him, had been kind of rude that first day? But it did matter.

Too, he had received another email from Janice. She had gone back to her light conversation, mostly chit chat stuff about her and her friends. Nothing more about the kissing.

She seemed to have twigged to his talk of TV and movies as she wrote a lot about that. Was she waiting for his reaction to her revelation? What should Mike send back? That he wanted to kiss her too? She had ended the email with 'Your friend' which was casual but still... Mike did a little skip and kicked at the gravel beside the road. It had been a pretty good day.

That evening on the porch Mike asked, "Gramps, would it be ok if I used the lawnmower tomorrow?"

Gramma looked at Mike behind Grump's chair. Mike smiled at her.

"Grass doesn't need cutting yet." Grumps offered after a 'hrmph' and a slow survey of the front lawn.

"I thought I might see if I could cut other people's lawns. Maybe make a little money." Mike had no intention of making money with the lawnmower, he had other plans.

Grumps raised one eyebrow and looked at Mike. "What are you up to?" He asked.

Mike just looked at him, opened his hands in front of himself then clasped them together again.

"You cut your foot off, don't be calling me for a ride home." The old man sat back in his chair.

Mike leaned back, looked at his grandmother and gave a single victory fist pump. She smiled and shook her head.

A Good Deed

Mike rattled the lawnmower down the driveway and around the curve onto the road. He hoped eight wasn't too early to cut Andy's lawn. He wanted to show his appreciation for what Andy had shared yesterday and this was the best way he knew how. Andy's yard needed some attention and Andy didn't seem able to do it himself. Too, Mike needed to get to the library, so he wanted to get an early start.

"Hey, watcha doing?" Andy came out on his porch a few minutes after Mike had started the mower engine. Mike hardly heard him over the roar, but Andy's waving arms caught his attention. Mike shut down the machine. "What the hell's all the racket for? Why are you on my lawn?"

"I thought I'd cut your grass, tidy up your lawn." Mike smiled at Andy. Andy was dressed in a saggy pair of pajama bottoms and a white, mostly grey, sleeveless shirt.

"All that friggin' noise? You trying to scare an old man into an early grave?"

"Mr. Andrews, I thought a lot about what you told me yesterday. I just want to say thanks."

"Couldn't think of a quieter way?" Andy looked from Mike to his lawn then back to Mike. "Well, I guess it could use a little trim." Mike laughed to himself, the grass was almost to his knees. "If it makes you happy." Andy turned and headed into the house.

Mike started the motor again. Andy called something else as the door banged shut but Mike couldn't hear it.

Two hours later the grass was cut and trimmed. Mike had found a rake in the backyard and used it to scrape at bare spots which he then covered with clippings and then raked again to work the grass bits into the soil. He returned the rake then surveyed the yard to see if he had missed anything. Andy came out of the house dressed in old jeans and a checkered shirt.

"Looks pretty good Doug." Andy reached out and

touched Mike's arm. "Never had a kid come and cut my grass before."

Andy reached a hand into his pocket and pulled out some crumpled bills. "Let me give you something..."

"Oh no," Mike stepped back, raising a hand in a stop motion. "I didn't do this to get paid. It's my thanks."

"Fer what? Saying some words to you? I ain't no charity case you know."

"Please just let me do this." Mike headed toward the mower. He wanted to get going to the library and he still had to take the mower back, clean it up and put it away.

"Well, ok but," Andy stuffed the money back in his pocket, "you'll have to let me buy you a beer then." The old man smiled wide at Mike.

"Sure, sure." Mike smiled back. "A beer. See you later Andy."

"Gator." Andy answered back and Mike left him looking around at his now tidy lawn.

Mike felt good as he put the lawn mower away, careful to clean it off and replace the old tarp over it in the barn. He then headed to the library and he couldn't help but look at Andy's lawn as he went by. It did look good, Mike felt pride in the work he had done. Somehow too, the old house looked a little brighter, the porch didn't seem to sag into a frown as much. Then he turned his mind to despatch riders.

Mr. Google turned up an unexpected Facebook page titled, Despatch Riders Canada. It didn't have a lot of followers but that didn't surprise Mike, how many despatch riders could there still be considering how much time had passed since the war. He posted a quick note asking if anyone had known his grandfather or his great uncle Wenner. He knew it was a stab in the dark, but he didn't have any other leads right now.

Mike decided to go home and work on the motorcycle while Grumps was at work. There was still a lot to do. He printed off instructions on how to clean a carburetor and hoped he was up to the task. He couldn't locate instructions for that specific motorcycle but thought he could figure it out.

Car Wash

While making his bed, Mike heard his cell phone chime. A message coming in. Expecting it to be an email from his parents or maybe Chuck, he was surprised when it was a response to his post on the Despatch Riders page. There were three altogether, but Mike recognized two of them as spam, simply trying to get him to buy something. 'Leaches everywhere.' He thought.

The third was from a man named Bruce Lapinski. He claimed to have known Wenner. Mike sent him an instant message with his email so they could correspond better. Before he had finished eating breakfast, with Grumps ensuring that Mike knew he didn't approve of the phone at the table, Mike had learned it was actually Bruce's grandfather who knew Wenner. He was also Bruce Lapinski, but since he wasn't very good with computers, grandson Bruce was helping him. They arranged for a video call the next day. Mike felt very excited.

Mike thought it was a bit funny, Grumps having so much disdain because of the cell phone at the table that he wasn't paying any attention to what Mike was really doing. That made it easier to plan right under Grumps' nose.

"What are you up to today Grampa?" Mike thought he might be able to calm some waters by engaging in conversation. Gramma gave him a funny look.

"Hrmph," Gramps said, nibbling on some bacon that he held in his hand. It was peculiar that no one else could break the rules but it was ok when Gramps did.

Mike was determined to remain positive. "That sounds interesting." He responded as though Gramps had actually said something. "I was thinking I would go for a swim today. Haven't been for a while."

"Oh, is Suzie working today?" Gramma asked, her eyebrows raised, and her mouth pulled into a little smile.

Mike felt the colour climb up his neck. Why did Gram

have to focus on that? "I don't know." Mike tried to be casual but he knew full well that she was working today. "Just thought I should keep in shape." He held up his arm and flexed his muscle.

Gramma just said "Boys." And shook her head a bit. Gramps just 'hrmphed' and chewed some toast.

"Can I wash the car?" Mike asked. He wanted to get an idea about what Gramps was up to. If he was heading out soon, he wouldn't let Mike was the car. If he wasn't, Mike would be stuck doing that task.

Again, Gramps just 'hrmphed'. Mike felt anger flare in his guts. Couldn't the man just communicate?

"That's a nice offer Mike." Gramma answered and Mike began to deflate. "Pull it onto the grass. No sense trying to wash it in the dirt of the driveway. You'll just turn that into a mud hole."

Mike peaked. She had asked him to move the car, drive the car. He had never done that and was excited for the opportunity. Sure, it would be only a minute or two but 'IT WAS DRIVING A CAR.'

"I'll move it." Gramps stated.

"Pshaw," Gram waved a hand at him, "let the boy." Did she know what it meant to him? Mike wondered. She had certainly shown in the past that she understood him.

"Yeah, Gramps," Mike offered, "I can do it. I'll do a good job."

"You better get at it." Gramma continued, "Gramps needs to go into town a little later." Again, she seemed to be reading Mike's mind.

"Alrighty then." Mike stood. He took the car keys from the hook by the door. He felt like he was walking on water as he picked through the gaggle of keys, locating the ignition key.

"Try not to hit the house with it." Gramps huffed around the toast he was chewing.

Mike tried to calm himself inside while he walked to the car. His heart was beating fast. His hand shook a bit when he reached to put the key in the door lock. 'Settle down. Don't do something stupid. It's just a little car driving. Who am I kidding? IT'S DRIVING A CAR!' Mike couldn't get his mind to focus. He sat behind the wheel and concentrated on his breathing. He felt his heartbeat ease off a bit.

He slid the key into the ignition, sat forward a bit and turned it. Nothing happened. The 'Check Engine' and 'Oil' lights glowed red on the dashboard but the car was silent. Then the radio blared to life. Mike jumped a bit, his heart hammering. 'Did I break it?' He wondered. 'No, something else. What did I forget?" He turned down the volume on the radio, jiggled the gear shift, and tried again. Still nothing. 'What, what, what?' Mike felt screaming in his head. 'Gas pedal? No, that will flood the engine.' He was about to go and ask for help when he remembered. 'The brake. You have to step on the brake to start the car.' "Frigging safety gurus." He muttered.

He pressed on the pedal and turned the key. The engine revved to life. 'OK,' he glanced over the dashboard and controls, 'how to do this? Think of the steps. Foot on brake. Shift into D. Foot off brake. Roll forward. Foot on brake. Shift into P. Turn off car. Easy peasy Japaneasy.' Too easy? Mike didn't want to make the experience too quick. Maybe he shouldn't just drive it straight forward. Maybe he should try to get the car a little closer to the house, the hose he would use to wash it, the plug in he would need for the vacuum to clean the interior? That would mean backing it up, turning the car, moving it forward, turning it more. More like driving.

Mike shifted into R.

Gramps stepped out the back door. Mike saw him.

The car lurched backward, turning hard. Mike jammed on the brakes.

Gramp's face contorted and he stepped forward, arms rising.

Mike shifted into D. The car started moving forward but Mike had forgot to turn the wheel. He began to turn it but stepped on the gas pedal accidentally. The car lurched forward, gravel kicked up a bit, and turned toward Gramps. He cringed.

Mike spun the wheel, tried to hit the brakes but stepped on the gas again. The front end rose, the car jumped forward, turned violently. Mike stomped the brake and the car slid to a stop, inches from Gramps but on the grass.

Mike shifted into P. The turned off the engine.

"You tried to run me over." Gramps was upset.

The back door opened, and Gram stepped out.

"What's going on out here?"

"He tried to run me over." Mike heard Gramps say as he opened the car door. Suddenly driving didn't seem like so much fun.

"I'm sure..." Gram started to say, and Mike spoke at the same time.

"I'm sorry. I don't know what happened. I didn't mean to..."

"Didn't mean to? Didn't mean to. Look you tore up the grass."

Mike looked at the marks the tires made in the grass. His heart was pounding, and he felt a lump of lead in his chest. "I didn't..." then Mike realized he was parroting himself and he closed his mouth and looked at the ground.

"Mike, what happened." Gramma's voice was calm, reasonable.

"I, I, I don't know. I guess my foot slipped or got mixed up or something."

"Can't even drive a car that little way." Gramps intoned.

"Well that certainly isn't going to help anything. Of course the boy didn't mean this." Gramma looked at Mike. "You have driven before haven't you?"

"I thought I could. It looks so easy."

"Alright, alright. Everyone's ok and the car's ok..."

"Lawn's destroyed." Gramps waved his hand.

"Hardly," Gram looked at the damaged grass. "It'll grow back in no time. Mike, go ahead and wash the car. I'll move it back when you are done."

"I'm sorry." Mike said as his grandparents turned to go

back in the house. He had managed to mess up something as simple as washing the car. Couldn't he do anything right? Mike banged his fist against his thigh then went and got the hose.

While he worked, Mike mused about how he would talk with his grandparents. He knew Grumps was going to keep working on digs about the slip up with the car. Gramma would be ok, she had put everything in perspective before going back in the house. No one was hurt and the car wasn't damaged. No injury except Mike's ego. He had thought driving was so easy.

By the time he was putting the hose and bucket away, hanging the rags on the line he determined he wasn't going to react to anything that Grumps said. Those were only words and words don't hurt...much.

He carried the vacuum into the house. "I'm done Grandma."

"Better have done a good job." Gramps was at the kitchen table, a bowl of soup in front of him. Mike could hear the spoon clink against the bowl and then Grumps slurped the hot liquid.

"I did Gramps." Mike offered. "I'm really sorry about the lawn." He heard the high-pitched, weaselly sound in his voice and hated that. He didn't like being on the defensive. "You can come check."

"And give you another chance to run me over?"

"Bert." Gramma shot at him. Her eyes were firm. "You know that was an accident. Stop making such a big deal out of it. Maybe if you took a bit more time with the boy, you would have given him some driving lessons."

Grumps huffed but remained silent.

"I'll come." Gramma offered. "The car needs to be moved back into the driveway anyway." She wiped her hands on her apron.

Outside Gramma stopped and made it obvious she was checking over the car. Mike felt good about that, he was proud of the job he had done.

"Very nice," She held one elbow in the palm of her hand, the other hand under her chin. "Very nice indeed young man. Even the windshield...haven't seen it so clean."

Mike felt good inside. "Just wait until you see the interior." He indicated the driver's door. All the doors and the trunk lid were open, airing out the interior.

"Wow," Gramma moved both hands to her face. "It sparkles. And the carpets are so clean."

"I even vacuumed the seats," Mike bragged, "I'm sure I even got last weeks farts out of the upholstery." Then Mike realized what he had just said. It would have been funny if he was talking to Uwe and Chuck but this was his grandmother he was talking to. "Sorry." He looked at her, trying not to smile, "Got carried away a bit there."

"Think I never heard something like that before? Been around men and kids my whole life. Farts can be funny. Been known to pass a few myself."

Mike felt his mouth drop open. He stared at his grandma. She smiled back at him then made a little farting sound with her mouth and rocked her hips. They both laughed.

"Alright, let's get this car back where it belongs." She jingled the keys then tossed them to Mike.

He caught them then looked at her.

"Well get in. This thing ain't gonna drive itself you know." She moved around to the passenger door, closing the others as she went.

Mike ducked his head, smiled, then climbed in behind the wheel.

"You follow my instructions and no one else needs to know." She nodded her head toward the house.

Mike nodded then started the car.

Moving it back to it's proper spot was uneventful, but Gramma kept up a constant stream of instructions, 'shoulder check, look in mirrors, easy on the pedals' Mike did as he was told and enjoyed the lesson. And not only because they were both defying Gramps. Gramma was nice, guiding, not blaming. Encouraging, not discouraging.

"Come inside and have your lunch." She said after they

climbed out of the car.

"Thanks for the lesson Gramma. Sorry about earlier."

"I know, let's just put that behind us. Can't un-bake that muffin so we have to find a way to live with it."

"OK if I go to the pool after."

"Don't see any reason why not."

Mike had his towel and trunks tucked under his arm. The day had gotten warmer and he was happy to be going to the pool. He was looking forward to talking with Suzie too. It wasn't until he was crossing the bridge over Catfish Creek and the smell of chlorinated water washed over him that he realized he hadn't even thought about Jeannie. Then he saw the bikes in the rack.

'Crap,' he thought, 'they're here.' Mike vowed he wasn't going to let Jack and Alan spoil his day or draw out his bad side. He was going to remain in control. He hadn't seen them for almost a week, it had been a good week.

When he stepped onto the pool deck, dripping water from his shower, he looked around for Suzie. He didn't see her. The lifeguard was Sean, Mike had seen him there a few times.

"Suzie not working today?" Mike intercepted Sean on his way to the edge of the pool. He tried to be casual in his comment, but Sean smiled.

"Not today."

"Tomorrow?"

"I don't know. Could be. I don't run her social calendar."

Mike thought it was best not to press any more. He jumped into the pool and did a few lengths just to warm up. He had gotten used to the pool being crowded and noisy. It was comforting in some ways, everyone having fun even though the splashing and dodging of swimmers was a constant interruption to his stroke practice. He tried to recall the coaching advice the Suzie had given him, focus on his form. He was disappointed she wasn't here, but it didn't have to be a total waste.

"Hey fish-boy." Mike stopped when he heard Jack's voice.

Clearing water from his eyes with one hand Mike treaded water with his other. "What do you want?" He didn't even try to keep the annoyance from his voice. The last thing he wanted was another encounter with Jack and his clown sidekick. He looked past Jack to see if he was alone. As usual, Alan was nearby. Mike noted that Jeannie was there too. She still looked beautiful even though her face was full of attitude. Mike pondered that it was peculiar that once you got to know people, they tended to look either more beautiful or ugly depending on their personalities and character. He remembered when he thought Jeannie was the most beautiful person he had ever met. Now she seemed only slightly better than mediocre. Jack just looked like crap.

"Just checking to see how you are. Been checking out your privates lately?" Jack looked back at Alan and both laughed.

"Why don't you just leave me alone?"

"Leave me alone," Jack mimicked in a high-pitched voice, "leave me alone. I am the champion of all girls and you should leave me alone."

"Jerk." The word was out of Mike's mouth before his brain even knew he was going to speak.

"What's that." Jack's head snapped toward Mike. "Got your big mouth going?"

Mike decided it was a good time to just disengage. This was getting ugly and he hadn't done anything to provoke it. 'Well,' he thought, 'I could have not come into the pool knowing these guys were here.' But then they would be controlling his actions and he wasn't going to give them that power. Mike gave a strong kick and propelled himself backward. He twisted to get into his crawl stroke.

Mike felt the water erupt around him and then there was a weight on him. He twisted and kicked away but hands grabbed him, an arm circled his neck. Jack must have jumped into the pool. There was another splash near him, probably

Alan jumping in.

Jack had him in a headlock. Mike felt himself sinking. Was he trying to drown him? A moment of panic gripped him, and Mike thrashed against the arm holding his head. He kicked out and shoved against Jack, trying to get to the surface. Hands grabbed at his ankles: Alan. Mike kicked again, hard, felt his heel connect with flesh. The grip loosened. Mike shoved against Jack again but didn't dislodge him. Then he felt real panic building in him. His arms and legs moved but with little effect.

Then his swim coach's voice came to him. "If you ever find yourself struggling with a drowning person, they have you in their grip, remember that the last thing they want is to go under water. Swim down and they will let you go." Mike knew he was a good swimmer and it hadn't been that long since he had taken a breath, so he still had enough air in his lungs to sustain him. He made his body straight up and down then pushed up on Jack and kicked his legs to take him deeper. The grip on his neck loosened and Mike swam free.

He kicked himself away from Jack and Alan and let himself come to the surface several feet away from them. His head broke the surface and he was facing them. He gulped in air, choked a bit on water that got sucked in with his breath. Coughing, he continued paddling away from them. He could see Jack's mouth moving but the water hadn't cleared his ears yet, so he had no idea what he was saying.

One of the good things about spending a lot of time in the water as a kid is you learn how to use the water to your advantage. He had been in innumerable water fights and had developed a precision technique to cup his hand so he could shoot water in a narrow stream. He did this now and aimed the stream right at Jack's face. The water hit him in the mouth, made him sputter.

Every time Jack cleared his face, Mike sent another stream to choke him up again. He saw panic build in Jack's features. He sent a few streams toward Alan as well, to keep him away too. And he heard some yelling.

"Hey, you," It was Sean, staring and pointing at Mike. "Stop that. No horse-play."

'Not horse-play,' Mike thought, 'Jack's more an ass.' But he held his tongue.

Mike felt his feet touch bottom. He sent one more stream at Jack and another at Alan, gaining him another call from Sean. Then he turned and waded to the shallow end of the pool. Jack and Alan followed him, shouting obscenities.

"You two," Sean pointed at from the pool edge, "out of the pool." Jack and Alan ignored him, kept heading toward Mike. Sean headed toward the shallow end.

Mike climbed out and headed to the shower room. He didn't feel like swimming anymore. He thought it was best that he remove himself before his anger flared up. He was still shocked that Jack had tried drowning him, if that was his intention. Mike glanced over his shoulder as he entered the doorway. Sean was between him and Jack, one hand on Jack's chest. Sean was speaking loud but Mike still couldn't hear him. He grabbed his clothes and towel and left without dressing.

Mike pulled on his t-shirt as he crossed the street. He thought he might be better heading into the park there rather than heading straight home. Jack and Alan would likely head that way once they got away from Sean. He would take a different route. While he walked, he towelled his hair then combed it out as best he could with his fingers. Then he began to shake.

He felt hot and ashamed that he was shaking, wondering why that was happening. Sure, he was scared, but only a bit. Jack was bigger but that didn't bother Mike much, he'd taken on bigger kids before and won. Not always, he's taken his share of beatings too. It wasn't even that there were two of them, Mike was certain Alan would run away the first time he got punched or if Mike got the best of Jack. Bullies friends typically didn't hold much loyalty when the cards were down. He was scared because this was the type of situation he had been trying to avoid, that had gotten him into so much trouble in the past, had helped erode his parent's marriage. He was angry because he was trying to do the right thing but feeling like a coward for doing it. Especially because Grumps wouldn't appreciate what he was doing, would only find some fault in Mike. But then he would do that no matter what Mike tried.

Behind him, Mike heard Jack and Alan come out of the pool. "Where is he?" He heard Alan ask. Mike moved closer to the river, putting bushes between him and them, hiding.

"Probably slithering home to cry on his mommy's titties." Jack said.

"Let's get him." Alan sounded a little hesitant, speaking quieter than Jack.

"He can't be far." Jack unlocked their bikes and they rode over the bridge, toward Talbot Street. Mike continued walking along the river, heading toward home but out of their view. If they managed to find him, he decided he would make sure they knew they'd been in a fight.

A few minutes later he heard bikes behind him, and laughter. He spun but it was just three girls riding through the park. Mike moved closer to the riverbank, into the full shade of the trees and bushes there. He sat down and watched the water sliding past. He waited for his heart to stop racing from being startled by the girls. He stared into the water trying to figure out what he had done wrong, how the day had come off the rails again. First the car thing and now this.

He saw a duck with four ducklings swimming in the river. They headed toward the shore. Mike watched them. Mama duck waddled up the bank, onto the grass. Mike stayed still, breathing through his nose. The babies followed, squawking and stumbling. The mama must not have realized he was there. She walked by him, close. Mike admired the sheen and colours of her feathers. Babies followed in a rough line.

The last duckling wandered close to Mike, pecking at the grass, then at his leg. It didn't hurt. Mike studied the small bird's soft looking down. Without thinking he reached out to touch it. There was a loud squawk, Mike looked to the sound. Mama duck was running toward him, wings and beak open.

She looked frantic, afraid for her child. Mike stood and backed away, hands out in front of him. Mama put herself between Mike and her baby, still squawking and holding her wings out. Mike backed away more. Mama duck folded her wings, turned to her baby, gave it a nudge with her beak in the direction of its siblings. She gave Mike one more squawk, tucked her wings, then resumed her waddle. Mike laughed once then turned and walked the other way.

A Chat with History

All the way to the library Mike thought about the chat he was going to have with Bruce and his grandfather. He hoped the guy was legit, not just some scammer. Mike felt confident that it was real but prepared himself for someone trying to take advantage of him too. He remembered to pack his ear buds to keep the noise of his call to a minimum. He logged into Skype and waited for them to connect.

About five minutes later his computer chimed that there was in incoming call. Mike hesitated a moment then answered. After a few more moments the video feed flickered to life and Mike saw a teen about his own age and a man who looked old enough to be his grandfather. So far so good. The old man squinted at Mike.

"You Wenner's nephew?" Bruce said. "Is this thing on?" He looked toward young Bruce then back at Mike. "Why isn't he answering?"

"You need to wait a bit Grandpa, I told you about the lag while everything gets sent through the internet. It's not like a phone where the sound goes immediately." Young Bruce gave Mike a glance that said 'hard to make them understand' but Mike also got the impression from young Bruce's tone that he was happy he could be helping the man out.

"Great nephew," Mike said, "I'm Wenner's great nephew. My Grandpa is his brother."

"What did he say?" Again, old Bruce looked to his grandson. "He doesn't look anything like Wenner. Is he a bastard? Ask him if he's a bastard."

Young Bruce took more of a lead in the conversation interpreting and relaying Mikes questions and answers and information between Mike and his grandfather. Mike was grateful for his help as the old man struggled with hearing challenges.

Grandpa Bruce had a son, now called Bruce Sr. The grandson was Bruce Jr. Mike wondered why families would name their kids like that, making things difficult but he wasn't really concerned. He wanted to learn about Wenner and that was what most of the conversation was about.

He learned that Grandpa Bruce and Wenner became good friend in England while they were training before shipping to France. After training they ended up in different units, but both were despatch riders. Bruce confirmed that he knew of Bert but had never met him. Wenner had talked about him a lot because they were very competitive, always trying to outdo each other. When Mike asked if Bruce knew how Wenner died, the old man grew quiet, his face went slack and his lower lip quivered. He looked straight into the camera as he spoke. Mike saw glistening in his eyes. It was clear he was back in the day he was speaking about.

"It was my fault." Bruce paused and looked down. Bruce Jr. reached toward him but the old man pushed his hand away and looked back. "I wanted to get together with Wenner. I had an eight-hour pass coming to me and I knew his unit was only a few miles away. It was his birthday and I had a bottle of whiskey to celebrate. I got hold of him on the field phone. He said he could only get a pass if he did a mission. He said he'd steal one from somebody else and meet me on his way back. He never showed up. I heard later he got killed. Read it in Dispatches. Again, the man paused but after a few moments continued. "If I hadn't asked him, he wouldn't have taken that mission. Will you tell his brother how sorry I am?"

They spoke for a few more minutes but it was mostly between Mike and Bruce Jr. Mike was able to get more information about their units and locations and learned that Dispatches were official reports describing heroic action involving the enemy. Mike wondered if he could get hold of the one Grandpa Bruce mentioned.

They ended the conversation with promises to keep in touch. Mike hoped they would, he got a good feeling from both. Perhaps too, Grumps would like to get to know the man. And he envied the relationship that Bruce Jr had with Grandpa

Bruce.

After they ended the call, Mike spent some time researching the Mention in Dispatches but didn't find anything specific.

That evening on the porch Mike told Gramma about the phone call.

"Grandpa Bruce said Wenner was mentioned in despatches. From what I could find out, that was usually a really good thing to have happen. It means someone did something brave."

"I remember reading some of those in the newspapers. I was always looking for your grandfather's name in them, or someone else I knew but I never did. It's comforting to know that Wenner was."

"There's a trunk in the barn with a bunch of military stuff in it. Maybe there's something in there."

"I don't think it would be a good idea to be getting into your grandfather's stuff without his permission. You know how he is."

Mike sat back, thinking. He now knew of two men who both thought they were responsible for Wenner's death, but he didn't have any details. The answer might be in the barn, but should he go in there looking when he knew Grumps wouldn't like that? Why did everything have to be so hard?

Digging Up the Past

"Gramps and I are going shopping in London today. Would you like to go with us?"

"And we're taking the car so you can't go hot-rodding with it." Gramps added. Gramma glared at him.

Mike thought that he would like to go, but spending all that time cooped up in the car with him? "Thanks, but I have some plans for today." He needed to get more work done on the motorcycle and he might have to do some rooting around in Gramp's old chest too. He still wasn't certain he was going to do that but he was pretty sure he would.

"Ok, there is some chicken in the fridge from last night. You can have that for lunch. Make yourself a sandwich if you like."

"Don't be getting into anything else. And leave my spicy mustard alone. Don't want some brat eating all my spicy mustard."

"Bert." Gramma glared at him again. "That is for everyone." To Mike she said, "You go ahead and have the mustard if you like." She glanced at Gramps then back at Mike. "Maybe you should eat all of it up." Then she winked.

"Hey." Gramps said.

"Ok, Gramma. I'll be fine."

The house felt empty once they left. With the sound of the car moving up the driveway Mike realized this was the first time he had been in their house by himself. He was tempted to go snooping around in Gramps' room but, once he was standing in the doorway, looking at the bedside table with its small library of western paperbacks, the bed, decorated with a cotton blanket that had a pattern of puffed balls of some sort, and the kitchen chair in the corner by the window, he felt like an invader. He turned away. The man deserved more privacy and respect than that.

He knew he was going to snoop into Gramps' war chest and that would be enough. And that was for a specific purpose, to help improve their relationship. Rooting around in the man's bedroom out of curiosity was just invasive, with a side of creepy. Mike knew he wouldn't like anyone poking into his personal stuff.

Mike headed to the barn. Today would be a perfect day to clean the carburetor. Mike needed to use a mixture of kerosene and acetone and the clerk at Canadian Tire had warned him to only use it in a well-ventilated area. He left the big door on the barn open to provide that. Before removing and disassembling the carb, Mike took photos so he would get all the parts back in the right places.

As he took it apart, the rubber seals disintegrated. Mike noted their sizes so he could make a trip into town to get replacements. He already had a cork sheet that he would use to make gaskets from.

The instructions he had were not specifically for this bike, so he had to wing parts of it. Since the bike hadn't been run in decades, Mike was aware that any residual fuel in it would have turned to lacquer and would be a gunky mess. He let the parts soak in his solution and, while he waited for them to clean, he pulled out the war chest.

Inside, the chest was tidy and organized. Again, Mike used his camera so he would be able to put everything back as he had found it. If Gramps never knew he had been in here, would it still be a violation? Just like the tree falling in the forest philosophical thought experiment from school, Mike had his own interpretation, 'If a grandson does something that Gramps doesn't see, is he still wrong?' Trouble was, the answer wasn't so elusive, it was a flat out YES.

There were photographs, a Union Jack flag, empty shell casings, letters tied into a bundle with some old string. Mike lifted these items out and set them aside. He felt reading the letters would be too personal, so he left them. Then there was a heavy cotton, green uniform shirt and pants. Both were neatly folded. Under those were several boxes. Mike lifted the lid of the first.

More letters, some news articles about the bombing of

London by the Germans. One of the articles had the photo of a soldier in the rubble of what looked to have once been a house. He wondered if the soldier was Gramps or maybe Wenner. There was a Toronto Daily Star newspaper dated May 7, 1945 announcing Germany Surrenders. The paper was old, cracked and brownish. Mike was gentle with it. Inside a box that had a lift off lid, Mike found a German luger. It was black and silver, silver where the black had worn off. It looked in pretty good shape. In another box Mike found a bunch of papers.

There was an old pay book, Gramp's discharge papers, a journal with about seven pages that had been written on, the rest was blank. The writing was messy, and the ink faded. Mike tried to read it but could only make out a few words here and there. Grump's wasn't much of an author apparently.

There was a paper that had been folded in four. Mike unfolded it, grimacing when it tore a bit along one fold. He didn't open it all the way to keep it from ripping any more. Under an official looking crest with a lion and unicorn It read:

By the KING'S Order the name of
Corporal Wenner Bryce Weinstein
Signals Corps
Was published in the London Gazette on
4 May, 1945
as mentioned in a Despatch for distinguished service.
I am charged to record
His Majesty's high appreciation.

It was signed, Secretary of State for War.

Mike read it twice. It was true, it was totally true. His uncle was a real war hero. He wondered what it was that the man had done to be distinguished like this. He found the answer in the next paper.

It was a typed form, a report, Mike assumed 'the

despatch'.

27 Apr 45. Cpl Weinstein was dispatched with troop movement orders for 125 Cdn Grndr. Cpl Weinstein failed to arrive destination. He was later found deceased, still in possession of his orders. Seven enemy casualties nearby.

Mike looked up. His uncle must have come across a German patrol, or they found him, or something, and then he killed them all. He must have got them all or the orders he was carrying would have been taken. No wonder he was mentioned in despatches. Mike chuffed a quick laugh as he thought, 'the despatch rider dispatched the enemy.' Then he thought about how young Wenner had been. Only a few years older than himself. There wasn't anything funny about that.

Mike read over the documents again, then packed everything back into the chest being careful to get it all in the same spot he had found it. Then he pushed the chest back under the bench where he had found it. Hoping Gramps would never find out that he had poked around in it, Mike went back to work on the carburetor. As he worked, he wondered why Grumps though he was responsible for Wenner's death. It had been the German's who killed him. What was Grumps thinking?

After making himself a quick lunch, Mike headed to the Canadian Tire to get the seals he would need. On his return he went back to the barn to make sure everything was where it was supposed to be. Then he headed to the front porch where he read his book until Gram and Gramps drove back into the driveway. He waved at them. Gramma waved back.

"I picked up some clothes for you. I hope you don't mind." Plastic bags rustled as Mike helped carry in the purchases from the trunk. Gramma seemed excited. "I thought you should have some new clothes for your big date."

"Gramma." Mike felt heat crawling up his neck.

"Doesn't the kid know we're on a fixed income?" gramps muttered.

"Now Bert," Gramma waved a hand at him. "It's not

like we're destitute and it was fun picking out a few things." She reached into one of the bags that had been piled on the table and pulled out a pair of jeans. She held them up, then against Mike's hips. "I think I got the right size."

"All the way back to London if you didn't." Grumps grumbled.

"Go try these on." She handed Mike a shirt as well.

Mike modeled the clothes for her, and she seemed quite pleased.

"Oh my, you are such a handsome young man."

Mike felt himself blush.

"Thank you, Gramma." Mike gave her a hug. "Thank you for the clothes."

Gramma pointed toward the living room where Grumps had turned on the TV.

Mike sighed but turned toward the room.

"Thanks Grampa. I really like these." Mike stepped into the living room so Grumps could see but he didn't even look at Mike.

Mike turned back to his grandmother and raised his arms. She just smiled at him. He headed back to his room to change again.

Gramps Gets Flushed

Mike woke the next morning feeling anxious about the upcoming dance. It was a nice feeling knowing that Suzie wanted to go with him. He had some nice new clothes to wear, but he still had to deal with the fact that he didn't know how to dance. That was on his mind when he walked into the kitchen for breakfast. Gram was at the sink, Gramps at the table, reading the paper.

"Good morning sunshine," Gram's voice was light, sing-songy. Mike wondered if Gramps was in a bad mood. "French toast?" She asked.

"Oui, oui, mademoiselle." Mike responded, "Pain perdu c'est bon." Mike wasn't certain how he had managed to remember that from his French class. He wasn't certain he had it right but who would know?

"Ne sois pas intelligent alec." Grumps rattled his paper.

Mike was surprised, the man's French accent sounded perfect. Not that he was any great judge of that, he didn't really like French class, but he did like the lilt when it was spoken properly. He wasn't entirely certain what his grandfather had said but assumed it was derogatory.

At the end of his linguistic ability Mike mumbled, "excusez moi, perdon."

"Perdon is Spanish. In French it's just excusez moi." Grumps looked over his paper at Mike. "Who says 'excuse me, excuse me?'" Grumps rattled his paper to make the corner that had curled down, snap up again.

Mike's face burned. He had only been trying to be light, and maybe a little bit funny, and now the morning felt like it was in shambles. This was going to be a long day. He sat down.

"If any of that means 'yes, I want some French toast', I am happy to deliver." Gram kept up her sing-song tone. She smiled at Mike and that lightened his mood.

"Yes, please Gramma." While Mike waited for his

breakfast, he stared at the newspaper between himself and his grandfather. How did he know French and Spanish? He must have picked that up in the war. The man was certainly full of surprises. Too bad they never seemed to be pleasant ones.

As he was mopping up the last of the syrup on his plate, with the last of his French toast, Gram said, "Gramps has some work to do on the car. It might help with your school if you get a bit of experience?" She looked at Mike. Her eyes were soft, and Mike realized she was being very careful in her choice of words. Her eyes flicked to Gramps then back to Mike and her chin hitched up a bit. She wanted Mike to help with the task, but she was trying to make it look like Mike was the one who needed help.

"Uh, yeah, sure," Mike really didn't want to go through another work experience with Gramps, but his grandmother was always so good to him, there was no way he would disappoint her. "That would be great. Would help a lot." Mike looked at his grandfather who had folded his paper by the side of his plate and was sipping the last of his coffee. "Would that be ok Grampa? What do we need to do?" Mike tried to get the right tone into his voice.

"You can come but we're speaking English. Verstehst du?"

Mike wasn't certain what Gramps had said, but the guttural sound of the words had him thinking it was German. He really had to hand it to the man, he was intelligent. 'But then why is he
so bad at relationships?' screamed in Mike's head. Maybe it was
just his relationship with Mike that the man wasn't any good at. Mike thought it was better that he
not say anything, since it would probably be the wrong thing so he just nodded.

When Gramps headed out,
Mike carried his dishes to the sink and kissed his grandmother. "Thanks Gramma, that was great."

"Be careful out there." she whispered.

Gramps was already in the car when Mike came out of the house.

He pulled the car forward, across the grass and into the scragglier grass at the edge of the brush.

"So, what we doing?" Mike tried to sound cheerful.

"Rad flush if you have to know. Kids always with the questions"

"Ok, sure. What can I do?" After he said it Mike realized it was another question.

"Get the hose and stay out of the way."

Mike ran to the hose, turned on the tap and made sure the water was running.

"Turn that tap off. Gotta hook up the flusher thing first."

Mike turned off the tap, feeling the heat creep up his neck. Was he going to be able to get through this? He carried the end of the hose to his grandfather.

"Don't just stand there," Gramps had raised the hood, "attach this thing." He held a plastic nozzle with a threaded collar on it. Mike screwed it onto the end of the hose.

"Should I get you a drain tray?" Mike had done this at school and knew you needed to drain the old coolant out of the rad before hooking up the back-flush valve to flush out the engine.

"What the hell for?" Gramps leaned over the front of the car, reached down between the rad and the engine. A moment later Mike heard liquid pattering onto the ground.

"Isn't that bad for the environment?"

Gramps just looked at him. Mike decided further conversation on that topic wouldn't be good.

The rest of the rad flush was quiet. Gramps told Mike to get the coolant from the trunk. When Mike got back to the front of the car, Gramps had put a large funnel into the oil filler hole in the valve cover. Mike wondered what he was doing.

When Gramps took one of the coolant jugs and was about to pour it into the funnel Mike decided that now was not the time to be quiet. If the man poured coolant into the oil, it would be a bad mistake.

"Gramps," Mike said, stepping close to the man and reaching for the jug of coolant, "I think that is supposed to go in the rad."

"Of course it is," Gramps pushed him away with his elbow, "what do you think I am doing?"

"But Gramps, that's not the rad. That's where the oil goes." Mike stepped in again.

"Of course it is," Gramps voice was firm but there was a peculiar look to his eyes, "you can't run a motor without oil." The man started tipping the coolant bottle again.

Mike felt panicked. He had to stop him but how?

"Here, let me." Mike tried to wrestle the bottle from Gramps. "Gramps held on tight.

What do you think you are doing? Let go of that."

Then Mike had an idea. He pushed his grandfather back hard enough to make him step back, but not so hard he would fall to the ground. Then he reached up and pulled down the hood.

"Ahh," he yelled, "my hand. My hand." Mike leaned over the hood, keeping his hand tucked under him. He hoped he was yelling loud enough to attract his grandmother.

"What have you done?" His grandfather sounded angry. "Stupid kids." As hoped, he set down the bottle and moved to open the hood. Mike heard the back door of the house click open then slam closed. Gram was on the way. Good.

"What's going on?" Mike heard fear in her voice. Then she was beside him. Gramps had released the hood release in the car was rushing to the front to release the safety latch. Mike kept up his yells of pain.

When the hood went up, Mike turned, keeping his hand close to his stomach. Gram was now beside him. Mike turned so Gramps wouldn't be able to see his hand, but she would. He looked at her, smiled a bit, then waggled his fingers so she would know he wasn't really hurt. No point in keeping her scared like this.

"What's going on?" She asked.

"Goddamn kids," Gramps was now as loud as Mike had been, "don't know what the hell they're doing. Just get in the way."

Gram looked at Mike who whispered to her, "He was going to pour the coolant into where the oil goes. I didn't know how else to stop him."

Gram's eyes widened in understanding. "Let me see that she said." reaching for Mike's hand. After a moment she announced, "Well, I don't think anything's broken. Think you two can finish this job and still have all your body parts intact?"

"Sorry Gram," Mike said, "I slipped. I didn't mean to alarm you, it all just scared me."

"Scared, shmared," Gramps harumphed. "Look what you did to my funnel." The plastic funnel had been crushed between the hood and the engine block.

"Sorry Gramps," Mike reached for it, intending to bend it back into shape but Gramps pulled it away.

"I'll do the work. Keep you from busting something else."

Mike felt relief when he saw Gramps put the funnel into the rad. Mike brought him the abandoned bottle of coolant then stepped back to watch the man work.

"He gets confused a bit sometimes." Gram had stepped in close to Mike, her words a whisper. "Good thinking." Then she was gone.

Mike stayed back, content on watching his grandfather work. After the job was done, Gramps looked over the engine, picked up the oil filler cap from where he had set it, stared at it a moment, rubbed his head, then tightened it in place.

Mike curled the hose and replaced it by the house.

Is Everyone Angry?

The next morning Mike checked his emails. There was one from Janice.

Hi Mike, I hope you are having good days. I am going shopping with my Mom later. I hope I can talk her into buying me a new outfit. What's your favorite colour? I went to see E.T. yesterday. Have you seen it yet? I won't say too much, so I don't spoil it for you, but I loved it. Maybe when you get home, we can go to a movie together? What kind do you like?

Mike sent a quick email back letting her know he likes science fiction and action movies best but that he can enjoy most. He was looking forward to seeing Janice when he got home but was feeling a bit guilty because of his date with Suzie and the fact he was still attracted to Jeannie. Girls were still so confusing to him.

He was a bit worried too. Tomorrow he was scheduled to work at the Legion, but he had to work with Eliza. That hadn't worked out too well so far, another person who just didn't seem to like Mike, no matter what he did.

"Gram," Mike said when they were having their evening tea, Jeopardy in the background, "have you ever really tried to get someone to like you but just couldn't?"

"Are we having a discussion about," she nodded her head toward the porch door.

After a moment Mike realized she was indicating Gramps.

"Oh. No. No. There's this guy I work with sometimes at the Legion. He's pretty surly. Hardly talks to me and, when he does, it's like he's angry with me."

"Maybe there's something you don't realize you did. Maybe he's angry about something else and he misdirects that at you. Maybe he's just like that."

"He's always nice to the customers. I haven't really seen him with any of the other staff except Sheila and he didn't seem angry then."

"You're a smart boy. I know you'll figure it out. Sometimes the best way to face a problem is head on."

The porch door banged open and the conversation ended.

Lying in bed Mike thought about what Gram had said. How could he meet this problem head on? He fell asleep thinking about it.

Facing Eliza

Eliza gave Mike a sideways glance when he first walked in, then busied himself with something that didn't need doing. There weren't any customers in the lounge. Gram's words from last night rang in his head, "the best way to face a problem is head on."

"Eliza," Mike felt a crawling in his skin, he didn't like this, but he was determined to see it through, "can I speak with you a moment while it's still quiet in here?"

Eliza looked at him, Mike thought he saw worry on the man's face. Then the skin tightened his lips into a snarl. "What?" It came out flat, he wasn't asking Mike to repeat himself.

"I feel like there's a conflict between us. Not sure what I've done to cause this, but I would really like to get it behind us. Can you let me know what's going on?"

"Well, if you want to open that kettle of fish, why are you even here?"

"To help out." Mike was a bit surprised by the question.

"I bin here a long time. Never needed no twerp kid to help me out. Think I don't know how to do my job?"

Did Eliza think Mike was here because he wasn't very good at his job? That would certainly explain why he was pissed off.

"No, I came to help out because I got myself into some trouble and I'm probably going to have to do some community service. This has nothing to do with you." Mike paused a moment considering his next words because they weren't exactly honest. He decided a little lie right now might be beneficial. "I actually think you do a great job. I've learned a lot from watching you." Mike hoped his words sounded sincere, they were partly true, Eliza was good with the customers.

"Well, if yer learning so much, maybe you should be

paying fer yer education."

'Ah,' Mike thought, 'it's the money thing.' Then he thought he might be able to distract the conversation and build the relationship.

"That sounds like a great idea. How be you keep my share of the tips? I don't have any other money to pay with since I do need to save for college."

Eliza just stared at him a moment, his face a bit squinty, his eyes hard. "You funning with me kid?"

"No," Mike softened his voice, "I think you are quite right. You are teaching me so I should make sure you get something for that. I don't have much, but I'll give up my tips. Totally worth it to me." Which wasn't a lie, there was value in what Mike was getting.

"Don't yer be whining to Sheila 'bout this."

"No, no, all will be good." Mike paused a moment then, when Eliza turned back to wiping something that didn't need wiping Mike asked, "What do you do when you're not working here?"

"Wadda ya mean? What do I do? I go home, wadda ya think?" Eliza had stopped his wiping and stared at Mike.

"Nothing," Mike glanced around, "just making conversation." Then the phone on the back wall of the bar rang and Eliza went to answer it. Mike turned toward the lounge tables looking for something to do.

A moment later he heard Eliza's raised voice, "He did what?" He couldn't help but turn toward it, and he saw Eliza with the phone handset pressed to his head. Mike tried to not hear the rest of the conversation but failed.

"Now why did he do that?" Eliza had gotten control of his voice and was speaking quieter, but it was still easy for Mike to hear him.

A moment later, "And what is that going to cost?" After another short pause, "Jesus." Eliza stared at the handset in his hand.

"Well, I don't know." and a moment later, "How the

hell am I supposed to know?"

Eliza set the handset into its cradle with a bang, "Goddamn kids." Then he went back to wiping what didn't need wiping, still muttering to himself but now so low Mike couldn't make out the words.

Mike wondered what that was all about. Somehow, he knew it had been a call from Eliza's home, but kids? He was almost as old as Grumps. Grandkids? Mike decided to get a bucket and clean under the bar again.

A little later Sheila entered her office, Mike decided he would go speak with her.

"I am having a bit of a time with Eliza. He seems angry with me all the time."

Sheila leaned on her arms; her hands clasped in her usual praying manner. "Eliza has his issues. It's nothing personal."

"I kind of feels personal. He's nice enough with everyone else."

"We spoke about this before."

"I know. I would just like to fix things."

"Not everything can be fixed."

"He asked me not to tell you, but I told him I wouldn't take any tips on days I work with him." Mike paused a moment then continued in a rush, "I'm not complaining, you see, I'm just saying, he can have my tips. I don't mind."

Sheila looked at Mike without saying anything. He chewed his lip a moment then said, "Don't vets get war pensions?"

"Yes."

"So why is Eliza still working at his age? Worried about the tips he gets."

Sheila's face went slack and she studied the desktop. "It's really not much of a pension, and its never kept up with inflation. Lots of vets struggle each month."

"Well, that's a jip." Mike stated.

"That it is." Sheila gave him a weak smile, "That's one of the issues the Legion tris to help with."

"I hope this helps a bit." He said, not knowing how to finish the conversation.

Sheila did. She said, "Well, I have work to do."

Mike headed back into the lounge. It was still quiet, so Mike wandered around, catching glimpses of Eliza now and then. There was something about the man, but Mike couldn't figure out what it was. Then it dawned on him once he moved a little closer. Eliza was scruffy.

Mike saw that the points of the man's collar were worn and frayed. There were a couple of light stains on his shirt and a white, jagged line near the hem of his pant leg. While Dan and Vic were always impeccable in their appearance, Eliza was a bit tattered. But this was only obvious on close inspection, the reason Mike hadn't noticed it before. Mike concluded that the man was more than struggling with his issues, he was poor. No wonder he was upset about Mike taking a share of the tips.

Mike wondered what he could do to help him without embarrassing the man.

The Dance

When Mike called for Suzie, she insisted he come in and meet her parents. Even though he was nervous, he did his best to be polite. Mr. Lucknow was a large man, beefy in the shoulders and a belly that extended past his belt. He held Mike at arm's length, "Well now, you're a bit scrawny but at least you're presentable." Mike had chosen to wear the new jeans Gram had bought him and the blue checked shirt.

"Dad, be nice." Suzie pushed at his arm. Turning to Mike she added, "he's not serious."

Mike smiled and shook the man's hand, trying to give it a firm squeeze like his dad had taught him but the man's hand was huge.

"Nice grip there Mikey." Mr. Lucknow turned their hands a bit and Mike had no choice but to let him. "You kids have fun but," He gave Mike's hand a little tug, "not too much fun."

"Dad!"

A bit later, while they were walking toward the arena Suzie slipped her hand into Mike's. It was soft and felt nice. Mike felt heat rise in his neck.

"Don't mind my dad, he thinks he's funny."

"I liked him." Mike looked at Suzie, "A father should look out for his daughter."

"Well, he's chased off a few boys." Suzie looked away, perhaps realizing what she had just said and what it might mean to Mike.

"Well," Mike gave her hand a little squeeze, "I'm glad he did."

The closer they got to the arena the more cars Mike saw parked along the street and the more people were walking on the sidewalks. Everyone seemed happy and excited and Mike couldn't help but get caught up in the feeling. Then he remembered that this was a dance and he really didn't know how. What was Suzie going to think of him when he did his little dance floor wiggle and nothing more?

When they entered the arena, the noise became overwhelming. People talking, laughing, kids running around playing and yelling, the sounds of the band warming up and everything echoing around the inside of the massive space. Mike had thought the Sales Barn was crowded; this place made that place look like a ghost town. Everyone had been right that this dance was a big deal. Mike didn't see anyone who he recognized. Suzie seemed to know them all.

The band was set up at one end of the arena and the food area was at the other. Around the perimeter of what would be the ice rink itself, tables and chairs had been set up leaving most of the ice area open as the dance floor. People were everywhere, the dance floor was crowded even though there wasn't any music to dance to yet, people were milling around greeting each other. Suzie reminded him that this was the only time most of these people got to see each other. There was lots of catching up to do. People were sitting at many of the tables and there were even people in the bleachers that surrounded the rink.

Suzie was greeted by so many people and she introduced them all to Mike but there were way too many names to remember. It was obvious she was well liked and well known from her work as a lifeguard, that would explain the kids. From school, that would explain the other teenagers. But she even knew the adults and they knew her. They got some surprised looks from the teens since they were still holding hands. Suzie didn't seem to care at all.

The aroma of sizzling burgers and hotdogs made Mike's stomach grumble. He remembered Gramma warning him about that and she had been right. Mike nudged Suzie in the direction of the food tables, and she headed that way but their progress was slow as she stopped and talked to so many people. Mike did his best to speak to each person as they were introduced but he found himself saying the same thing over and over and it began to feel a bit phoney. He didn't know what else to say though. He hoped he didn't sound too foolish.

Then he saw a familiar face.

It was more the golden curls that he recognized but when she turned toward him it confirmed that Jeanie was there. She looked at Mike, smiled, looked down at his hand still holding Suzie's. She gave a little smirk then turned away. Mike felt embarrassed but wasn't certain why. He wasn't Jeanie's boyfriend; she had hardly shown any interest in him at all, but he still felt uncomfortable at her seeing him with Suzie. Why were relationships so difficult? He wondered again why he even cared what Jeanie thought.

Then the guitar twangs and unconnected drum sounds were interrupted by "1, 2, 3, 4" and the band broke into How Do You Like Me Now, a fast country tune.

Suzie said "Toby Keith" and looked toward the band, her feet tapping, hips swivelling.

Approval and claps rose above the music for a moment then a rush of people moved to the dance floor. The party had begun.

Suzie looked toward the dancers, bouncing on her toes. She looked at Mike and he knew she wanted him to lead her there. He was too nervous. He held his hand to his stomach and looked toward the food area. Feigning needing to eat would buy him some time. Suzie looked disappointed but nodded her head.

As they continued weaving their way toward the food Mike cast glances at the dancers hoping to memorize some moves. There were people jiving, swinging and twirling, others were line dancing in familiar routines, others were just dancing. Mike had seen enough dance movies, Footloose and such, and knew what all this was. In his mind he could picture himself deft in fancy movements but, when he had tried in the privacy of his bedroom, he wasn't as smooth or coordinated as he was in his mind. Dancers made it all look so easy. He did see some who didn't look very experienced, but they were still smiling, having fun. Maybe he should stop worrying about what everyone else was thinking and just enjoy himself. He hoped he could do that.

After they got themselves a burger and cob of corn Mike looked for an empty table. He didn't see any. There weren't any for just two people. There were a few for four but mostly they were large tables with eight or ten chairs.

Suzie led him to a table that was already occupied but had some empty seats. "Anyone sitting here?" She asked. She had to speak loud to be heard over the music.

"You." A man who looked in his forties said, smiling at them.

Suzie tried to introduce Mike, she knew these people too, but he couldn't catch any of their names. He smiled and sat down.

Suzie sat and turned toward the music. Her feet were bouncing, and her hands were clapping. She was into the party. Mike watched her, the smile on her face, the excitement in her eyes and he realized she was beautiful. Where he had thought her to be a bit plain when he first met her, her eyes close together, now that he had had some time to get to know her, he realized how foolish he had been to make a judgement about her earlier. He was glad to be here with her.

Then he saw Jack on the dance floor dancing with a girl Mike hadn't seen before. There was no stumbling or fumbling going on, Jack spun his partner with confidence and grace. Mike's desire to dance in front of these people disappeared like an ice cube on a hot grill. He ate slow, trying to ignore Suzie's frequent glances.

When the song ended a man in a suit jumped on the stage and spoke into the microphone. He introduced himself as the evening's MC and welcomed everyone. He frequently asked everyone if they were having a good time and the crowd roared to every instance. He reminded the parents that the children's and young teens parties would start at eight thirty in other rooms and could they ensure all the youngsters were escorted out of the main arena at that time so the real party could begin.

Suzie leaned toward Mike and said, "That's when the bar opens."

The MC talked briefly about there being spot dances coming up and a dance off later in the evening. He closed with "Aylmer may be a small town, but we know how to have big fun." The crowd roared even louder than it had before. The band began again, another fast song but rock and roll that Mike recognized, Tarantula by Smashing Pumpkins. Again, Suzie looked at Mike. He ducked his head a bit and bit into his cob of corn. Mike did find his foot tapping to the rhythm of the song.

Mike allowed the atmosphere, the sounds, the aromas to engulf him. Everyone seemed to be having a good time, everyone except Suzie. She spoke with people and smiled but Mike felt he was letting her down. He had invited her to this dance and now he wasn't dancing. He vowed he would get up for the next one.

When the song ended the lead singer announced, "We'll slow it down now so the old people can have a chance to dance." This was followed by a round of cat calls and shouts of 'we'll show you old.' But it was all so good natured that Mike was certain it was a ritual. As the strains of Waltz Across Texas were picked out on guitar Mike groaned. He had worked himself up to dance with Suzie and now it was a slow dance. What was he going to do? He had at least done some wiggling to fast songs, he had never, ever danced a slow one.

When she looked at him, he couldn't say no. He rose slow, pushing his chair back with the back of his knees. Maybe he could fake an injury? No, he would just have to do this. She smiled and it was so beautiful that Mike couldn't help but feel a little good at the core of his dread. She reached out her hand and he took it. It still felt so soft and warm in his.

"Look Suzie," Mike said as they worked their way into the crowd of couples swaying on the dance floor, "I really haven't done this before."

She looked at him. "Really? Thought I couldn't tell?" She turned toward him and stepped close. "Its easy." She moved his hand to her shoulder, "Here." She put his other hand on her hip. "Here. Now just follow me."

Not too certain what 'follow me' was, Mike watched her. When she stepped toward him, he stepped back, when she stepped back, he stepped toward her. "That's right." She encouraged. "Relax, this is supposed to be fun."

Mike felt the heat rise in his neck and cheeks. "It is," he said, "because I'm with you." Mike saw her reaction and knew he had come up with the right words. He watched her feet and worked to match her steps. By the end of the song he thought he was doing pretty good. Sometimes he stepped in when she did or stepped away when he should have stepped in but Suzie guided him with gentle tugs and pushes and words of coaching and encouragement.

"That's it, smooth. Follow the music. Twist your hips. You sure you never did this before?" She spoke soft, close to his ear and her puffs of breath sent tingles through his body. He really started to feel comfortable. As the final strands of the music played out Mike was struck from behind.

He turned, ready to apologize for bumping into someone but it was Jack and their collision had been no accident. "Bitey Mikey. Just wash those feet and can't do a thing with them?" Jack gave a little two step flourish that Mike was certain was in reference to his own hesitant and uncertain dance skills. He had a cruel smile on his face.

The next song started, Footloose, and Jack spun his partner away and into the crowd.

Mike felt the heat rise in his neck again and his vision narrow. He had gone from feeling so good dancing with Suzie, he really had been dancing, to finding the rage racing through his mind. Why did that asshole have to come and spoil things? Mike took a step in the direction Jack had disappeared but then he thought 'why would I let him spoil my good time?'. He felt the flare of anger recede and turned back to Suzie, ready to go and sit down again.

Suzie had other plans. She was already dancing to the music, encouraging Mike to join her. She looked so happy that Mike couldn't say no. He started his wiggle dance, tapping one foot twice then the other, swinging his arms to each side, low, close to his body. He really wanted to kick it into the wild, free, dance moves from the movie. His mother had dragged him off the couch when they had watched it, encouraging him to dance with her but even then, in the privacy of their living room, he hadn't ventured any more than his wiggle dance. The people on the screen were having so much fun, enjoying the music, revelling in the contortions their bodies could work through and we he was such a slug.

Suzie smiled at him and Mike felt the heat burn in his neck and ears. Was she mocking him? Then she took a step toward him, leaning back, then a step back, leaning forward. At the same time she swung her arms, making the flare of her dress billow out. Mike realized she was showing him some dance steps. He mimicked her and they moved in unison briefly. Then she changed it up a bit.

Mike was able to follow her lead, his initial steps each time uncertain and clumsy but then smoother, steadier. As they danced, she seemed to grow even happier and that made Mike happier. By the end of the song Mike was moving in perfect unison with her through their brief routine. He no longer wanted to sit down and that seemed to make Suzie even happier.

Two songs later she had led him through some jive steps, swings and reels. Mike felt the sweat dotting his forehead and dripping down his back. He was pleased that it was from excursion, not embarrassment. When the next song started Suzie took his hand and lead him toward their table.

"I need a break." She slumped into her chair, fanning her face with her hand. Her chest heaved as she drew in large breaths. "That was fun. You did great." She leaned toward him her mouth open in a smile that showed her teeth.

Mike leaned forward, mesmerized by her lips, the lipstick glistening, little beads of sweat above her upper lip, clinging to the fine hairs there. Mike started to lean closer, opening his mouth a bit, turning his head to accept her kiss. She sat back with a sigh and closed her eyes a moment. Mike almost fell forward then realized it hadn't been her intention to kiss him. He felt blood rush to his face. She didn't seem to have noticed his advance.

Suzie opened her eyes and said, "I need something to drink. Would you get me a pop or juice or something?"

"Sure." Mike stood. His legs felt weak. Despite all the walking and swimming he had done over the past few weeks, the dancing used his muscles in a different way. He headed toward the food area.

He was almost to the food table when he felt a poke in his side. He turned to see the kissing girl and her sister. He couldn't remember their names, so he just said hi.

"You remember me?" The kissing girl asked and giggled.

Mike scrambled through his mind for her name, but it eluded him. "How could I forget," then he remembered she was Janice's cousin, so he finished "you're Janice's cousins."

She looked a bit disappointed but smiled and added "Maybe we can dance later?"

The other sister said, "We saw you out there." Pointing toward the dance floor with her head.

"Oh yeah." Mike didn't know what else to say. He looked toward Suzie to see if she could see him but too, he supposed it was alright for him to know some people here too.

Then the server at the food table asked what he wanted and by the time Mike turned back to the two girls, they had gone. He shrugged and headed back to his table.

He had two more dances with Suzie before the M.C. announced it was time for the youth to head to their separate parties. He thought he was doing well dancing, even though he still fumbled a bit and bumped other dancers sometimes. Maybe he wasn't the only one bumping, maybe they were bumping him too. He decided to just be careful and not worry about the other dancers so much. He was really having a good time.

After the kids left, the noise level changed, the energy in the room changed. Suzie leaned across the table and whispered, "Now you'll see some stuff." There was a huge shift in the crowd as the booze table opened, and people rushed for drinks. "Would you like a drink?" Suzie asked.

Mike looked at her and she winked. He had only ever drank alcohol once before, him, Uwe and Chuck has snuck some beers from Chuck's dad. Mike thought it was bitter but drank the whole bottle in little sips. Uwe pretended he was drunk, but Mike had wondered what all the fuss was about. He didn't feel any affects from it. He knew some of the kids at school bragged about getting bombed on the weekends and he was curious about that, what it was like, but not so curious that he had tried.

"I better not," he responded, "my grandparents are coming and I don't need to be in any more trouble with Gramps."

"Do you mind if I have one?"

"No, I guess not. What about your parents? You said they were coming."

"They are here. I'll only have one and I'm almost old enough. I don't hide stuff like that from them. They are ok as long as I don't get stupid about it."

"Wow, nice parents."

"They would know anyway, small town." Suzie gave a quick shrug, then stood, "I'll be right back."

The band was on a break, but a DJ had taken over the stage. He put on 'Old Time Rock and Roll' and Mike found himself bouncing in his chair to the tune. He felt a tap on his shoulder.

He turned and it was Jeanie. "Come dance." She said.

Mike looked toward Suzie, but she was lost in the crowd. Would she mind? Mike wasn't certain but thought one dance would be ok.

"Sure, but just one. I'm here with someone," He found his voice lowering at his last words. "she'll be right back." He wanted to show off some of his new moves to Jeanie.

The dance floor wasn't too crowded, since so many were still in the crowd waiting for their first drinks, but Jeanie still danced close. She kept reaching for his hand, then letting it go as she twirled, then stepped in close and bumped hips. Mike was uncertain how to respond to that, he hadn't done any dancing like that before. He just did the best he could hoping he was impressing her a little bit. He was still attracted to her, but he was uncertain too. As the song wound down, he looked toward his table but Suzie hadn't returned yet.

"One more?" Jeanie stepped in close to him.

'Why not', Mike thought. Suzie still wasn't back, was probably talking to everyone. Another fast song started. During the song Mike saw Suzie return to the table and then look around. He assumed it was for him and when she looked his way, he waved at her. She lifted her glass toward him and gave him a funny smile. Then the song slowed down and Jeanie stepped in close taking one hand and putting her other around his waist.

Not expecting this, Mike did his best. He was uncomfortable being this close to her even though feeling her sway against him felt nice. Then he stepped on her foot and he cringed and stepped back. Jeanie pulled him close and kissed him full on the mouth.

Mike was surprised and befuddled and before he regained his senses, he felt himself accepting the kiss then he remembered where he was, who he was with and what was really going on and he pulled back. He immediately looked toward his table. Had Suzie seen that? She was looking right at him and her eyes were hard.

Mike pushed Jeanie away, she looked shocked and stepped back, hands up in a 'what?' Gesture. She moved her hands to her hips as Mike headed toward his table.

"Suzie, I," Mike was speaking before he got to the table. Suzie turned away. "didn't know she was going to do that."

Suzie looked at him. There was an empty look in her eyes. "You looked like you were enjoying it."

"She took me by surprise." Mike sat, reached across the table. Suzie pulled back.

"If that's what you're looking for you should go dance with slut queen." Suzie waved a hand in the direction where

Mike and Jeanie had been dancing. "I thought you were different than that."

"I am different." Mike had raised his voice to be heard over the music but at the same time he spoke the song ended. Heads at the tables around them turned in their direction. Mike gathered himself then spoke in a lower tone. "I didn't start that." Mike felt a bit guilty since he had in fact thought about kissing Jeanie, just not tonight. He realized Suzie was feeling hurt and betrayed, how girls had made him feel in the past. How could he make this right? "Look Suzie," she had looked away again. She looked like she was on the verge of crying. Did he mean that much to her or was it the shock of what she had seen? "Please look at me." She turned toward him but didn't look him in the eye. "I came here with you, asked you to go with me because I like you, want to be with you."

Suzie's eyes snapped to his and he realized what he had said. "Not like that. I want to spend time with you. I thought she just wanted to dance."

Tears welled in Suzie's eyes. "You don't want to be with me like that?"

Mike sighed. This was so complicated. Again, he was in that place where no matter what he said it would be the wrong thing. Of course he would like 'to be' with Suzie, what sixteen year old boy wouldn't? She was beautiful, smart, had a great sense of humour but if he said that he would look lecherous. If he said no, she would think she wasn't attractive. He had been trying hard not to think about those things about her, pushing raging hormone thoughts away but she was throwing them up at him. Was she struggling with hormones too? Probably.

"Right now, I want to spend time with you, dance with you, talk with you, get to know you." He saw her eyes softening a bit. "That other stuff? Sure, if it feels right for us, when it feels right. Right now, I don't want THAT to get in the way of THIS." He waved his hand between them. "Can you understand that?"

The band had returned to the stage and they started

into Honkey-Tonk Woman. Suzie leaned closer so he could hear her. "I think so. Sorry if I'm being a jealous idiot."

"Would you like to dance?"

"No kissing?"

"Just dancing."

"Then no." But Suzie was smiling, and she got out of her chair. She took his hand and led him onto the dance floor. Mike felt light, she had been thinking of kissing him?

Part way through the next song there was a commotion at the entrance to the arena. People there started clapping and cheering. Others joined in. The noise grew so loud that the band stopped mid song with a couple of flat string twangs. Mike strained to see what was going on.

Suzie touched his arm. "It must be Mr. and Mrs. Fixit."

"Who?" Mike still couldn't see what all the commotion was about, but the crowd had started to part.

"Mr. and Mrs. Fixit. Not his real name but that's what everyone calls him." Suzie rose on her tippy toes and stretched her neck looking over the crowd. "Yup, I see his silver hair."

"Who are they?"

"Well he's the maintenance guy at the public school, fixes everything. We've called him Mr. Fixit as long as I can remember."

Mike stood and stretched himself up to see over the heads and raised clapping hands. A chant had risen that soon drowned out the band. Once the voices synchronized with each other Mike made out what they were saying. "Fix It, Fix It." There were even some fists being flung into the air with each chant.

The band had given up their song and the crowd roared when they began picking out the opening strains of Can I Have This Dance. Mike thought it odd that a ballroom dance song would get that sort of reaction when it had all been country and rock so far. There was a ripple in the crowd as people moved backward. Mike pushed forward so he could see why the crowd was making space on the dance floor. Everyone began clapping their hands to the music. Mike couldn't help but join in. Finally he was close enough to see.

Grumps and Gram stood in the centre of the open area. A spotlight shone on them. Gramma glittered in a sequined dress that reached the floor. Her hair was up with cascades of curls trailing from a loose bun. She had woven something sparkly into the strands. Gramps wore a dark suit with a dark blue double stripe made of some sort of shiny materiel running up the outside of the legs. His shoes gleamed. His shirt had frills on the chest and something that had been woven into the frills reflected the light. His jacket matched the pants, dark with dark blue circling the cuffs. His frills matched her hair. They both smiled and bowed and waved at the crowd.

Then they turned and faced each other, his hand on her hip, the other holder her hand above their shoulders. She placed her hand on his shoulder. The crowd roared their approval. Together they stepped to the music. Mike realized there was a slit in Gram's dress all the way up to mid-thigh that allowed her to move without restriction. They moved without a hint of the arthritis and aged joints that was always emphasized at home by the tapping of his cane. They danced, moving as one. In, out, step together, step apart, turn, twirl, spin, dip, without hesitation. Mike saw the years fall away, the age and lines and experiences peeled back to reveal two teens falling in love, beginning a life together.

Mike felt a hand slip into his. He turned and smiled at Suzie.

"Aren't they amazing?" She whispered as though her words might interrupt the flow of movement of the two dancers.

"They are beautiful." Mike stated. "They are my grandparents." Mike realized that despite all the challenges Grumps had presented him so far this summer, he was proud of the love these two people had maintained for each other. Sometimes it was hard to see, like when Grumps stumbled in after an afternoon drinking at the Legion or when he was calling about 'women's work' from the kitchen door, but it was real. So real it could be felt by everyone crowded into this building. Despite the frustrations he had endured trying to build a relationship with such a stubborn man, he loved his grandfather. Now he wanted to show that man how he felt, the same way Gramps was showing Gram how he felt about her, in public, in front of the whole community, without embarrassment or hesitation, and Mike was certain how he could do that. He would do that a little later. For now, he only wanted to do one thing. He tugged Suzie toward the dance floor. She followed.

Taking Suzie in his arms in much the same way Gramps held Gram, Mike did his best to mimic their movements. He knew he was stumbling, fumbling, un-coordinating his way through the dance but he didn't care. He was having fun and Suzie seemed to be too, she was smiling and gently guiding him. His grandparents looked at him, smiled, Gramma nodded letting Mike know she approved. Then everyone began dancing to the ballroom tune. All the time the spotlight remained on the glittery couple occupying the centre of the floor.

When the song ended the room broke out in clapping and cheering. Mike found it hard to believe so many people could be happy for each other, just enjoying the sense of community. He had never seen that in the city.

Then the band began playing 'In the Mood', fast and jazzy. Mike moved toward his grandparents intending to invite them to his table. Just before he got to them the crowd parted again leaving Gramps and Gram in the centre of the clearing again. Gramps was shaking.

Mike thought he might be having a heart attack, or a stroke, and he pushed past the few people still in his way. The crowd began clapping to the music, stamping their feet and chanting again. "Fix it, Fix it."

Gramps removed his jacket, and someone took it from him. He ran his fingers through his hair, making it stand up in a maniacal way, a wide-eyed Einstein kind of look. Then he began to dance, waving his arms and stomping his feet. Gram swayed, lifted her dress a few inches and kicked out in a quick step. The crowd roared their approval and then the whole floor began jumping. Suzie turned Mike toward her, and they joined in.

"Wow you two." Mike grinned across the table at his grandparents. They had all sat down following the fast dance. "You never mentioned you were, like, the Dance King and Queen. You're like a couple of celebrities"

Both seniors were breathing hard, Gramps leaned an elbow on the table. As people walked by they greeted the two and lots of shoulder grips were given.

"We just like to dance. We told you that." Gram puffed. "Unfortunately, those will likely be the only ones we have in us tonight. We aren't twenty-one anymore."

Gramps just looked around, nodding at greeters, smiling. Sweat stood out on his forehead. Mike had noted that when they had left the dance floor, Gramps had been leaning heavy on his cane. It was as though the dance had been a painkiller for him. Without the motion, he was back to his arthritic self. "Get me a beer." He nudged his wife's knee.

Gram looked at him a moment then reached for her purse and stood up. Mike stood too. He couldn't get the beer for his grandfather, but he could accompany Gram through the process. As he stepped around his chair, he felt a hand on his shoulder.

"Doug, glad to see you made it." Dan, the Legion bartender stepped in close. Mike saw Gramps look his way. "And you brought such a pretty date." Suzie looked away blushing.

"Uh, yeah, Dan. How are you?"

"Always a good time at these dances. So much livelier than the Legion lounge."

"Yeah," Mike was feeling uncomfortable, as though he had been caught doing something wrong. He glanced at Gramps. He wasn't smiling and he was staring at Mike. There were creases across his forehead. "I'm just helping my Gramma here."

Mike followed his grandmother, heading toward the bar

area.

"Uh oh," Mike touched Gram's elbow, "I think my cover is blown."

Gramma looked at him and smiled. "Did you think it would last forever? You forget, you are in a small town. I'm surprised you've maintained it this long."

"Do you think he will be mad?"

"Your Grandfather?" Gramma stopped and looked at Mike, "You've deceived him. How would you feel?"

"But I didn't do it to hurt him."

"Still, you've been hiding the truth from him."

Mike thought about all that he had been hiding, working at the Legion under an assumed name was just one thing. All the research into Gramp's war past, the work on the motorcycle, contacting his brother's old war buddy, he figured Gramps had a right to be upset. It was also time to come clean on all that stuff and hope that once Gramps understood why he was doing what he was doing, it would make everything ok. Or at least better than it was right now. He could settle for that.

Back at the table Mike found it hard to look at his grandfather. The courage he had felt a few minutes earlier had drained away in the face of reality. He fidgeted and asked Suzie if her drink was ok. She took a sip and nodded at him. Mike was certain everyone at the table could feel the pressure he felt under. Conversation had dried up.

The rest of the party continued unabated. The band rocked out fast tunes and the dance floor bobbed and jittered, always crowded.

"What's the matter, Doug." Gramps spoke as a song ended. "Feeling a little exposed?" He had paused before saying Doug, gripping Mike with his squinted gaze. The lines in the man's face had never seemed so pronounced to Mike.

"I can explain." Mike reached out a hand and Gramps flinched away. Mike pulled his hand back. He hated how his voice had sounded, high pitched, like a whining kid. He paused and coughed then continued in his normal voice as the band started into a new song. "But not here. Tonight, but not here."

Mike turned to Suzie. "When we leave here tonight, I would like it if you would come home with me."

"I don't think..." Her eyes grew wide and Mike realized how what he said sounded.

Mike interrupted. "Not like that. There is something I need to show my grandpa. I think it would be better if you were there." Mike looked down then back at Suzie. "It would make it easier for me."

"Okay." Suzie drew the word out as though she wasn't too certain it was a good idea.

"And then I'll walk you home." Mike didn't add 'if I can' since he wasn't certain how Gramp's reaction to his big reveal was going to go, but he thought it.

As the evening progressed Suzie and Mike had more dances. He grew more confident in his own ability and really began to like the slow dances, how Suzie felt pressed against him, the touch of her skin, her scent. When she laid her head on his shoulder, he felt electricity course through his body. He nudged her head with his chin, and she turned to face him. Then they were kissing. Mike had thought there could be no more glorious an experience than when he had been lip-locked with the kissing girl. He discovered he had been wrong.

He felt himself falling into the softness of her lips, the gentle way she flicked her tongue into his mouth. He could taste the beer she had been sipping all evening and somehow, now, it tasted wonderful. He felt himself responding and pressed his mouth firmer to hers. She pulled back, breaking the contact, breaking the dance. She raised a hand to her mouth.

"I'm sorry Mike." Suzie looked around as though emerging from a daze. "I shouldn't have done that."

"Why?" Mike reached for her hand, but she pulled it away.

"I don't want you to think...I'm not like that. Let's sit down."

Not understanding Mike followed her back to their

table.

Grandma smiled across the table at Mike. Then she winked. She had seen. Is that how it had been for her and Gramps? Finding that magical, wonderful, amazing feeling on the dance floor? Discovering that the person they held in their arms was someone they wanted to share so much more with? He could understand why they still danced. It would be like a celebration of their love.

Suzie sat staring toward the dance floor, but Mike was certain she wasn't seeing any of the people gyrating there. He was certain she was looking there so she wouldn't have to look at him. Was she struggling with her feelings, emotions? Was she ashamed to be seen kissing him? Somehow that didn't feel quite right. Then he remembered the "Suzie Lucky Now" nickname she had been saddled with.

"Suzie," Mike leaned toward her and touched her hand. She continued to look away. Mike just waited. After a few more moments she turned to him. He touched her hand again. She allowed him to take it. He held it in both of his. He stared into her face until she looked at him, into his eyes. "That was a most amazing experience for me." He saw confusion darken her features. "That kiss. I never thought it could feel like that. I want you to know how this looks from my side. I don't care what others think or say, I really like being with you. If it ends now, our relationship I mean, I am really glad I got to have that kiss from you. It will be the one that I measure all others from. I just want you to know that."

He saw tears well in her eyes then she blushed, raising a hand to her face she said, "Oh Mike." Then she leaned toward him, laid her head on his shoulder, her hand gripping his as though he was the only thing keeping her from falling. Mike felt that jolt of electricity again. This time he just held her. And it felt right.

Spot Dance

"Alright everyone." The DJ called out. "It's time for our spot dance." The crowd grew excited. "Get your special someone onto the dance floor. The spot prize is fifty dollars." The crowd cheered and many couples moved onto the floor.

Mike looked at Suzie and she back at him. He nodded his head a bit and she smiled. She led him into the crowd as the music started. Mike knew that whatever couple was on or under the lucky spot when the song ended, would win the prize. The floor seemed so big.

While they were dancing, Mike looked around to see if he could find a likely spot for the prize. There weren't any marks on the floor that he could see, maybe they just chose a random location. It would be great if they won, he could use the money to replace some of his savings that he had spent on Gramp's motorcycle.

Then he noticed the stars that had been hung from the ceiling. They looked like cardboard cut-outs that had been covered in tin foil to make them shiny. He saw one that was a different colour. He checked around to make sure, yes, just one of that off colour. He knew that would be the spot dance location. He steered Suzie toward it. When the song ended, Mike and Suzie were underneath the darker star.

"Alright everyone, hold your position." the DJ called through his mike. "Jackson here," he indicated the man standing next to him, "will find the lucky couple."

Mike looked up as Jackson headed into the crowd. People chattered and oohed and aahed as he approached, then passed them. Mike looked up at the star he was certain marked the right spot. When he looked down, he saw that Eliza was beside him, about two feet away. Standing beside him, holding his hand, was a short, tired looking woman. Mike guessed it was his wife. Both were dressed in slightly worn, tired looking clothes. The emotion that Mike had felt yesterday realizing that war veteran was spending his retirement years working because his service to his country wasn't being properly recognized, welled up.

Jackson was still approaching but only a few couples stood between him and Mike.

"Eliza," Mike whispered.

When the man looked at him, Mike reached out, pulled him closer, then guided Suzie into Eliza's spot.

"Mike," Suzie started.

"Hey," Eliza said at the same time.

"And here's the lucky couple," the DJ announced as Jackson stepped up to Eliza and his wife.
"Fifty smackeroonies."

The crowd started to break up, now that they didn't have to hold their spots anymore. Mike was smiling. Suzie gave him a little shove. "What did you do that for? WE could have won."

Mike replied, "We did."

Eliza looked at Mike, then at the cash Jackson had pressed into his palm, then back at Mike. There was a stunned look on his face. Mike smiled as he snapped a sassy salute toward him.

Mike led Suzie back to their table. He would tell her why he did what he did once they sat down.

The Dance Off

Despite her earlier proclamation regarding only having a few dances in them, Mike watched as his grandparents danced a few more times. Each time it was slow, and the crowd gave them extra space on the floor. They were delightful to watch. It was obvious, however, that Gramps was in some discomfort. His limp was quite pronounced.

The DJ broke into Mike's thoughts. "And now's the time you've been waiting for. Grab your partner, get on the floor," changing his tone to that of a wrestling ring announcer he cried out, "let's get ready to stumble." He dragged out the lllll, bringing his cry to a dramatic crescendo.

Mike looked at Suzie, he didn't understand.

"It's a dance off." she explained, "Everyone dances, if you get tapped on the shoulder, you're out and have to sit down. Last couple standing, wins."

"Wanna go?" Mike asked. He was feeling good with the dancing he had learned and making Suzie happy made him feel happy.

"No," Suzie batted a hand at him, "No point. Your grandparents always win."

Mike thought for a second then said, "So what? It'll be fun."

He reached out and took Suzie's hand. That electric shock ran up his arm again. It was entirely pleasurable. She resisted a moment then followed him onto the dance floor. It was crowded.

'Blueberry Hill' by Fats Domino started and the crowd groaned. Before Fats got to "Blueberry Hill," the needle scratched across the record and Staying Alive, by the Bee Gees, blasted from the stage. The crowd roared and everyone danced.

Mike and Suzie began to jive, and Mike watched the rest of the crowd when he wasn't concentrating on not stepping on Suzie's feet or bumping into too many people. As couples were tapped by Jackson, they left the dance floor.

Next came, 'Twist and Shout' by the Beatles and everyone began to twist. Except Mike, he had no idea. He looked at Suzie and she pointed at her feet. Mike watched a moment then mimicked her squishing a cigarette butt motions. After a few moments he felt himself moving with the beat of the song. Then he felt a jab in his side. He looked and saw Jack dancing close to him, arms and elbows waving. The look Jack gave back made Mike certain the poke hadn't been an accident.

Mike renewed his dancing, determined to at least, be on the dance floor longer than Jack. He had to admit thought, Jack was doing a pretty good job. The song twisted on.

Jack poked Mike two more times, each harder than the time before. After the second, Mike turned to Jack. Jack stopped dancing, dropped his arms and stood there in an open invitation for a fight.

"Mike," Suzie said quietly from behind him.

Wanting nothing more than to punch Jack right in the face, Mike forced himself to settle down. He turned back to Suzie and started dancing again. Just before the twist ended Mike felt a tap on his shoulder. He spun, ready to parlay with Jack, but it was Jackson.

"Sorry man," Jackson said, giving him a little head nod.

Mike took Suzie's hand and lead her from the dance floor. He felt a burning in his chest when he saw Jack was still dancing.

Sitting down, Mike scanned the dancers for his grandparents. He saw them jiving to 'Rock Around the Clock' by Bill Haley and the Comets. They were really boogying, and Mike hoped Gramp's knees would hold up.

The floor only held three couples, one of them Jack and Jeannie. Then the third couple was tapped out. Mike saw Jack move close to Gramps and then, in a wild flay of arms and legs, Jack bumped Gramps, knocking him to the floor. The whole crowd gasped. The music stopped mid-note.

Mike stormed out of his chair and ran across the floor.

He hadn't decided if he was going to light into Jack or help his grandfather, but he knew he needed to get there fast. His vision focussed on only the two combatants. How could Jack have done something so underhanded?

Mike saw his grandfather raise his hand in a stop motion.

The old man got to his feet without assistance. He moved slow; Mike could see the cords in his neck stand out with the effort to gather his feet under himself. He brushed off his pants then looked at Jack.

Jack looked back, a look on his face as though the incident had been by accident. Mike wasn't certain what was going to happen next, there was no way he was going to let Jack and his grandfather fight.

Gramps gave Jack a little bow then raised a finger into the air, his forefinger, and gave it a spin. The crowd cheered. Gramps turned to Gramma as the song began playing where it had left off. Both couples returned to dancing.

Not expecting that reaction, how could Gramps not know that Jack's actions had been on purpose? Mike stayed where he was, about ten feet from the dancers. Gramps had a bit more pronounced limp, but was still very graceful. Mike felt so proud of the man.

Then Jack moved in close again, making the same move. Mike started forward but was too far away to stop what was about to happen. As Jack's foot moved in to tangle the old man's again, Gramps spun Gramma the opposite way, raised his foot in a natural motion and kicked Jack right in the crotch with his heal. Jack fell in a heap. The crowd ooohed. The music continued and Gramps and Gram finished the dance as though nothing out of the ordinary had just occurred.

The crowd closed in, clapping and cheering, embracing the old couple. No one stopped to check on Jack. After a few moments, Gramps went over to Jack, offered his hand so the teen could get to his feet, leaned in close to him. Mike was certain he said something because Jack's face turned red. It was an ashamed red, not an angry red.

Back at their table, the large trophy occupying a good portion of it, Mike spoke to Gramps. "You guys were great out there. Never knew you could dance like that. But when Jack. . . you handled that so well. Right in the knackers," after a pause Mike continued, "What did you say to him when you helped him up?"

Gramps' brow was still damp from the exertion of the dance off. He gave it a wipe with his sleeve then said. "Fool me once."

Mike sat back. He had heard that phrase many times, so he knew the whole phrase, 'Fool me once, shame on you. Fool me twice, shame on me.' Gramps had known the knock down had been intentional. Mike reached out hand hugged his grandfather. The man hugged him back.

The Last Dance

All too soon the band was announcing the last dance. Mike asked Suzie if she would join him.

"Okay but," then she touched her lip and shook her head.

Mike understood.

When the dance ended, the lights were turned up. The crowd had diminished throughout the evening, people departing when they had had enough or when other deadlines pressed on them. Mike looked around the table making sure no one had forgotten anything.

"Would you like a drive home with us?" Gramma asked. Gramps looked at her, his eyes narrowed. He had refused Mike's offer to carry the trophy for them. Mike presumed he was still angry about Mike working at the Legion.

"Sure, but there is something I need to show Grampa when we get home. I would like Suzie to be there too. Is that ok?"

"I think that will be just fine."

The Big Reveal

The closer they got to home, the more Mike felt the burning in his stomach. He hoped his big reveal would have the desired effect but with Gramps, you just never knew. There had been the hug after the dance off, but then those narrowed eyes when Gram offered the ride. No one spoke much, Mike was too tied up in his worry. The trophy stood on the backseat, between Mike and Suzie. When they arrived home and Gramma shut the car off, the darkness that engulfed them felt like it had weight.

"What I want to show you is in the barn." Mike said. Gramps just hrmphed.

"Are you sure?" Gramma said as she climbed out of the car. There was a worried look on her face.

"Positive." Mike tugged the sliding door open, reached in and snapped on the lights.

"What's he up to?" He heard Gramps ask as he strode across the barn to the darkened stall. Mike reached up, twisted the fluorescent tube. It hummed then blinked to life, flickered a moment then blazed. The tarp and what it concealed cast harsh shadows, starker than Mike remembered from any of his hours working out here.

Gramps and Gram came into the barn. Gram held Gramps' arm. Gramps leaned on his cane. Suzie followed, looking around the barn's interior.

"What have you done?" Gramps' jaw was firm, his mouth squirmed as the words came out. Mike noted the concern and worry on Gram's face. It was now or never.

"Gramps," Mike's mouth was dry. He swallowed, trying to work up some moisture, "we have been together here for more than a month now. I have tried to do things that would make you happy. I know I have made some mistakes along the way..."

"I'll say." Gramps muttered. He looked like he wanted to step forward but Gram's hold on his arm restrained him.

Mike ignored the comment and continued. "but I have been trying."

"I'll say." Gramps muttered. A twisted smile accompanied a quick glance toward Gram. She gave him a stern look.

"All I wanted to do was build a relationship with you. Have some grandpa grandson moments like we see on tv, but nothing I did seemed to help. I have learned a lot about you Grandpa, from working with you, working here in your space, and from the library."

"And from the Legion it turns out." The sneer had returned to Gramps mouth. "Snooping in my business."

"Not snooping Grampa, learning. Trying to learn about you, how to make you happy," Mike's voice broke as he felt a ball of emotion rush up his throat, "how to get you to like me."

Mike saw a pained expression grow on Grandma's face as though she too was just learning how important this was to Mike. Despite their many conversations and her strong support for his efforts, at least the efforts he had shared with her, had she missed just how important Grandpa was to Mike?

"So, I have taken the one thing that you retained from the war, from a time when you seem to have found some sort of happiness, and I have worked on it. I don't know why you hide it out here under this old tarp," with a flourish Mike pulled the tarp off the motorcycle, "but it's time it was honoured."

Mike heard gasps from both Gramma and Gramps. Suzie stood in silence behind them not understanding what was going on.

"What have you done?" Gramps took a step forward, his words drowning out Michael final ones.

"I've restored the motorcycle."

"You, you, you've wrecked it." Gramps eyes blazed, his voice was a roar. Gram and Suzie cringed. Mike felt his vision narrow, a crawling sensation in his crotch, Gramps' twisted face filled his entire view. "You had no right...what have you done."

Mike resisted the temptation to run. He hadn't known

exactly how Gramps would react; he had imagined everything from elation to some words about invading Gramps' space but he was not prepared for the naked anger he felt flowing toward him. Instead of retreating, backing down, Mike charged forward.

"I did what Wenner would have wanted."

Gramps was silent, stood still, his face lost all expression. After a few moments he said, "and how would you know about that?"

"I know a lot more than you understand Gramps. I haven't been wasting my days, I've been studying the war, researching what you did, what you were asked to do. I've been trying to understand what it must have been like to be facing the things that you faced back in those days." Mike felt tears burning in his eyes. He wasn't certain if they came from fear, from uncertainty, from the less than positive reaction from Gramps but he wasn't going to let them stop him.

"I know Wenner was your brother, that you were both despatch riders. Mostly I know that you both loved the motorcycles, loved each other, and you were fiercely competitive with each other. And I know that something happened on Wenner's last mission, where he got killed, and you think you are responsible somehow."

Mike knew from Gramps' stunned look that he had surprised the old man with how much he knew. He felt no comfort in that but, now that he was on this road, he was resolved to see it to the end. Even if it turned out to be a dead end.

"Grandpa, I don't know what happened that day, but I do know that letting this motorcycle rot out here in the barn isn't going to change how you feel about it all. There was a reason you brought this machine home and I think it was to somehow honour Wenner, remember him, come to grips with how you feel. I don't think that has happened but that is what I have tried to do. I know I disappoint you a lot, have made some pretty stupid choices and decisions but fixing up this motorcycle is not one of them. I just wish we could have done this together, grandfather and grandson."

Silence descended on the small group in the barn. Mike felt his energy drain out of him as his last words faded into the quiet of the stall. Somewhere deep in one of the timbers, a piece of wood settled, a minute air bubble collapsing perhaps, generating a click that would normally have gone unnoticed but sounded more like a rifle shot to Mike. Mike studied his grandfather's face. The muscles there were moving, his eyes twitching, his mouth almost opening then closing, the chin moving back and forth, it seemed that a lifetime of emotions, moods, and feelings were roiling in competition and confusion.

Then the old man shuffled forward. He gave his elbow a little flick and Grandma let it go. Mike stepped aside to let him pass. Gramps stopped in front of the motorcycle and stood there looking at it. Then he reached out and touched the handlebar. Then his legs gave out and he collapsed to his knees.

Mike stepped forward fast enough to take much of Gramps' weight, helping to ease him to the ground. Gramma rushed forward but Gramps raised a hand to stop her. "I'm ok, I'm ok." Mike felt vibrations in the man and realized he was crying. Kneeling beside him, Mike put an arm around his shoulders and gave him an awkward hug. He expected the man to shrug him off but he didn't. Mike was about to start explaining his motives again when he heard the old man speaking in halting, quiet words, not much more than a whisper.

"It was my mission. Message to the front. But Wenner took it, always having to outdo me. When he didn't return, I went and followed him. He was in a ditch, under his bike, "Gramps patted the front tire, "this bike. He must have run into an enemy patrol. He was dead but his despatch was still there. Pinned under his bike, he still killed those Krauts. It should have been me." Then his body quivered and sobs erupted. "It should have been me." Grandma moved forward and knelt to comfort her husband.

Mike patted his grandfather on the shoulder then stood.

He walked over to Suzie, she reached out her hands and Mike took them.

"I'm sorry about that. Didn't think it would go like this."

"Mike, this is amazing. I think you have done something profound here. You worked on the motorcycle?"

"Yeah, just cleaned it up mostly. Had to replace a few parts." Mike realized that some of the stains he had cleaned off might have been Wenner's blood. That thought brought the experiences of the war very close to home for him.

"You fucking young arse. Look what you've done." Gramps' voice seemed loud enough to rattle dust from the rafters. Mike turned and saw his grandfather coming toward him, brandishing his cane like a sword. Gram was behind him, reaching toward him, a stunned look on her face. "I'm going to teach you to mess in my stuff."

Mike stepped back in surprise, accidentally pushing Suzie back as well. Too late he realized he had trapped them both in the stall across from the motorcycle. Mike raised his hands.

"Grampa, wait." Mike didn't know what had taken his grandfather from the quiet reminiscing to this rage and he wasn't sure what he should do next. He certainly didn't want to get struck by that cane, even in the hands of an older man it was going to hurt, but he didn't want Suzie or his grandmother taking any of the rage either. Should he scramble over the stall wall? Would Gramps follow him?

"Don't you call me that you little Nazi. You don't deserve to call me that." The cane whipped back and forth as though to slice Mike in half. "I'll show you what you deserve."

Mike feinted to his right then rushed left when Gramps lunged. Then he was behind the man, between him and his grandmother. He saw enough space to get himself between Gramps and the barn door. He rushed toward that opening.

The cane swung around and struck Mike across the head. He stumbled, raising one arm in a late defense.

"Ha, ha. Felt that, didn't ya?" Mike spun to face his grandfather again, hoping to be able to see and fend off any more attacks. The expression on the man's face was terrifying. His eyes were jittering back and forth, he licked his lips as though looking at a juicy steak. Mike was certain he wasn't facing his grandfather; something was possessing the man. Something quite insane.

Mike recalled the article he had read in one of Gramps' Legion magazines, a magazine in the workbench drawer only six feet away from him. It had listed some of the symptoms of PTSD which included recurrence of traumatizing events, Gramps had called him a Nazi; and, in rarer cases, complete breaks in psychosis. Was he witnessing one of those right now? He recalled that these reactions could be triggered following recollections of traumatizing events. Had he caused this reaction in Gramps by reminding him of Wenner and the war? Cripes, could he never make the right choice? All he wanted to do was please the man and now he had guided him into a full mental breakdown. What to do, what to do? What had the article said to do, had it said anything? At least Gramps was still focussed on him. Mike backed toward the door as his mind scrambled to figure out what to do.

Behind Gramps, Gram was reaching for him, calling his name. Suzie had stayed deep in the stall. She looked scared. Mike felt horrible for the situation he had set up. His back came up against the door. It was closed. It opened in. If Mike was going to open it, he was going to have to move closer to Gramps, into cane striking range.

Instead he fell to his knees, put his hands on his head and said, "I surrender, I surrender" and he braced for the blows. After a moment Mike looked up. Gramps was standing there, the cane above his head and a bewildered look on his face.

Gramma touched him on his shoulder, "Bert," she began. Gramps spun, the rage returning to his face as he spun, the cane wielded back a bit more. Mike realized he was about to strike her. Mike rushed forward and grabbed the cane. He didn't want to fight with his grandfather, but he wasn't about to let him hit Gramma either. Gramps turned back toward him, twisting the cane, trying to free it. Mike held firm.

"You stop that." Mike yelled and was rewarded with a look of shock on the man's face. "What do you think you're doing?" Mike felt the effort Gramps was putting into freeing his cane waver. "Get a grip. You are acting like a miserable old man intent on destroying everything around you...just like Hitler. Is that who you are? Hitler?" Spittle flew from Mike's lips, he realized how angry he had become. He was on the verge of giving into his anger, his frustration, his fear. He was going to hit this man and it was going to feel good.

'No it won't.' A voice flared in his head, 'it will feel good for a moment and then you will have to deal with it.' Mike felt his anger rush out of him and tears build in his eyes, a ball of emotion grow in his throat and he wondered if they were both going off their nut. Then he reined himself in, thought about the kiss that Suzie had given him that evening, how he had felt as they danced, how nice it was to have her body swaying against his. Now he knew what to say.

"It wasn't about you." And Mike shared the story Bruce had related. "He took the dispatch so he could go to his birthday celebration."

"Gramps," Mike steadied his voice, spoke as calm and quiet as he could, "she needs to dance." He looked toward his grandmother, her eyes were wide, her mouth slightly open and quivering. Mike knew she was scared. "She waited for you then, she's waiting now. Don't make her wait any longer. Dance with her, that's what you do."

The look of shock on Gramps' face faded into one of confusion. His eyes still rolled but had become less jittery. His mouth relaxed from a grimace to a silent 'O'. Then he turned back to his wife, lowered the cane, dropped it to the floor and he moved forward, snaking one hand around her waist, the other taking her hand. He stepped in close to her and began the rhythmic moves he was so good at. Mike could hear him humming a quiet tune. His wife moved with him.

"Oh my God Mike," Suzie skittered up to Mike, "that was amazing." Her voice was quiet, a smile on her face. "You handled that like a pro."

"I don't think I've ever been so scared." Mike whispered back. "It felt like I was totally losing it." Mike lifted the latch on the barn door and opened it a crack. He looked toward his grandparents. Grandma nodded at him, 'it will be ok now' she seemed to be saying. He watched them for a few more minutes.

"I better get you home." Mike took Suzie's hand and lead her through the door.

"Will they be alright?"

"Yes, I am pretty sure Gramps' moment has passed."

"What was all that about?"

"Let me tell you..." They walked along the dark, dusty driveway and Mike talked.

A Gramps Moment

The next morning Mike paused before entering the kitchen. He knew Gramps was up, he had peeked into his bedroom where the bed was neat and tidy. He could hear Gram working at the sink. Not certain what to expect, Mike took a big breath then walked into the rest of his life.

"Good morning." He tried to sound as cheery as he could, but Mike was scared, a huge knot inside.

"Good morning Mikey." Gram sing-songed. "Hungry?"

Mike glanced at Gramps who was reading the paper as though it was just another day.

"Sure," Mike looked at Gram for some sort of clue as to Gramps' disposition. She just shrugged at him.

"Toast?"

"Sure." Mike pulled out a chair from the table.

Gramps looked up. He wasn't smiling. He stared at Mike while the young man sat down. Mike stared back not certain if he should say anything. Not certain what to say. He had laid awake a long time after walking Suzie home, wondering what would happen now. There was a tremendous sense of relief now that he had revealed everything to Gramps. There were no more secrets to protect, but had all his efforts only served to further erode their relationship? Suzie had seemed excited about what he had been up to, had said Gramps should appreciate the lengths he had gone through to please him. Mike still wasn't certain the man was capable of appreciation. Mike was certain too that one of Gramps' big challenges was a raging case of PTSD, there had been a lot of evidence of that now that Mike had the advantage of hindsight, along with Gramps' fugue slip-ups last night. But that was really a matter for professionals, not a sixteen-year-old.

"We need to talk," the old man spoke. His mouth barely moved. "about the rest of your summer."

Mike glanced at Gram, but she just raised her hands and shook her head, she had no idea what was coming. Mike braced himself. Was he going to be told he had to leave? That he was being banished? Where would he go? His parents were still in Mexico and him going there was not an option. He couldn't go home and stay by himself, although that would be preferable to remaining here with an unresolvable relationship. His mind raced over his possible future. And just when things had been looking pretty good in some areas. Suzie had given him a pretty nice kiss when they said good night, pressed herself against him, hugged him tight.

"You have really overstepped your bounds," Gramps frowned but his voice was calm. "Messing with the motorcycle, all of my stuff." The man paused when Gram slid a plate with two pieces of buttered toast in front of him. He looked at the toast, then at her, then back at Mike. "And all the lies. The poking around in my life, the sneaking around at the Legion, the who knows what you've really been up to all the days you spent in town."

Gramps spread jam on the toast. The silence that had fallen after his words hung heavy, disturbed only by the crunch of the bread under the swipe of the knife. Mike wanted to defend himself, reiterate why he had done what he had done but every time he opened his mouth, words refused to come out. They were tangled in a jumble of thoughts and emotions and feelings. Everything Gramps had said was true, he had messed in his stuff when he knew he shouldn't, he had lied even though he had been careful to keep it to mostly withheld truths, he had snuck to work at the Legion, purposely keeping it from Gramps, even sneaking out the back door when Gramps had come while he was working. He had even spent his own money for the parts for the motorcycle. He had done these things but for what he thought were the right reasons. Didn't that count for anything?

And then there was what he had said last night during the big reveal. He had said some nasty things, even called Gramps Hitler. Did he remember that? That whole part of the evening was a big fog to Mike with certain parts of it appearing in clarity then falling back into the dimness.

"I think I have every right to be angry with you." Gramps set down the knife. "It seemed every time I laid down a rule you immediately moved to violate it."

"I..." Mike started but Gramps cut him off.

"But last night you asked me a question."

'Oh no,' Mike thought, 'here comes the Hitler question.'

"You asked me what Wenner would have done."

The apology that Mike had been preparing in his head, died on his tongue.

"Wenner would have brought that motorcycle home, cleaned it up, then rode it until the tires fell off."

Gramps took a bite of toast and chewed it while Mike pondered what he had said. Gramps raised his eyebrows as though waiting for Mike's response. Mike had no idea what to say. Wasn't certain where Gramps' last words were leading.

"I'm not sure what to say." Mike stated after glancing at Gram.

"Does that bike run?"

"Almost." Mike leaned toward Gramps. "It turns over well, but I can't get it to actually start."

"Stutter cough?" Gramps said it more like a statement than a question.

"Yeah, like it's going to start but doesn't."

"Ha," Gramps hit the table with his hand, "you young pups think you know it all with your internet and wooshywisms on your fancy phones." Eat your breakfast then I'll show you an old D.R. trick." The man was smiling.

Gram placed Mike's toast in front of him. He hardly felt like eating now, there was a wave of excitement that had passed from Gramps to him. He could imagine how Wenner had felt facing his brother so many years ago.

"Go on," Gramps pointed at him, "eat up. Some stuff you need to hear first." Gramps leaned forward on his elbows, pushing his plate toward the center of the table with his forearms. "Some stuff you said last night makes sense. Some of it was pretty mean. I ain't no Hitler."

"I'm sorry…" But Gramps cut him off with a wave of his hand.

"Needed to be said. I know I've been a bit hard on you," Mike resisted the urge to chuff, "I think you kids today get molly-coddled too much, makes you into a bunch of wimps. And ya don't have much respect either." The man paused a moment, "At least that's what I thought. Last night when I almost," he looked toward his wife then back to Mike. He raised one hand as though brandishing his cane. "You know." Another pause. "You brought me back. A lot of it is fuzzy but I remember that. God knows the last thing I want to do is hurt someone. Enough of that in the past." Mike was certain he was referring to the war but maybe last night hadn't been the only time he had been violent since those days. "Anyway, maybe I got some stuff I need to be working on. I just want you to know that."

Mike licked his fingers. "Sure Grampa." He got up and headed into the bathroom to wash up. When he came out Gramps was by the back door. There was a glint in his eye that Mike had never seen before. He looked mischievous, a young kid with a secret that was itching to be told. Mike followed him out. Gramps talked while they headed toward the barn.

"We were always worried that someone would mess with our bikes, needed to make sure the Krauts couldn't use 'em, so, Wenner and I started switching around our fuel lines whenever we parked 'em. I expect that's why you couldn't get it to start. To the untrained eye, everything looks fine but the carbs ain't getting no fuel." Gramps limped and leaned on his cane but the pace he had set had Mike almost running to keep up. "We even fashioned our own clamps to make the switching easier, no screwdriver needed."

Gramps went straight to the bike. He started to crouch beside it, winced then motioned Mike over. "Get down there. Reach in by the carb." He pointed.

Mike did as he was told without saying that he knew what a carburetor was and where it was. He was enjoying this moment with his grandfather and he wasn't going to say anything to spoil it.

"Pinch that clamp there, and that one there." The old man squinted as he pointed. Mike saw what he needed to do. He remembered noticing this arrangement of hoses before. They had looked normal to him. "Switch them around."

Mike did as he was told. He thought this was a pretty clever trick, so simple, yet effective.

"Now kick her over." Gramps stepped back so Mike could straddle the motorcycle. "Crank that throttle, get the gas flowing."

Mike followed the directions. He stomped down hard on the starter pedal. The engine spun but didn't start.

"Again." Gramps sounded excited.

This time the engine sputtered a bit, the same as the best effort Mike had gotten so far.

"Again, put your back into it." There was a laugh in his tone.

Mike stomped hard, twisted the throttle and the motorcycle roared to life. A plume of white smoke erupted from the exhaust. Mike looked back at it.

"Don't worry about that." Gramps was smiling, fairly bouncing. He had to yell to be heard over the noise of the motor.

Mike twisted the throttle and the engine revved. The cloud of smoke settled around the motorcycle.

Gramps gave a little cough. "Maybe we should move it outside. Get some air." Gramps headed to the door and pushed the sliding door full open. He waved at Mike.

"I don't know how." Mike called.

"What?" Gramps cupped a hand to his ear.

Mike squeezed the left handlebar lever, the clutch. It didn't feel right. He pressed on the shifter with his toe, but that didn't feel right either. And there was the lever beside the gas tank that Mike didn't know what it was for. This was all different from the dirt bike.

"I don't know how to drive this." Mike yelled.

"Oh," Gramps looked surprised, "It's a suicide clutch

so remember to keep your foot on it." The man waved at him again as though his explanation would solve any knowledge issue. 'Suicide clutch,' Mike thought. 'I want to ride this thing, not kill myself.' He looked down at the foot pedals and the lever mounted on the side of the fuel tank.

"Where's the clutch?" Mike yelled back.

Gramps looked at him a moment as though digesting the question along with his toast. Then he shook his head and limped toward Mike. "I thought you kids new everything from your phones. Here, let me have her."

Mike stepped off the motorcycle and stood by to help Gramps straddle it. Gramps waved him away. "I can do this." Gramps settled onto the saddle then leaned the bike to the left and flicked the kick stand up with his right foot. "Maybe you can help steady this a bit." Gramps looked at Mike. "It's been a while." He revved the motor, placed his left foot on the foot pedal, pressed down with his toe, shifted the gear leaver with his right hand, revved the engine a bit and the machine moved forward. He guided it through the fog that had gathered in the barn and out the door. Mike ran behind him.

Outside, Gramps stopped the bike, shifted the shifter again, then set the kick stand. He looked back at Mike and the man was beaming. "Need my helmet."

"In the saddlebag." Mike opened the side bag and pulled out the leather helmet and goggles. Gramps looked at it, then pulled it onto his head, fastening the chinstrap. Gram stepped out the back door and stood on the step with her hands on her hips.

"Back in a flash." Gramps said, kicked up the stand, shifted and revved the motor. Then he was moving down the driveway, a small cloud of dust spurting away from the tires. In a moment he disappeared around the bend that turned into St Andrew Street.

Mike stood in the cloud of settling dust. He marveled at how his Grandfather had changed so much in such a short period of time. He had been more like a kid, a teenager, climbing onto the motorcycle and puttering off. In the distance he heard the engine blat and Mike couldn't help but smile. Had he finally done something right? Grandma crossed the laneway and stood in front of him.

She placed her hands on his shoulders and pressed her forehead against his. "I haven't seen him like this for a very long time. Sometimes when we dance, I get glimpses, but you have coaxed some spirit out of him and that is a wonderful thing. Thank you." Then she hugged him. Mike let her squeeze him. It felt like it should last forever.

He heard the engine sound increasing, Gramps must be coming back. Mike heard a siren whoop once and saw blue and red lights reflect off the large tobacco barn that stood beyond the bend in the driveway. Then Gramps roared around the bend, sped toward him, tires throwing up the dust cloud again. Right behind him was a police car, lights flashing.

"Oh Gramps." Mike said and stepped aside as Gramps brought the motorcycle to a stop where he had been standing. Gram moved with him, moved behind him, her hands returning to his shoulders.

The police car stopped about ten feet away. After a moment the engine died. By the time the cop opened the door, Gramps had dismounted the motorcycle and removed his helmet. Officer Campbell tugged his hat onto his head as he approached them.

"Can you believe this?" Gramps waved a hand at Campbell then indicated the motorcycle. "My grandson did this."

Mike noted that this was the first time he could remember Gramps acknowledging their relationship.

"She's a beaut. Registration and license?" Campbell asked.

"I know I shouldn't have it on the road. That's why I only went a little way. Mikey here put so much work into restoring her, there is no way I couldn't acknowledge that. I couldn't resist."

"Mr. Weinstein, I could site you for...,"

"But you won't." Gramps gave a little laugh and raised

himself on his toes. "'cause you love this bike too." He gave Campbell a little point with his finger. He looked at Mike then added. "Pretty amazing."

Campbell looked at Mike then back at the motorcycle. He tipped his hat back on his head a bit and put one hand on his hip. "You did this?"

"Well," Mike felt a bit embarrassed now that the spotlight was on him. "I cleaned it up a bit."

"A bit?" Gramps went into a long spiel describing what Mike had done, pointing out the parts that had been replaced. Under Campbell's questions, Gramps revealed the history of the motorcycle and it returning to Canada, his relationship with his brother, his trick for securing the bike. He beamed throughout his tirade of words and giggled a few times. From the nature of Campbell's questions, it was clear he was interested.

"Well Mr. Weinstein,"

"Please, Bert."

"Alright, Bert. If you want to ride this thing on the roads, you need to put plates on it. And, you need to have an operator license too. Otherwise, keep it in the laneway here."

"Yup, yup. Sure, sure." Mike continued to marvel at Gramps' good spirits.

"Officer Campbell," Gram spoke for the first time since he had arrived. "We will do as you ask."

Campbell tipped his hat at her. "Mrs. Weinstein." Then he looked at Mike. "I need to speak to you." And he gave his head a little jerk in the direction of his car. Mike felt that uncomfortable feeling again in his balls, but he nodded and followed the policeman behind the cruiser.

"You surprise me. What you've done here, and at the Legion, makes me think you really aren't involved with the stuff at Trucker's Haven. I'm going to review my notes on that. Can you keep your Grandfather from breaking any more laws?"

"Sure, yeah, maybe." Mike fumbled for the right words. "I'll try."

"Alright, you do your best and I'll do mine. Together we'll protect that old veteran from himself."

"Sure. Of course." Mike felt free again. Campbell was telling him he was going to drop the charges, at least that was how Mike took his words. He wasn't sure how well he could control Gramps, but he thought he could.

"Good." Campbell said then turned toward Gramps. "And get yourself a proper helmet, this isn't 1940 you know." But he was smiling.

Gramps waved at him. Mike stepped aside as the cruiser backed down the laneway then looked at his grandparents. They stood there smiling, Gram behind Gramps, her hands on his shoulders, Gramps looking at the bike, smiling.

"Woo hoo." Gramps said, rubbing his hands together. "Your turn Mike."

Mike couldn't help but feel that he had been right after all, this was going to be his best summer ever.